THE TEMPESTUOUS VOYAGE OF

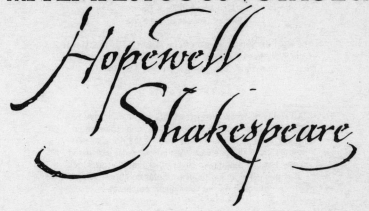

Hopewell Shakespeare

Sophie Masson

A division of Hodder Headline Limited

A Catalogue record for this book is available from
the British Library

ISBN 0 340 86581 4

Typeset in Bembo by Avon DataSet Ltd,
Bidford-on-Avon, Warwickshire

Printed and bound in Great Britain by
Clays Ltd, St Ives plc

The paper and board used in this paperback are natural recyclable
products made from wood grown in sustainable forests.
The manufacturing processes conform to the environmental
regulations of the country of origin.

Hodder Children's Books
A division of Hodder Headline Limited
338 Euston Road
London NW1 3BH

If you'd like to contact Sophie Masson, go to her website at:
http://www.northnet.com.au/~smasson

Contents

Thule, the period of cosmography,
Does vaunt of Hecla, whose sulphureous fire
Does melt the frozen clime and thaw the sky;
Tricnacrian Etna's flames ascend not higher:
These things seem wondrous, yet more wondrous I,
Whose heart with fear does freeze, with love does fry.

The Andalusian merchant, that returns
Laden with cochineal and china dishes,
Reports in Spain how strangely Fogo burns
Amidst an ocean full of flying fishes.
These things seem wondrous, yet more wondrous I,
Whose heart with fear does freeze, with love does fry.

Anonymous, 1600, *Thule, the period of cosmography*
(or furthest point on the map).

Part One

The White Ship

One

'Get here at once, you wretched boy! At once, do you hear!'

No fear, thought the boy in question, pressing himself against the dusty stones as Mistress Cecelia Page's shrill wrath filled his ears. He could picture her face going the loud, extravagant hues of a fop's costume: crimson and scarlet and purple, with livid streaks and patches.

'Come here, you cream-faced loon! Lily-livered wretch, hence! I know where you are, 'tis no use hiding like a plague rat in a drain! Come here, so's I can tan your wicked hide for you!'

In the shadows, the youth grinned. It was plain Mistress Page had no idea where he was. Or else his hide would already have been tanned redder than Master Walter Page's fancy Spanish boots. This hidey-hole in the cellar was one he'd discovered himself, and whose existence she did not suspect.

'Hopewell Shakespeare, listen well!' Her voice had gone suddenly from bellowing to deadly quiet. 'I shall count to three. If you're not here when I finish counting, you are out on the streets for ever. And I shall be writing to your father, whatever happens.'

Hopewell winced: Mistress Page's wrath was like a summer breeze compared to the tempest of his father's anger when he found out what a ne'er-do-well his youngest son was. Robert Shakespeare, Worcestershire farmer and Puritan worthy, had high expectations of all his children. For Puritans were the most earnest of all God's people. Hard work, that pleased God, they said; obedience, and Sabbaths kept holy and quiet and good works: those saw you on the narrow road to Heaven. But the broad road to Hell – well, that was lined with disobedience, flightiness, music, plays, colour, fun, cakes and ale.

Alas! These were all things Hopewell loved dearly, and plays above all. It was not that he wanted to upset or offend his parents, for he loved them. But he could not help his own nature. He couldn't be a Puritan if he tried.

From the moment of his birth, Hopewell had caused trouble for the good name of the Shakespeare family: at least that was how his father put it. That, and the shameful reputation of their fortunately very distant relative, the notorious playwright and actor William Shakespeare.

Mistress Page's voice broke into Hopewell's thoughts. 'I am starting the counting, Hopewell. *One . . .*'

What to do? Mistress Page had said his father would be told, whatever happened. Father had been so relieved that the Pages had agreed to take him as an apprentice. Hopewell's mother had been pleased too. Less stern, softer, more imaginative than her husband, she had nevertheless worried about her youngest child. When they heard about this, they would both be very upset and disappointed. *And* he would get a beating from Mistress Page, too.

'*Two . . .*'

Hopewell made up his mind. He would run away. He was tired of the boring, backbreaking chores of the wheelwright's workshop, where as the lowliest apprentice, he also had to do the lowliest tasks. Not for him the slavery of a snivelling apprentice, and the dull career of a wheelwright! He wouldn't stay in this place, neither. He'd go down to the docks, get work on a ship going to Virginney, maybe, to the New World, where riches were to be had, just like that, he'd heard. Or on one of the privateers that sailed the Spanish Main and captured ships laden with gold. Like the legendary privateer Captain Richard Wolfe, master of the *Golden Dragon*, who'd been the most famous man in England at one time.

'*Three!*'

Aye, he'd make his fortune, so he would, and spite the lot of them when he came back with gold at his wrist and velvet and silk on his back! He'd always had a yearning for travel and adventure, unlike his boring brothers who thought their little green corner of Worcestershire was the be-all and end-all of the world. London to them was another world. But Hopewell had learnt that boredom could live in London too, as much as in the country. Only at the Globe Theatre, his favourite place in all of London, could he dream of real excitement and adventure. Well, things would change!

'That's it, Hopewell Shakespeare!' He could hear her panting with fury; heard her turn on her heel and clump up the stairs from the cellar. He heard her lock the door up the top. It didn't matter. There was another way out to the street.

He'd need some money in front of him. He could hardly ask Mistress Page for his wages. But what about Master Page? There was more to *him* than met the eye. Hopewell had found this out quite by chance. A few weeks ago, when he'd slipped along to the Globe to meet up with his sweetheart Annie, Hopewell had caught sight of Master Page there. It was a shock: but soon Hopewell realized the wheelwright hadn't seen *him*. But he'd stored the knowledge away for possible future use. Mistress Page disapproved of the theatre. She was not a Puritan, and neither was her husband, but nevertheless she thought the theatre was not respectable. There would be hell to pay if she found out her husband went there on the quiet.

Hopewell smiled to himself. Truth to tell, Mistress Page had never been to the theatre, but she was sure she knew all about it. All sorts of unsavoury people went there. Assignations were made, loose women were on the lookout for men, all sorts rubbed shoulders with you, there were pickpockets, and plague, and Heaven knows what else. Actors were liars, anyway, she proclaimed. They pretended to be what they were not: boys dressing up as girls, poor men dressing up as courtiers and kings, and all sorts of other mischief. How could you trust such a place, or the people who worked there, or went there?

Yes. He'd just have to mention what he'd seen, and Master Page would hand over his wages, Hopewell was sure.

All was quiet. Hopewell crept out of his hole. He unloosened a stone in the cellar wall behind which he kept his few treasures. These were four jet buttons with gold trim, splendid things he'd saved painfully for; and a blue ribbon which he had bought as a birthday present for Annie, who was turning sixteen that week. He put them all carefully in the drawstringed purse he wore at his waist. He looked around the cellar for the last time, stretched happily, and wriggled out through the other side of the hole, into the alleyway behind the shop.

Free! He was free! The sun was shining, he had a fortune to make, he would no longer be tied down to drabness and boredom. They'd see, all of them, that he wasn't a ne'er-do-well, a mere dreamer, but an adventurer, a man of action!

First things first. He had to find Master Page. And he thought he knew just where the wheelwright might be at this time of day: in the Gadfly Tavern, with his cronies.

Mistress Page did not like it. 'Gadfly is as gadfly does!' she would snort. 'I'd gladly swat the lot of you buzzing fools, that's for sure!' But Master Page took no notice. Once a week, he met with his friends at the Gadfly, and nothing Mistress Page said or did would stop him. She might unwillingly put up with the Gadfly; but she'd never, *ever* forgive him the Globe. Maybe, seeing that was so, Master Page would give him more than his wages, to keep him quiet? Yes. With all that, Hopewell could easily buy himself the necessaries for his journey, and then more. Perhaps, if he had money enough, he'd buy a jacket, of some rich and shiny stuff, and get those buttons sewn on it . . . He'd get barbered, too, and fresh-pomaded, and smelling sweet as a rose, go and visit Annie. They'd go walking somewhere nice, and he'd tell her solemnly he was going to seek his fortune, and she'd cry a little, and cling to him, her eyes big and brimming. He'd prevail manfully over her tears, though, and part from her with sweet and tender words, words such as he'd heard at the Globe . . . 'Goodbye, sweet love,' he practised to himself as he trotted along the street, 'goodbye and may flights of angels guard you from all harm . . .' Oh, he could feel the tears starting even now. It would be such sweet, sweet, sorrow . . .

Alas! Reality can be a very bad stage manager indeed. When Hopewell reached the Gadfly, he found that Master Page was not at his accustomed bench with his accustomed cronies. What was more, the landlord stared at him suspiciously, and asked brusquely if Hopewell had been given a holiday by his employer. Hopewell fled, not stopping for breath until he was sure there was no hue-and-cry after him. He had no desire to be asked any more questions. Runaway apprentices were often severely punished.

Now what was he to do? He had no money. Only the jet buttons were of some value. For an instant Hopewell's bright nature drooped a little and his shoulders slumped. Then he straightened up. Never mind. He'd go and see

Annie, and explain his predicament. She'd lend him some money, perhaps, even: she always had spare. Then he'd go to the docks and offer his services. They were always after crew, weren't they? He would find a likely ship's captain and tell him that he was Will Shakespeare's cousin, or nephew or some such; that would impress them. He'd done it before, after all: Annie believed it fervently, he thought, with all the hero-worship of her sweet little heart. Amongst the other 'prentices who were good patrons of the Globe too, Hopewell had often strutted in the reflected sunlight of Will's glory, though he was careful to do it away from the ears of the Pages, who knew the full truth.

Two

Annie's mother, Widow Frail, whose name belied her appearance, owned a busy laundry not far from the Globe. It was hot and noisy, smelling of steaming clothes, yellow starch, and sweat. Not a place where one could easily imagine Annie, with her crushed-flower skin and gentle blue eyes. Indeed Widow Frail had great hopes for her only child, hopes that extended far beyond laundry fumes. Annie always had pretty clothes and had been coached in pretty manners and sweet speech by a tutor who used to teach minor noblemen's children. That is, until his carousing ways could no longer be ignored even by huntin' fishin' gentlemen whose idea of an education was swearing in Latin. Under Widow Frail's gimlet eye, however, the tutor had not dared to drink anything more enervating than lemon-barley water, and Annie had certainly learned some manners above her station: and no swearing in Latin, either.

Widow Frail had her eye on a good marriage for Annie, not to a nobleman or even a gentleman, for such did not like to sully their hands with trade. No; what she had in mind for Annie was a good solid merchant's son, heir to a business that would fit in with her own, perhaps: a tailor, or weaver, or dyer, or some such. She was certainly anything but sympathetic about penniless, heedless 'prentice boys courting Annie.

So Annie and Hopewell had had to keep their affections secret; hence the meetings at the Globe. That had been Annie's suggestion: she was even more affected by Hopewell's namesake's stories than her sweetheart was. She loved the intrigue of being, as it were, in a drama of their own. 'Star-cross'd lovers are we,' she'd said, dreamily, to Hopewell one day, echoing a line from *Romeo and Juliet*, and Hopewell had squeezed her hand, whispering, 'So we are, but the stars can be tempted off their paths, my honey-dear.' He was quite proud of that line – it wasn't in the play, but had popped out of his head unexpectedly. But Annie had just nodded, not seeming to realize those weren't William's words, but her sweetheart's. She had grown quite annoyed when Hopewell had tried to tell her, hushing him with fierce looks, saying she could not hear what the actors were saying, with him gabbing on so.

Hopewell skulked past the open door of the laundry. Good. The Widow Frail was there: busy boxing the ears of some hapless new girl who had not double-starched a ruff, or some such. It was likely Annie would be at home, in the walled garden perhaps, reading one of her many picture-books, hopefully without her maid Joanie. But it would not matter even if she was. Joanie loved a star-crossed lover as well as anyone, and she easily fell in with their plans.

Mind you, in the last couple of weeks, there had been a little coldness between Hopewell and Annie. Annie had proven a little elusive, and argumentative when she wasn't elusive, and so there hadn't been any Globe-trotting. But Hopewell was confident it would easily be sorted out. Things usually were, in his experience.

He scrambled up the garden wall, and peered over. Yes, Annie was alone. She was sitting under the apple tree, turning the pages of a book. In her red and green gown, she looked as flushed and sweetly round as one of the tree's own rosy fruits. Hopewell smiled, and softly sang a song from Annie's favourite play, *As You Like It*:

'It was a lover and his lass,
With a hey, and a ho, and a hey nonny-no . . .'

Her head jerked up from her book, her bright blue eyes startled. She dropped the book and came running.

'Oh, Hopewell, what are you doing up there!' she said, anxiously.

Hopewell looked proudly down at her. 'Do not be afraid, my sweet, I'd jump as high as the moon for you!' he said, and sprang lightly and gracefully to the ground – only to trip over a loose stone and sprawl in a most undignified heap at her feet.

'Oh, Hopewell,' repeated Annie, wringing her hands, 'what on earth are you doing?'

'What does it look like, Annie?' he grumbled as he got to his feet. He fumbled in his clothes for the ribbon; alas, it must have fluttered out when he'd jumped. He looked around for it, but could not see it.

'Hopewell, maybe you'd better . . .' His sweetheart was looking decidedly green around the gills, he thought, a little puzzled.

'Annie, what is wrong?'

'Nothing, nothing . . . just . . . I . . . Mother might come soon and I . . .'

Hopewell took one of her hands and looked into her face. 'Do not fear, sweet Annie. I will soon be gone. I have come to bid you goodbye, my sweet, my rose without thorns.'

She snatched her hand away, so quickly that a pin in her sleeve scratched Hopewell's wrist. 'Ow!' he said, reproachfully, sucking at the little wound.

But Annie took no notice. Her eyes shone with quick tears. 'I knew it,' she whispered, turning her head away, 'You have found another, and no longer love me . . .'

'Oh no, no, that's not it at all!' cried Hopewell in dismay. He had his speech ready. This was not her cue!

Annie drew herself up. 'Please, Hopewell,' she said, in a low, tragic voice, 'do not say to me that I am fair, and that your heart is wounded sore at having to choose between us. Just leave me to my pain, and my sorrow, as black as it is endless . . .'

Hopewell stared like a mooncalf. The bewilderment was strong in him, even more so because he had the strong suspicion that Annie was enjoying herself making this heart-rending speech. Before he could utter another word, however, his sweetheart lightly kissed her own fingers, and fluttered them towards his forehead.

'Farewell, then, sweet friend,' she said, and Hopewell saw that the tears were falling as softly down her cheeks

15

as the words fell from her pretty lips. 'May the angels of God keep you from harm, and give you wind for your sails as you set forth on your voyage away from me . . .'

'What the—' She had used some of his own words! He caught himself up, and went on, desperately, 'I'm off, Annie. Off on the—'

'I know, I know, sweet Hopewell. You are of Will's blood. You do not wish to wound my heart,' she said, infuriatingly. 'May the angels of God—'

'Heaven help us, woman!' Hopewell stuttered. 'I'm off to sea. To make my fortune, see? So's we can . . .'

But Annie wasn't listening. 'Farewell for ever, sweet friend,' she murmured. Slowly, tragically, the very picture of a spurned but dignified lover, she turned away.

At that moment, the door into the garden opened with a great rush. There stood a tall, stout young man, holding an elaborate nosegay of flowers. A fur-lined cloak, flung over sober dark clothes, and sensible, good-quality shoes made him look much older than his age, as did the fatuous smirk he wore on his face.

'Sweet Mistress Annie—' he began, then broke off abruptly as he caught sight of Hopewell.

In an instant, Hopewell understood. Annie was being courted by this rich fool! What was more, she had hoped Hopewell wouldn't find out. That was why she had been so nervous. She had hoped to get rid of him before this ass-head arrived!

'On guard!' he shouted at the startled stranger, drawing his sword. 'On guard, you blackguard!'

'What the . . .' the stranger stammered, dropping the flowers, and backing away. Menacingly, Hopewell advanced. Annie flew at him, with a furious passion.

'Don't you dare, Hopewell Shakespeare! Put up your sword! Leave him alone! Go away! It is over between us!'

'I say . . .' began the stranger, protestingly, but neither Annie nor Hopewell took any notice of his intervention.

'It was over long ago!' shouted Annie. 'It was your fault!'

'*My* fault?' Hopewell put his sword up. 'My fault, Annie?'

She waggled a finger at him. 'You see! You don't even know what I'm talking about! That proves it!'

'Does it?' said Hopewell, thoroughly fuddled.

The other youth coughed, and said, weakly, spreading his soft white hands, 'Er, perhaps I had better . . .'

'No!' retorted Annie, glaring at him now and not just at Hopewell. 'You will stay here, Master Giles. Until I tell you you may go.'

She sounded just like the Widow Frail. Master Giles blushed, but stayed put.

Annie flashed out at Hopewell, 'Two weeks ago, you did not answer my question – what you would do to keep my love – you did not answer because—'

'Because I did not hear you,' groaned Hopewell. Too late, he had remembered how the coldness between him and Annie had started.

'You did not hear me because you never hear me! You were off wool-gathering! In your dreams! As usual!' She frowned. 'Do not bother arguing, my friend. It is no use!'

Hopewell shook his head. 'No, it is not,' he agreed, sadly. Then he rallied. 'It was at the Globe you asked me. You don't like me talking during the plays . . .'

'Ha!' Annie tossed her head. 'It was not during the play, but after it. You were mooning still, staring at the stage. I knew then I came second, no matter what happened.'

The injustice of it stung Hopewell. 'It was always the Globe this, the Globe that, with *you*, Annie!'

'No,' she said, sharply, casting a sideways glance at her coxcomb of a suitor. 'It was *you* dragged me there, Hopewell. The Globe – what do I care about the Globe?'

He could only goggle at her.

Clearing his throat, Master Giles began, 'I say, I—'

'Be quiet,' said both Annie and Hopewell, together. Annie whirled on Hopewell.

'Master Giles is from a good family. He is wealthy, reliable, sensible. He does not spend his time dreaming of what can never be. He has offered for my hand in marriage, Hopewell. And I have accepted.'

Master Giles smiled at this. 'Yes, I am very—'

'Shut up,' said Hopewell, softly, dangerously, 'you yellow poltroon, you lily-gutted fool, you ass-headed, coxcombed gull.' He turned to Annie. ''Tis your mother wants this, isn't it? I'm not good enough for her.'

'Or for me,' said Annie, defiantly, though a tear glittered still in her eyes. ''Tis enough, Hopewell. You'll never do any good. You'll never know what the world really is. You'll never know what a woman wants. T'isn't enough to dream. You should forget dreams. The world is real.'

'Hark at her,' he said, sharply, 'and she sighing after words and dreams in a play!'

'I've done with all that,' she said, softly. 'Life is serious, Hopewell. It is a thing for a man. And you are just a boy, though you are past sixteen. You will always be just a boy.'

It was too much. Hopewell gave one last reproachful look, snorted twice to show what he thought of her, and strode manfully away from her and the anxiously-smiling Master Giles. He intended to go out of Annie's life in a blaze of tragic glory, but it is hard to do that when you must scramble like a thief over a wall.

Out in the street, he stood for a while and mopped his brow. Heaven help us, what traitors women were! She had meant all along to play with him, Hopewell, whilst always keeping a weather eye out for a rich man. But she had thought to put the blame on him. He thought of what she'd said when he first came over the wall, her evident anxiety. She'd been glad, he thought, glad that Hopewell had given her a way out which would rebound on him, rather than her. He shook his head. Well, rather Master Giles than him, then! He was welcome to Annie Frail, who'd turn into her own mother soon enough!

As he thought these vengeful thoughts, though, a funny forlorn feeling came over him. He saw Annie and himself at the Globe, cheering and laughing and crying. That would never happen again. Never. And he couldn't even remember it fondly any more, not after what she had said, disowning their times together at the Globe.

He was on his own now. Truly on his own. Nobody to care for him, nobody to know his dilemma. He couldn't tell his parents, the Pages were out of the question, and now even Annie had rejected him. Lord, what will happen to me, he thought, in a brief instant of panic. What . . . what if nobody wants me at the docks, either? What if I end up without anything, forced to work like a slave, like . . . like Meggie, the little street-sweeper near the Globe?

It was a horrible moment. But an instant's thought soon comforted him. He was nothing like Meggie. He had style, cleverness, hope. She had nothing except her broom. He had a future. She did not. Yes. No point moping about the past. One had to look to the future. He was sure of it. Sure.

Three

They say that when you think of the devil, you always
see his tail. And so, when you think of a street-sweeper,
you are bound to see her broom. In Hopewell's case,
you are bound to *trip over* her broom.

For the second time that day, Hopewell found himself
sprawling at the feet of a girl. Furious, muddy, he hauled
himself up again. 'You could have looked where you
were going, Meggie!'

She stood her ground, though she looked a little
scared. Long orphaned, Meggie had been working since
she was eight or nine. She was big-eyed, mop-haired
and thin as a half-starved cat, looking not her true age
of sixteen, but rather closer to twelve or thirteen. But
she seemed to like Hopewell, possibly because like her,
he loved everything that went on at the Globe, but more
likely because the young man was not as cruel to her as
most of the other 'prentices, and had even been known
to give her a kindly word or two. Indeed, only a couple
of weeks before, he had rescued her from a threatened
beating, by a dyer's 'prentice who was always too big for
his boots. Hopewell was handy with his fists, and had
acted instinctively when he came around the corner to

see the other 'prentice standing over Meg. Now he half wished he hadn't done it, because she would think he'd always be her protector. And he couldn't be. She had to survive as best she could. Everybody did, in this cruel world.

In any case, he found Meggie disturbing. It was not because she was a girl; she was too thin, too small, too nervous, too ugly for him to even think of her as a female. It was because just as a stray cat, despite her sticking-out ribs and staring fur, can remind you in a jungle instant that she is of the race of tigers, there was a kind of wildness to Meggie which made most people – apart from the dyer's apprentice, who'd been drunk, anyway – tread warily with her. Some people even said she was a witch, and called her Megwitch. Hopewell had no patience with such talk, but there was no gainsaying the fact that Meg was a strange and unusual little body.

He looked at her now as she cringed a little away from him, and felt his anger ebbing away. 'You should look where you put your broom,' he said to her, but kindly now. 'Some would not take very happily to ending up in the mud.'

Meg shook her head. 'Forgive me,' she muttered. Hopewell thought he could see tears in her eyes. He sighed. 'Never mind. Just be careful next time.'

She looked at him, and he caught a puzzling flash of a fleeting expression in her eyes. But before he could work out what that expression had been, she said, 'Where are you going, Hopewell? There's nothing on at the Globe, this time of day.'

Hopewell glanced past her, at the great polygon structure of the famous theatre rearing up to the sky, its bright yellow flag fluttering in the light breeze that came off the river. He felt a sharp pang. If he did what he meant to do – and he had to, now – when would he ever see the Globe again? 'I . . . I just felt like taking a look,' he muttered.

Her face brightened. 'I will come in with you.'

'You . . .' Hopewell began, then seeing her determined expression, he sighed. 'If you must.'

She clutched her broom. 'I will say I need to sweep the yard, if anyone asks.'

Hopewell shrugged, and hurried across to the entrance of the theatre. Though there was nothing on for a couple of hours or so, it was busy. People were coming in and out, carrying things, chatting, generally bustling; and nobody paid the pair of them the slightest attention.

The Globe was the best theatre in London; others, like the Fortune, tried to imitate it, but this was the best, no doubt about it. It was so big that nearly three thousand people could fit in it, in differing degrees of comfort. The most expensive seats were in the private boxes, but the covered galleries that ran along the three sides of the stage were quite comfortable, too. Sometimes, young bloods would pay extra to sit on hard chairs on the stage itself, peer at the actors, pass rude comments and generally make nuisances of themselves. But the majority of people, including Hopewell, of course, bought the cheapest places of all: standing-room only in the groundlings' yard in front of the stage. There, you were jostled, elbowed, you had to watch your purse carefully: but did that matter, if you could get a clear view? And Hopewell had become very good at using his elbows, his feet and his height to obtain the best vantage point.

He looked up at the stage. Supported on its twin pillars, it was like a world in itself. Up above it were the Heavens, where stage machinery, concealed by an upper balcony, could be used to magical effect. Below the stage was the place actors called Hell: a trapdoor through which people could disappear at given moments in a play. In between the two was the stage floor itself, the middle-earth where human passions, tragedies and dreams were played out, just as in the real world. Hopewell sighed, remembering . . .

Remembering Puck, skipping to the edge of the stage, squinting slyly into the upturned faces of the 'groundlings' amongst whom had been Hopewell and Annie. He whispered the words of Puck's final speech, from *A Midsummer Night's Dream*:

'If we shadows have offended
Think but this, and all is mended.'

Beside Hopewell, Meggie took a firmer grip on her broom. Her eyes glittered. '*That you have but slumbered here,*' she broke in quietly, continuing the quotation, '*While these visions did appear . . .*'
Hopewell glanced at her, then away.

'And this weak and idle theme,
No more yielding but a dream . . .'

24

A dream! No one wanted those, did they? His glance fell on the upstairs balcony. A sharp pain gripped at him. He remembered clutching Annie's hand when Romeo called up to his ladylove Juliet as she stood there on the balcony.

'But, soft! What light through yonder window breaks?
It is the east, and Juliet is the sun . . .'

They had been true to each other, those two. Nothing could break their love; not even death could part them. Unlike Annie, whose eyes had overflown with tears at the sight of the lovers' fate, but who had thrown over her own lover with happy abandon, when money hove near! Hopewell gritted his teeth. What if Juliet had done the same? What if she had married Paris, as her parents wanted, instead of staying true to Romeo? What then? Poor play indeed that would have made!

This time, he did go, sweeping out through the entrance with Meg hurrying after him. He was done with it all, he thought, done with London, done with faithless women. He strode off away from the Globe, towards the river, but Meg kept following. At last he stopped, and whirled crossly on her. 'Go away, Meggie. Leave me be.'

The street-sweeper looked at him consideringly, her head on one side, her eyes narrowed. Her earlier timidity seemed to have fallen away. 'Hopewell, that is not the way back to the Pages', she said. 'Have you run away from the Pages?'

Hopewell started violently. He stared at her, unable to say a word. How had she known? He thought uneasily

25

of her witchy reputation. He didn't believe in it, but . . .

She smiled, a little bitterly. 'You don't want to tell me,' she said. 'You think I might tell Master Page. But I keep my mouth shut. How many times have I seen you going to the Globe, for instance, with that girl, Widow Frail's girl? But did I tell the Widow? No. I'd *never* tell.'

Hopewell had a sudden vision of the street-sweeper making her offended way back to Master Page's house, and telling him that she'd seen his runaway apprentice. She said she'd never tell, but he'd had one example already today of the treachery of women, and so from now on he'd do best not to trust anyone of that sex, especially not a witchy little creature like her. Anyway, all going well, he would be well away by the time the wheelwright and his wife came puffing and snorting like dyspeptic dragons down to the port, looking for him, but you never knew. His mind whirled. He put on his best borrowed feathers of pretty speech.

'Meg,' he said, beckoning her closer. 'There's something I must tell you, my sweet friend.'

My sweet friend? That was a master stroke. Meg's thin cheeks would have pinked with pleasure, if you could have noticed such a ladylike thing as a flush on her tough, pale skin. She came closer, her eyes Globe-bright.

'There is a burden on my shoulders,' declaimed Hopewell, quite enjoying his own words. 'Dark things are in the offing, my dear friend.'

'Dark things?' whispered Meg.

'Dark things,' repeated Hopewell, nodding his head gravely. 'Desperate things,' he added, after a pause. 'I go in secrecy, to the very doors of danger, Meg. So, will you let me pass? More, will you keep your lips sealed for my sake, come what may?'

Meg nodded, speechlessly. Her thin cheeks were scarlet, her eyes very bright.

'I go on the high seas, to balm my heart and make my fortune. Seek not to follow me, for where I go, no sweet maid may follow,' said Hopewell, with what he thought was a suitably manly look of secret sorrow. He put a hand gently on Meg's arm. She started wildly, like a surprised cat, throwing off his touch.

'No sweet maid may follow,' repeated Meg, in tones that suddenly made Hopewell feel most uncomfortable. 'I will keep your secret, Hopewell. Always.' Meg looked up into his face, for one instant, and then she sighed, deeply. 'I must go,' she said, quietly. 'There is work to be done.' And, shouldering her broom, she trudged away, without another word or look, leaving Hopewell standing there in a mixture of bewilderment, unease, and relief.

Lord, he'd be glad to be out of London, if only not to have to clap eyes on Meggie again. For he had the terrible feeling that he had stirred up something in her fierce little tiger's heart that would not easily be laid to rest. His skin prickled for an instant, and then he shrugged, well pleased with himself again. He was fairly sure now that Meggie would rather be racked than reveal to anyone that she had seen him, and where he had gone.

Hopewell had been to the port several times before. He liked to watch the ships being loaded and unloaded, and the strange sights that you saw down there sometimes, especially the men of all sorts of colours and shapes and dress. Once, he'd seen an Irish chieftain disembarking with a gaggle of bodyguards, or *gallowglasses*, as they were called. They had been an extraordinary sight, in their animal skins and tattooed faces and great gold and silver jewellery, as outlandish as Red Indians, with a superb pride of bearing that had amazed Hopewell. For it was as though they did not realize they had come to the hub of the world, and should feel grateful for being there. No, it was more as if they felt they graced London by their presence, and took the crowd of onlookers for admirers. Not that Hopewell or anyone else there that day begrudged them their bit of foolishness: for with an elegant flourish of his hands, the chieftain ordered his gallowglasses to shower coins on the crowd. Hopewell had got himself a scratched face and bruised shin as well as a handful of coins, scrabbling among all that rowdy lot. Still, he'd come down a few more times after that, hoping the wild Irish might turn up again to distribute largesse: but in vain. Mind you, he hadn't been the only one.

Today, unfortunately for his empty pockets, there were no wild Irish in sight. Perhaps it was just the time of day, or perhaps it was a quiet day, but the port was not very busy. There were a few ordinary-looking ships unloading cargo of a rather prosaic kind; sacks of grain, bolts of cloth, bawling, yelling livestock. None of the ships looked as if they had come from far away, or were heading far away. They seemed solid, settled, boring. Sensible. Without any dream quality at all. Working on them would be like working for the Pages. No.

Hopewell sauntered along, hoping to find something better. A man hoping to mend a broken heart, or a man in search of a glittering fortune – he wasn't sure which of these pictures of himself he preferred – must have a ship to suit his destiny. A galleon of life, he thought to himself, superb and proudly dignified, as would his life be from now on. Not some broken-down old nag of a thing that limped up and down the Thames carrying unglamorous goods. A ship, he thought, seeing it in his mind's eye, a ship of rare power and majesty. It would be a vast, castled galleon, of rare scented wood; with pure, white, silken sails; and a figurehead on it of a lovely lady with the fairest hair and the bluest eyes. It would carry gold and jewels and costly perfumes, and always glide before the wind like a great white bird. Inside, it would have a cabin like a palace just for him, with rare and costly hangings, and golden plate, and cages full of exotic birds singing in strange tongues . . .

'Cousin dear, will you buy my goods . . .' a whining, decidedly unexotic voice interrupted his gorgeous thoughts. Hopewell turned to find a dirty, snotty beggar child with a basket of shabby trinkets on her arm. 'Pretty gewgaws, just for you . . . or your lass, coz . . .'

'I need nothing,' said Hopewell, superbly, striking a pose and playing up to his vision of himself. 'And I have no lass, for she proved untrue. I just have my courage, and boldness, to set out on adventure.'

The beggar child looked at him and grinned. 'Well, good luck to you then, coz.' And with that, she thrust something at him – a scrap of dirty mirror. Startled, Hopewell could do nothing else but take it. 'I have no money to pay you,' he warned, but the girl shook her head. ' 'Tis a gift; a pretty gift, for a pretty boy, coz!'

Hopewell coloured just a little. Decidedly, he was having a lot of success with the ragamuffins of the female persuasion today! 'Wait,' he said, kindly, 'there might be something I . . .' He turned to fumble in his purse – and discovered it had been expertly cut, and the jet buttons vanished. He spun around back to the girl – but of course she had disappeared, in the seemingly supernatural way of her kind.

'Oh, curse it, and double curse it, caught by the oldest trick ever!' he shouted, incensed, and flung the glass she had given him into the mud, earning himself several curious looks from passing sailors. He stood there fuming for a moment, then stooped down, picked up the looking glass, wiped it carefully, and put it in his pocket. His buttons, which he could have sold, were gone. But you never knew. Perhaps he might be able to exchange the bit of glass for something useful, like food.

Food! He was aware now that he was hungry, very hungry. He badly needed something to eat. All these emotions had given him a huge appetite.

He looked up the docks. A short distance away was a sailors' tavern. Oh! For a jug of ale, and a meat pie, fragrant with herbs, Hopewell thought hungrily. But how could he get them? He could throw himself on the charity of the landlord . . . or find some sympathetic soul who might help. Well, it was worth a try. He squared his shoulders, and strode over to the tavern.

Four

Inside, it was very noisy, and close, with a thick fug of stale smells of all kinds, river water and sweat and beer and stewed meat. A few dozen men and fewer women were packed in like sardines around the wooden tables, yelling and laughing and singing and fighting. No one took any notice of Hopewell whatsoever as he approached the rough wooden counter where the landlord, a grizzled, brawny man with the tattooed arms and raffish look of an ex-pirate, was busy pouring brimming jugs of ale.

'Master,' said Hopewell, rather hesitantly, 'I wondered if . . . I am looking for work on a ship . . .'

He'd intended at first to ask the man if by his charity he could spare some food, but had made an instant decision that that would probably be the wrong move. As it was, the landlord merely laughed. His small eyes wrinkled up into glittering slits, his mouth was full of yellow teeth. Looking around at the other men around about the counter, as if appealing to an audience, he drawled, 'You ever been near water, son?'

'I can swim,' said Hopewell, drawing himself up.

'Very useful,' observed the landlord, nodding his head

wisely, but with a glint in his eyes which made Hopewell very annoyed indeed.

'I'm a true-born Englishman, and I want adventure, to capture Spanish gold, and bring honour and treasure to my country,' said Hopewell, hotly. The landlord laughed again, and most of the crowd laughed with him.

'Wouldn't we all,' said the landlord, languidly, at last. 'But those days are over, son. The Spanish are wise to us. It's a much harder life, being a privateer, than it used to be. You should have been born ten or fifteen years ago, if it's adventure and honour and treasure you want. Now . . . well, hard-headed business rules. And runaway 'prentice boys, landlubbers like you with stars in their eyes, are no use to real ships' masters. Best forget your dreams, and go back to your master, before it's too late.'

Hopewell coloured, and swallowed. Was it as obvious as that? He glanced around at the circle of faces and saw no sympathy there, only amused contempt, rather fuddled by carousing. He lifted his head high, but his voice came out a little stammering. 'Very well then, if that is what the spirit of England has become. If we are no longer a band of brothers, we happy few, we . . .'

Gales of laughter interrupted him, for in his agitation, Hopewell had quoted half-remembered words from one of Will Shakespeare's most popular plays, *Henry V*. Hopewell blushed as the landlord, still chuckling, said, 'You're no King Hal, son, rallying the troops!'

'Not even a Pistol or a Nym, I should think,' said a customer, grinning villainously, making everyone go off into peals of laughter again. Pistol and Nym were crowd-pleasing rascals in the very same play; rallying the troops was certainly not their strong point.

'Best be on your way, boy,' said the landlord, not altogether unkindly. 'And a word to the wise. If you want a job on a ship, best forget that fancy speech of yours. Good enough on stage – but not in real life, friend.'

Hopewell gave him a disdainful look. Without another word, he turned on his heel and went out. But their raucous laughter followed him, ringing in his ears.

It was well and truly dusk now, and a fog had come down over the river. The water slapped against wooden hulls, seabirds were roosting for the night. The port looked bleak and sad. Not a place for dreams. Hopewell walked blindly along, stomach growling, head whirling. The landlord's words had stung him. It was not only the fact that he'd so easily seen that Hopewell was a runaway apprentice; it was those other words, about him being of no use. What did that man know? Nothing. He wasn't a ship's master, not even a sailor; he was just a landlubber himself, the owner of a dirty, smelly tavern. What would he know? Nothing! He had no idea of Hopewell's qualities, of his strength, his courage, his willingness. Best forget your dreams indeed! He was the second person today who'd said that to Hopewell. They had no idea. If you forgot your dreams, you forgot your soul. Yes, indeed! Hopewell marched along with renewed vigour. He'd show them! He'd show them all! He would! He'd . . .

'Oof!' Absorbed in his thoughts, he'd cannoned into

someone hurrying from the opposite direction. He glared at the person. 'Really, sir, you should be . . .' Then he stopped. This was certainly no ordinary sailor, no rough Thames boatman either, but an extraordinary-looking man, one about whom something indefinable clung, some presence of greatness, some glamorous quality that made Hopewell catch his breath. He looked more closely at the stranger. He was tall, well-formed, clad in rich, fashionable, black, silk clothes, his feet shod in boots of the finest white leather. He had black hair shot through with silver, a curled beard that was equally frosted, and a hard, still face that must have been very handsome when younger, but though still striking, was now scored with the marks of old scars, and fine wrinkles. He wore two or three fine rings on strong wide hands whose bones were almost painfully prominent; and his long-lashed eyes were of an amazing colour, a kind of grey-brown, the colour of a winter river, with not a trace of age in them. At his side he carried a sword of unusual shape and size, encased in a finely decorated scabbard. He was a total stranger; and yet, there was something familiar about him to Hopewell, something he couldn't quite place.

'Forgive me, friend,' said the stranger, speaking in a well-modulated, rich voice that held the suggestion of laughter in it. 'I was so intent on my way that I did not see you looming there in the dusk.' He spoke to Hopewell in a way no one had spoken to him before – in the manner not exactly of an equal, but with respect, and courtesy. It was so unexpected, so pleasant, that Hopewell found himself stammering heartfelt apologies.

The man nodded, gently. 'You look all in, my friend. What can be the matter? Can I perhaps be of any help?'

Hopewell was astonished, and warmed by the real interest in the man's tone. But he was a little wary, nonetheless. The stranger saw his hesitation, and smiled, a little sadly. 'Do not fear, my friend. Your secret is safe with me. I have kept many secrets in my time. Many secrets indeed. Too many for my own good.' He paused. 'Perhaps you know who I am?'

Hopewell looked at him, the familiarity gnawing at the corners of his mind, and also the sense of that quality about the man, the presence of greatness. He said, 'I . . . I am sure I do, sir, but your name . . . it escapes me.'

The man sighed again. He looked out at the river, and Hopewell saw muscles tightening at the sides of his mouth.

'I am Richard Wolfe,' he said.

Hopewell stared. His heart lurched. He gabbled, 'Captain Richard Wolfe? The great Captain Wolfe?'

'You do know me, then,' said Wolfe, with a kind of weary dignity. But a little smile played around his lips.

'Oh, who does not know of Captain Richard Wolfe and his ship the *Golden Dragon*!' breathed Hopewell. 'All London knows of you; nay, not only London, the whole country! The very barbarous Scots in their savage lairs must hear your name, and tremble, sir!'

Wolfe smiled slightly. 'A pretty conceit, boy,' he said. 'But, alas – the fame you speak of – 'tis long gone . . .'

'Oh no, sir!' said Hopewell, fervently. 'The fame I speak of lives for ever! It still clings to you, sir! Golden as your ship! I can see it!' Indeed, he thought, that was what the quality that clung to the man must be – the aura of fame, the golden nimbus of great deeds. Softly, he went on, 'I have heard wondrous things of you, sir. I have heard of marvellous battles at sea with the Spaniard, and booty captured beyond compare; I have heard of countless enemy ships being sent to the bottom, and the *Golden Dragon* laden to the gunwales with Spanish gold! I have heard of our great Queen herself receiving you in private audience, and of the useless fulminations of Spanish Philip! Oh, sir! You made the name of England ring golden and clear on the wide wild seas, and the very waves themselves still proclaim your glory!'

Wolfe regarded Hopewell thoughtfully. The muscles around the side of his mouth trembled into a small, sad smile. 'All gone,' he said, softly. 'Yes, I served my country well . . . but my country did not serve me well. I had to go to foreign lands to be received with any degree of respect. Ah! Drake may well have made his fortune; but Richard Wolfe, who was greater by far than he, was hounded like a dog!'

Hopewell said nothing. There was a depth of angry sadness to the man's voice which was unlike anything Hopewell had never heard before. Wolfe pushed a hand through his hair and went on, lightly, 'But that is all old history too. The future is before me again!' He peered at Hopewell. 'What is your name, friend?'

Hopewell drew himself up. His heart took up a steady tabor – rhythm, thump, thump, thump thump. 'My name, sir, is Hopewell Shakespeare.'

'Hopewell *Shakespeare*,' repeated the privateer. 'Ah. I understand.'

Hopewell knew at once what the man meant. A blush of sheer pride and excitement flamed through him. 'He is my cousin, sir,' he said, keeping his voice steady. 'My distant cousin,' he added, with a cautious honesty.

'Not so distant, then,' said Wolfe, smiling; and Hopewell flushed again at the compliment.

'I love fine words, and writing, sir,' he said. 'It may be in the blood.' He waited, breathlessly, thinking that something good was coming, and he was not disappointed in that, for Wolfe, smiling, said, 'I am glad of that, for I need someone just like you, with words in his blood, to make his fortune.'

Ha! thought Hopewell, if only all those doubting Thomases could have heard that! No dreams, no fancy speech, a word to the wise, hmmm! What did they know, those fools?

Wolfe went on, 'Do you know Latin, or Greek?'

Hopewell's face fell a little. But he rallied bravely. 'A little, sir,' he said cautiously. Of course he had only a few scraps of Latin, such as he had remembered from petty school and the grammar school where he'd gone for only a year before being expelled for his laziness. Greek he had none; but he was sure something would occur to him, when the time came. He could read well enough in English, which was more than most apprentices could do; his father had made sure of that.

'Well, that is all to the good,' said Wolfe, 'for indeed if you had said you knew it well, I would not have believed you. If you had said you knew it not at all, I would have taken you for a dullard, who could spin no pretty words. It is not Latin or Greek I need.'

'*Sir?*'

'Pray call me Captain, or Master,' said Wolfe, with a humorous twitch to his lips. 'I am not yet knighted.'

'Oh, but, sir . . . er, Captain, you soon will be, I am sure!' exclaimed Hopewell. 'You have long been gone from public view, but now you are back, things will change, I am sure. And with the favour of the Queen—'

Wolfe made a sudden, impatient gesture. His eyes had gone as cold as the Thames. 'Perhaps,' he said, forbiddingly, and Hopewell understood that there was to be no more mention of such things; but what did it matter? Life was opening up before him. Fortune was really smiling on him.

'So,' said Wolfe, smiling again, 'you truly want to make your fortune?' Hopewell nodded eagerly. 'Well, then,' the privateer went on, 'do you want to sail the seas with Wolfe of the *Golden Dragon*?'

'Sail the seas on the *Golden Dragon*?' Hopewell could hardly bring out the words. 'Oh, sir, I did not know it was still . . .'

'I have refurbished her, and she is equipped for perhaps her greatest voyage, the greatest adventure of her entire career,' said Wolfe, abruptly. 'We will be sailing shortly. It is a small and hand-picked crew I have for this voyage, Hopewell. And I should like you to be in it.'

'Oh, sir! I . . .' Hopewell could not finish his sentence. Blood roared in his ears and flooded his body with red light. Wolfe leaned towards him. 'We need men of strength and courage, who know how to keep their mouths shut and their hearts open,' he said, quietly. 'Do you have that in you, Hopewell Shakespeare?'

'Oh, sir . . . er, Master Wolfe, it is all I have ever wanted, to sail the seven seas with merry sailors on a privateer's ship, it has ever been in my dearest dreams, to bring honour and glory back to my country, and . . . I know how to keep my mouth shut and my heart open . . . and I will do anything . . . anything . . . to . . .' Hopewell couldn't say any more, he was suffocated with joy, with a flooding happiness, with an excitement that was so great he thought he might die from the thrill of it.

'Good. Good.' Wolfe paused. 'Now, Hopewell. Are there any folk here in London whom you need to bid farewell?'

'No, sir . . . er, Captain . . . but my parents . . . I should write to them, so that they—'

'You are not to tell them where you are going,' snapped Wolfe. 'You are to say only that you have found employment with a ship's master, and will be gone on a long voyage. You will tell them not to fear for you,' he went on, seeing Hopewell's expression, 'for you will be quite safe. And well rewarded. Very well rewarded indeed. But I would prefer it if you did not tell them more than that. Do you understand, Hopewell?'

Hopewell nodded. 'Of course, Captain Wolfe. I understand.'

'Very well.' Wolfe looked hard at him, then smiled, and clapped him on the shoulder. 'You'll do,' he said. 'I am glad to have met you, Hopewell Shakespeare. Come with me.'

Five

Wolfe did not say any more to Hopewell, but hurried along, humming instead under his breath. Hopewell did not mind; he felt almost as if wings had sprouted on his heels, like a veritable Mercury. All unease was banished in the splendid thoughts that rushed and washed over him like a great, sweet, golden wave. Captain Wolfe was glad to have met him! He had chosen him to be in his hand-picked crew! Hopewell would make his fortune! He would sail on the *Golden Dragon*! He would become a privateer, and return laden with gold and jewels! He would fight a dozen, a hundred Spaniards, and be covered with honours by the Queen! He would land on wondrous faraway islands of silver sands and azure skies, and learn a dozen strange languages! He would return and buy a grand mansion in London and become known as the second greatest privateer after the great Captain Richard Wolfe! Ah! His famous cousin, Will Shakespeare himself, would come knocking at the door of his mansion, and humbly ask him for details of his travels, to embroider into his plays at the Globe! And he would say, ah he would say, with a kind of graceful condescension, 'Yes, Will, *you* adventure in your mind, but I, I have been on *real* adventures!' As to Annie, she would likely come to him on bended knees and beg him to look kindly on her again, but he would look masterful and mysterious, and speak of the sweet, dusky maidens he had met on his voyages . . . and she would be jealous, oh, so jealous, she who would only be that fat fool's bored wife! She would stamp her feet, and her face would grow red, and her eyes bulge, and then he would dismiss her from his presence, just like that! And then, he'd go courting someone far better, a beautiful, noble lady with—

'Here we are.' Wolfe's voice cut into his dreams. Hopewell blinked. Here they were indeed. There, in front of him, bobbing gently on the tide, was the famous pirate ship, the *Golden Dragon*, lit up with torches and flares, with sailors swarming all over it, getting it ready for the voyage.

A tiny dismay somersaulted in Hopewell's breast. The ship was smaller and shabbier than he had expected. In his imagination, the *Dragon* had had the grandeur and terror of its namesake, huge and mighty, with golden timbers and terrifying fire-red sails. But this dragon looked more like the laidly worm of the old stories; not a splendid, graceful thing, but a small, plain galleon which had seen better days. It was about a hundred and twenty feet long, dark and unpolished, with a height at mainmast of about ninety-two feet. It had a large sail area, but the sails were of a rather greyish canvas rather than the splendid red silk Hopewell had imagined. Only the figurehead, a snarling golden dragon's head, freshly painted, was everything Hopewell could have wished for, and suited the saturnine splendour of her master.

'Isn't she a most beautiful sight, Hopewell . . .' Wolfe's face had softened as he looked at his vessel, and Hopewell said eagerly, 'Oh, yes, she is a most gallant ship, and sturdy.'

'She is, that.' Wolfe's face softened with a kind of love. 'She has been in many adventures, boy, and ever acquitted herself nobly. She has not been to sea for a while, for I had to keep her in dry dock, till I could . . . till I could have enough to deck her out again. But now she is worthy again, and strong, for this the finest of all our adventures together!'

'Yes, Captain,' said Hopewell, his spirits rising again. What did it matter if the ship had the elegance of an old earthworm? What mattered, indeed, was her reputation, and that of her master. And that was indeed no made-up story, but simple truth.

At that moment, a man detached himself from the crowd of sailors who were busily loading the *Golden Dragon*, and came towards them. Small, brightly dressed, with crooked teeth and a villainous scar on his right cheek, he had a surly, discontented face and flat, dark eyes, and the smallest, whitest hands Hopewell had ever seen on a man. Hopewell disliked him on sight. He seemed to return the compliment, for his gaze at Hopewell was distinctly unfavourable.

'Davy,' said Wolfe, with a sardonic glance at the two of them, 'this is Hopewell Shakespeare. He is coming with us.'

'I have already hired a galley boy,' said Davy. 'And we do not need any more powder monkeys.' In contrast to his appearance, he had a deep, melodious voice with strong Welsh intonations in his speech.

'Is that so? You had not hired a galley boy this morning.'

'I found one, just now. Kit Sly by name. He came to me for work.' He shot an unfavourable look at Hopewell.

Wolfe smiled. 'Let us hope his work is more felicitous than his name, then, Davy.'

'Names mean little,' said Davy, stolidly.

Wolfe laughed shortly. 'My poor friend! And you a Welshman! Where then is the poetry in your soul?'

Davy did not answer. Wolfe sighed. 'In any case, Hopewell is to be part of the crew, for I have decided. He is just right, Davy.'

'Ah,' said Davy. He looked Hopewell up and down, with unmistakable contempt, and Hopewell flushed bright red, as much from sudden panic as from anger.

Wolfe laughed softly. 'Davy, Davy, you must trust me.' A complicated look passed between the men, and Wolfe's tone changed, became hard and menacing. 'Hopewell *must* come with us.'

The other man stared back at him, his face still, his eyes unreadable. At length Davy nodded, rather curtly. 'You are the captain, Dick. You will know what is best.'

'I am glad you remember that,' said Wolfe, still in that hard tone. Then he went on, his voice softening, 'And *I* do not forget what I owe you, Davy; I do not forget that you are a partner in this great enterprise of ours.'

'That is well,' said Davy Jones, stolidly. His eyes were still on Hopewell, and the young man thought: He

44

dislikes me. Why? It is almost as if he does not want me on the ship. What has he got to lose with me coming aboard? And why did Captain Wolfe say I was just right? What sort of work does he have planned for me? But he said nothing, and after a moment of scrutiny, Davy Jones looked away.

'Everything is ready, Dick,' he said to Wolfe. 'We can be on our way at any time, as soon as the wind is with us. There's just one thing that I—' Catching sight of Hopewell's openly curious face, he growled, 'Get you gone, boy. Captain Wolfe and I have things to talk about, things not for your ears.'

Hopewell glared at him, and looked questioningly at Wolfe, who smiled a little, and handed him a couple of silver coins. 'Here. If you want to eat, or to send word to your parents, Hopewell, now's the time.'

'Oh sir . . . Captain . . . thank you.'

'Don't thank me. Be back here before dawn. We may well sail on the morning tide, if there's a good nor 'easter wind to speed us on our way.' And he turned away to speak to Davy.

Hopewell stood irresolute for an instant, his fingers clenched around the coins; then catching Davy's black look at him, sauntered off, pretending to take a great deal of interest in the ship, his head aching with questions. Pretty soon, though, the pretence of interest became real. He watched the busy activity on the ship with growing excitement; the loading of barrels of food and water, of live chickens and goats and sheep, of gunpowder and ammunition, of all kinds of household implements and items, the readying of armoury and galley and bilge and decks. This sturdy little ship was going to be his world for weeks, perhaps even months, maybe even years – who knew? And the people on board her, the crew, would become closer to him than anyone else in his life before . . . How strange to think that, how exciting to be on the edge of this great adventure! Where would they be going? Wolfe had not said, exactly, but it must be a fair distance, to judge from the supplies – they must be sailing to geat treasure, to the New World, somewhere . . . . How odd it was, to look at the ship bobbing on the greasy river water, close to shore, and think of her out on the high seas, frail as a walnut but gallant with human endeavour, gallant as the spirit of her master!

Oh! Hopewell frowned. Why, *why* did a great man, a captain as noble and brave as Richard Wolfe, have to rely on such an ill-featured ruffian as that Welshman! Yet he'd said it had been a hand-picked crew. So he must have picked Davy. And if so, why? He would bear some watching, Hopewell thought.

'Here, kitty, kitty . . .' Hopewell jumped at the voice behind him, and turning, saw a skinny young boy dressed in ill-fitting rags, pouncing on a small cat as thin and unprepossessing as he was. Succeeding in his task, the boy stood up, the unprotesting cat under his arm, and grinned at Hopewell. Hopwell looked back at him without much favour.

He had a narrow, pinched brown face, all except for the colour the typical face of a London street urchin, and bright, but expressionless hazel eyes. His black hair was closely, and badly, cropped, with almost bald patches in places, as if someone had taken a vengeful set of shears to it. As probably they had, to get rid of the armies of lice that had likely lived in his hair! His ears were small and close to his skull; his full lips were set in a friendly line and his voice was high and squeaky. 'She's comin' with us, this one. Master Jones says she be a good one for a ship's cat!' He looked curiously at Hopewell. 'You be for the *Golden Dragon* too, friend?'

Hopewell did not like the familiar way in which the boy spoke to him. He said, a touch frostily, 'I was hand-picked by Captain Wolfe, yes.'

'Ah!' said the boy, nodding. 'And I be hand-picked too, by Master Jones! I be the galley boy with the cook, Master William Gotham!' He stroked the cat, and gave Hopewell a sidelong look. 'What's your name, then, Master Hand-picked?'

'Hopewell Shakespeare,' said Hopewell, shortly. The boy nodded, seemingly not impressed by the name or its associations.

'Me name's Kit Sly,' he said. 'And this is me first sea voyage. You a greenhorn too, like me?'

Hopewell raised an eyebrow. 'I've been hand-picked by the Captain,' he repeated, frostily.

'Yes, I know, my friend,' said Kit cheerfully, 'but happen that's because we're both greenhorns, eh? Now, if you will forgive me, Hopewell Shakespeare, I have to get kitty settled into her new quarters.' He spoke as if Hopewell himself had held him up instead of the other way around. Hopewell opened his mouth to say something cutting to the cheeky galley boy, when he realized he was speaking to the empty air. Kit Sly had vanished.

Hopewell stood looking after him for an instant. Then he shook himself. He had a couple of coins to spend on some good food, a letter to write, and some sleep to catch before dawn. Before the adventure of his life really began.

Six

Hopewell had never been on a seagoing vessel before. On a barge, yes, and of course on the fast little skiffs that hurtled up and down the Thames, for the waterway was by far an easier road in London than the traffic-choked narrow streets. Now he stood with his feet firmly planted on the red-painted deck of a real ship, of the kind that was making England both rich and feared. He took a deep breath. He, Hopewell Shakespeare, would soon be of that dashing race of men who pluck riches from the sea, and who cruise the great oceans of the world, looking for adventure!

A sudden swell in the river below caused the ship to lurch alarmingly, and Hopewell almost fell over, earning himself a very ripe curse from a sailor who was just at that moment trying to get past him with his back bent under a huge barrel. Stammering excuses, he righted himself and stepped back, cannoning straight into Davy Jones.

'Dick, Dick, what've you done, taking this flummery-footed landlubber with us now,' grumbled Davy in his beautiful voice, scowling horribly. 'You'd best learn to get some sea legs soon, boy, or by God's bones, once we're at sea, you'll be pitchin' headlong into the waves!'

It sounded like a threat rather than a warning, even though Wolfe, following him, laughed heartily.

'Better flummery-footed than leaden-heeled, Davy,' he said. Turning to Hopewell, he said, 'So, boy? Spent a good enough night? Ready for everything?' He looked bright and cheerful this morning, even in the grey, dawn light, and there was a suppressed excitement in the way he moved.

'Yes, sir,' said Hopewell, who had, actually, spent an atrocious night catnapping fitfully on a pile of straw at the back of a tavern. But who cared about broken sleep when you were set to make your fortune? 'Oh sir,' he went on, clasping his hands together, 'such a great adventure I have never yet been in! To sail the vasty seas, with a captain frank and bold, and a crew of honest men of our own isles, is that not every man's dream?'

'Does he not speak well, Davy?' said Wolfe. When Davy only grunted, Wolfe went on, smiling, 'Davy's a man with a head hard as oak, but a heart of pure gold, Hopewell, and you'd do well to remember that.'

'Yes, sir . . . er Captain Wolfe,' said Hopewell, his eyes meeting Davy's expressionless glance.

Captain Wolfe said, 'The wind is just right, and the tide, Hopewell. We sail this morning – to the Lost Island!'

'The Lost Island, sir?'

Wolfe smiled. 'Yes.' A pause, then he went on, 'Come, Hopewell, you have not seen all over the *Golden Dragon* yet, have you?'

'No, sir, but I should love to,' said Hopewell, eagerly.

'Hmmm,' said Davy, turning away with a disgusted look.

He'd thought last night it was like a little world, and indeed it was, or like a floating, noisy village, complete with domestic animals. Hopewell was all eyes and ears as he followed Wolfe through the ship, through main deck and gun deck and foredeck and fo'c'sle and down even to the hold, to oversee that everything was correctly stored and stowed. And if this was a village, then Wolfe was its lord, a lord, by all that Hopewell could see, obeyed without question, and with respect.

At length, after a long tour of inspection, they went back to the half-deck, where was the captain's cabin. Having seen the cramped sailors' living quarters on the gun deck, where men slept on the floor, rolled in blankets, when not on their duties, Hopewell was expecting a palatial space: and hoping that he would be accommodated there too. But the cabin they entered was a very different thing to what he had imagined. Compared to the wheelwright's own chamber back in London, for instance, it was certainly nothing to crow about. Indeed, it was only just a little bigger than Hopewell's own poky little broom closet of a room, back there at the Pages'. It had very little furniture, apart from an oak table with a small mountain of papers neatly stacked on it, and a three-branched candlestick; a high-backed chair, two narrow curtained beds built into the wall, and a storage chest. That was all. No rich and costly hangings, no golden decorations, no exotic birds in cages calling out greetings in strange tongues. The only concession to decoration was one picture on the wall, a rather nice picture, to be sure, showing a magnificent galleon with bright, red sails, flying serenely across a calm blue sea: obviously some flattering artist's attempt at depicting the *Golden Dragon*. No picture of Wolfe's patron, if he had a patron; no picture of a ladylove, or of the Queen.

He glanced over rather nervously at the privateer. Captain Wolfe had gone straight in to sit down at the table, pulling the stack of papers towards him, and appeared to be deep in contemplation. Hopewell shifted from one foot to the other, wanting desperately to speak but afraid to.

'Sir,' he began, hesitantly, at last. 'Why does Master Jones mislike me so much?'

Wolfe looked up. He spoke without heat. 'Mislike you, Hopewell? Now why would he do that?'

Hopewell stared at him. Was that not the question he himself had asked? Confused, he managed to say, 'I . . . I have no notion why he should, sir.'

'Why, then, you do not need to concern yourself with it, do you?'

'No, sir, I suppose I do not. But I rather fancy that . . .'

Wolfe gave a sigh, and pushed back his chair. 'Butts are for filling with malmsey,' he said. 'And fancy is for milk-fed girls. If you understand that, Hopewell, you will get on in my ship.'

'Yes, sir,' said Hopewell, rather dashed. He was silent a moment, then burst out with, 'I am very grateful to you, sir, for your kindness and your gentleness. I had no notion that Fortune would smile on me this way.'

Wolfe regarded him without speaking. Then he passed a weary hand through his black hair, and gave another deep sigh. 'You speak well, Hopewell Shakespeare,' he said, very quietly, turning back to his papers. 'But you speak too much.'

After that, how could Hopewell ask him anything? He stood in an agony of embarrassed indecision, wondering if, after all, he had made the right choice in accepting Wolfe's offer. The memory of Wolfe's strange questions before, and Davy's odd reactions, assailed him with renewed unease. What did the privateer *really* want from him? Yet, was that not a discourteous thing to think in itself? So far, the man had behaved to him with courtesy and discretion, and there was nothing to suggest anything untoward. And he had told him he would make his fortune. Perhaps he was to be his cabin boy, his personal servant? Even a cabin boy could make a fortune, on treasure voyages. Hopewell had heard that Sir Francis Drake's cabin boy, for instance, had become immensely rich through the trips he'd made with the privateer. Hopewell was lucky, unbelievably lucky, to have been chosen like this by the great Richard Wolfe! In any case, what was there for Hopewell to return to in London? At the very least, a stiff fine from the city authorities and a beating at the hands of the wheelwright before being made to return to his apprenticeship; at worst, gaol. He couldn't return to Worcestershire, either; no, no, imagine how his father would make his life miserable, even if Hopewell should *want* to get the mud of his native fields on his boots again! So, really, there was no choice.

'So you're still here.' Wolfe spoke so suddenly that Hopewell actually jumped.

'Sir, I . . . Forgive me, I . . .'

The captain steepled his fingers. 'I told you, no *sir*. Hopewell, you must be hard of hearing.'

'No, Captain, sorry.'

'Are you not wondering why you are here? What your duties are to be?'

'Captain, I . . .'

'Of course you are. And so you should know.' The Captain leant back in his chair and looked seriously at Hopewell.

'They are to be what you are asked to do, no more, no less.'

'Sir . . . I mean, Captain, I thought perhaps . . . a cabin boy . . .'

'I have no need of a cabin boy, Hopewell. And I do not think you want to be a servant, do you?'

'No, but . . .'

'I want you to do as you are told. To keep your ears and eyes open. To trust me at all times. Is that understood?'

'Yes, sir . . . er . . . Captain. I understand.'

Wolfe smiled, a warm smile that lit up his whole face.

'Good. Hopewell, I am indeed glad you do. Now, in a ship, all hands must be prepared to work at whatever is needful; no man may count himself separate, not even the captain, at a crunch. And we have a smaller crew than is normal, Hopewell, for several reasons. So that means everyone must show extra willingness. Do you understand, Hopewell?'

Now, in London, Hopewell would have regarded such a speech with great suspicion, as presaging a dreadful amount of work for himself; but here, everything was different.

'Captain Wolfe,' he said, 'I will do whatever is asked of me, for I am in your debt.'

Wolfe waved a gracefully dismissive hand. 'In all this, Hopewell, I want you always to keep sight of this: your part in our great enterprise is essential.'

Hopewell beamed with pride, and put his hand over his heart.

'Captain, I will do *whatever* is needful. This I promise solemnly.'

'Good.' Wolfe turned away rather abruptly. 'Do you not wonder where we are headed, Hopewell?'

'Yes, Captain, I do, but I trust that you . . .'

'We are going to find the Lost Island, Hopewell. The Lost Island, that lies in the western seas, a long way beyond Ireland.' He smiled. 'You look blank, Hopewell. I presume you have not heard of the Lost Island.'

'I have heard of enchanted isles, Captain, and blessed isles,' said Hopewell, eagerly, 'but never lost ones. Who lost it, sir?'

Wolfe gave a bark of laughter. 'We did, Hopewell, we did!'

'*You* did, sir?'

A black frown. Hopewell winced. 'Sorry, Captain.'

'It was not we, we personally as such, Hopewell, who lost it, but us: the human race, do you understand?'

'Ah . . . I think so, Captain.'

'You don't *look* so, Hopewell. No, don't protest, and

don't try to talk. The Lost Island was lost to human view hundreds of years ago, and though many have been the times that seagoers have looked for it, never have they found it.'

'Is it lost for ever, then?'

'Do you think I would be looking for it if that were so? Are you more of a fool than I think you are?'

'I don't know, sir . . . er, Captain,' said Hopewell, humbly, though he seethed inside.

'The island is ruled by a man they call the Lord of Alchemists,' Wolfe said, abruptly pushing away the chair and standing up, 'and he is the greatest magician that has ever been. It would be nothing to him to make the island disappear like mist, for ever. But that is not what he does. Every so often, the island appears out of the western sea, and he who finds the path to it will be given the greatest fortune that has ever been seen in all the days of the world. A fortune beside which the fortune of the greatest king on earth is nothing but a pile of pebbles.'

Hopewell opened his eyes wide. 'The Lord of Alchemists must indeed be a very great magician, Captain.'

'He is indeed,' said Wolfe, coming so close to Hopewell that the youth could smell the other's sweet, hot breath. 'And a cunning, devious one. Many people have tried to find the Lost Island and failed, because they did not understand the mind of its lord. But I once knew a man, a philosopher, who was starting to see into the mind of the Lord of Alchemists. By years of patient research and long study, this philosopher had discovered that the Lost Island would once again be found, in our time, in a certain year, on the very night of the midsummer moon.'

'So he went there, sir, and was given a great fortune?' Hopewell breathed.

'The fortune he was given,' said Wolfe, showing all his teeth, 'is one, alas, that we are all heir to.'

'It was . . .'

'Death,' said Wolfe. 'The philosopher I knew – he died. His was a fortune rejoiced in only by worms.'

'Oh, Captain! That is a terrible sadness!'

'For him, indeed; but not for us: because the year that he spoke of was *this* year. If death's greed had not snatched him, Hopewell, he was going to sail, in my very own ship, to the western sea this year, Hopewell, and find the Lost Island, and the Lord of Alchemists.'

'But instead he died. And so *you* are to go on his great undertaking!'

The grey-brown eyes regarded Hopewell steadily. 'You improve, boy. Before he died, he gave me something. Do you know what it was, Hopewell?'

'He gave you his study, sir, his research, so that you could go to the Lost Island in his place!'

'You are not, indeed, a fool, Hopewell.'

A warm glow of pleasure filled Hopewell. He smiled modestly, and said, 'Sir . . . I mean, Captain, did the philosopher write down exactly what one must do when one finds the Lost Island, and how the fortune is to be gained?'

'He did, Hopewell, he did.' The gaze rested on him again, thoughtfully. 'But I thought that what he said was impossible. Now I know it is not so. I know because of *you*, Hopewell. And you are of the most supreme importance in this great enterprise we are on.'

At that very moment, there was a loud knocking at the door, and Davy's voice calling out, in his mellifluous tones, 'Dick, it's time! We sail!'

Wolfe smiled at the thunderstruck Hopewell. 'Sit down. I'll be back,' he said, and strode past him and out of the door, leaving Hopewell alone in the cabin.

Seven

Hopewell did not sit. He stood quite still for a moment, trying to fully grasp the import of all that Wolfe had said. But it was all too much; lost islands, Lords of Alchemists, dead philosophers, midsummer moons, great fortunes. 'It is as if,' he said aloud to the timber walls, 'as if I, Hopewell Shakespeare, have taken root in some strange old romance, in some outlandish play.' And yet it seemed more real to him than anything that had ever happened to him before, like something he had waited for all his days. His old life, the wheelwright's shop, the London streets, Annie, even the Globe – it seemed to be like a kind of dream, a shadow play in a cave, far away. Now he was out in the sun of the extraordinary. A great thrill rippled through him. 'I will be the hero of this romance,' he declared to the patient walls, 'because it is I who has shown Captain Wolfe that finding the Lost Island was possible!' How this had happened, he had no idea. But it was enough that Captain Wolfe had said so. 'Oh, I will serve him to the end of my days!' said Hopewell, fervently, 'he is a man of great and noble renown!'

Under his feet, suddenly, the ship rolled. Hopewell

clutched at the table to get his balance, causing a tremor to begin in the mountain of papers on the table, which rapidly became an avalanche as papers snowed in all directions. Hopewell scrabbled around trying to gather them all together, and in his panic, managed to rip one sheet of paper which was lying under the others. He pulled it out, his heart hammering. What would Captain Wolfe say? To his relief, the sheet was quite blank; it had obviously been an endpaper to what looked now to him like an unbound quarto book. Hopewell screwed it into a ball and hid it in the breast of his doublet. Now to make sure all the other bits of the book were in order . . .

He leafed through it, trying to make some sense of it, but soon gave up. It seemed to him to be a very dull thing indeed, without illustration or decoration, written in a crabbed, close Latin of which he could only make out one word in a hundred, and that one word to be boring. Fortunately, its pages had been carefully numbered, so that he was able to get it back into its right flow, and place the whole thing neatly on the table.

When he had finished, he wiped his brow. Phew! He pulled out the chair to the middle of the room and sat down, demurely putting his hands in his lap, so that he looked a very allegory of Obedience. Not a second too soon; for in the next moment, Wolfe and Davy came into the room.

Hopewell saw Wolfe's quick glance towards the table, and the thought struck him that the Captain would have been none too pleased if he had known what had happened. But the privateer said nothing about it;

presumably he was satisfied all was as it had been. Instead, he waved a hand towards Hopewell, and said to Davy, 'See, my friend, what a good boy he is. A veritable angel, would you not say?'

'The very mock of an angel, and more like a dawcock on its perch, to me,' said Davy Jones, sullenly. 'Is he going to be here all night, Dick? Or is he, perchance, to drive me from my own bed?'

'Now, Davy, would I do that to you? Of course, he will sleep in the men's quarters. He will not be worried about that, will you, Hopewell?'

Hopewell felt dashed, but nodded. Davy, sitting down with a proprietorial sigh on one of the beds, said, with heavy amusement, 'Oh, it doubts me that he will worry overmuch about that this night. If he sees more than the inside of a bucket tonight, I'm a Dutchman.'

'That you're not,' agreed Wolfe, with a humorous lift of his eyebrows directed as much at Hopewell as the first mate. Hopewell had been listening to this exchange with growing dismay. It gave him an uncomfortable feeling, being discussed as if he had no more animation than a plate of beans. He thought a little resentfully about what Wolfe had said, that he was of supreme importance to this great enterprise. Shouldn't that mean he should have been treated with more . . .

Wolfe had been studying his face. 'Hopewell,' he said, quietly, 'why don't you get up on deck. It's your last chance to see London, my friend.'

'Oh, yes . . . of course . . .' Hopewell backed out of the cabin, uncomfortably aware that Davy Jones was still regarding him with that sardonic air.

* * *

Once up on deck, however, he quite forgot his discomfort. London on a bright clear summer's morning, from the deck of a privateer's ship, a brisk wind billowing the sails! What a marvellous thing! What a wonderful sight! What a glorious feeling! Hopewell gripped the rails, knuckles white with excitement, as the great city that had been his home, the very bounds of his world for the last few years slipped away, slowly, as the ship, guided by its pilot, made its way down the river. The traffic on the waterway was intense; rash or skilful boatmen shot across their path from time to time, ferrying passengers to and fro; barges laden with goods cruised ponderously, gallants called out greetings and curses they could not hear. On land, the crowds surged and bustled, seemingly not at all interested that the *Golden Dragon* was leaving port, heading out on the tide to sea. How could they carry on living their dull, little lives in their bounded, little world? Hopewell could not understand it. Even Will Shakespeare, with his mind seas and airy adventures created out of mere words, seemed one to be pitied, stuck as he was in the centre of a circle of bounded worlds: the world of his plays, the world of the Globe, the world of London. But he, Hopewell, was bursting all those bonds, emerging into limitless, real adventure.

Even the motion of the ship, he told himself, was not unpleasant, but only slightly disturbing, something he would soon get used to. Hah! Flummery-footed landlubber, he thought, remembering Davy's words; that's not me, no, sir! Solid earth is for stolid fools!

Alas! Hopewell's splendid assurance did not survive the day, nor the emergence from the estuary into the sea as the *Golden Dragon* tacked down towards the south coast. As Davy had prophesied, he spent what seemed like hours throwing up into a bucket, swaying unhappily on the lurching floor of the sailors' quarters, to the accompaniment of the odd catcall and jeer. Nobody else, not even Kit Sly, seemed to find the sea at all of a trial. The men not on duty spent their time playing at dice and cards, drinking and singing songs, until one by one they dropped off to snoring sleep. But Hopewell could not sleep; not only was his stomach aching and his throat burning, but he had serious doubts about the wisdom of his course of action. Banished here like the lowliest sailor, what could he do to help Wolfe, even if he understood what Wolfe really wanted him to do? It had sounded like some kind of spying – but spying on what, or on who?

Finally, not long before dawn, Hopewell knew the worst of the sickness was past. But he could not bear to be trapped down below any more; he needed fresh air, or he would die, he thought vaguely. He dragged himself over to the ladder and crawled feebly up it, emerging at length on to the main deck into a night so blackly profound that, disoriented, he thought at first he was asleep. It was that time of the night that is darkest of all; the young moon had set, and thick clouds veiled the faces of the stars, whilst all around the black, black sea stretched in all directions. Dark sky, dark horizon, dark sea, heaving in darkly unstable billows. But at least the air was clean and cool, the wind rushing softly past his face.

He crawled along, feeling his way cautiously, his head whirling with emptiness, his eyes useless in this thick dark, until he came to what felt like a solid wall, probably that of the foredeck, which he could rest against. There were sacks already leaning there in the corner, and he crawled in amongst them like a dog looking for a warm nest; and there, sheltered in the warm darkness, he could hear nothing but the creak of timbers and sails, the slap of the sea against the sides of the ship, and once or twice, the muffled step of the watch.

His limbs relaxed as drowsiness invaded him. Then all at once, a voice seemed to come at him from beside his head, and he started, for it was Davy's, speaking not in his usual unfriendly tones, but with genuine pleasure.

'Here you are,' the man said, 'and here I am.'

Hopewell was just about to reply, when another voice spoke; a voice he did not recognize at all. It was a light, thin voice, with a slight trill of laughter in it. 'Here we are,' it agreed. In his hiding place, Hopewell stiffened. Without knowing quite why, he did not call out to them, or make his presence known in any way, but listened closely, hardly daring to breathe, wide awake now.

'We'll have to be careful,' Davy said. 'He suspects something, of that I am sure.'

'You will have to keep close watch on him. If he knows, all is lost.'

'We will have to wait to act, though. And that may be dangerous.'

'You are right. We must wait,' said the light voice. 'Surely you are not afraid, my friend?'

'It is easy for you to speak thus,' said Davy, in his old

64

sullen tones. 'But you do not have to share a cabin with him, and have him watching you like a hawk, night and day . . .'

'Take care the mouse does not fall under his claws, then.' The light voice had that trill of laughter again. 'Now, my friend, are you sure of . . .'

The voice dropped to a whisper, so low that Hopewell could hear nothing more, then there was the sound of footsteps hurrying away. Hopewell waited till no more could be heard. His heart was thudding so hard behind his aching ribs that he thought it might become detached from its place and drop down into his empty stomach. His first suspicions had been right! The first mate of the *Golden Dragon* was a scoundrel. He was plotting some kind of mutiny. Davy Jones would not let Captain Wolfe win the fortune of the Lost Island.

Somehow, he and his fellow conspirator, or conspirators, were going to try and get it for themselves. What a traitor the man was! Hopewell remembered Wolfe's words at the quayside, when he had reminded Jones that he was a partner in the great enterprise. Obviously it was not enough for the greedy Welshman. But what were they going to do? And when? Was this what Wolfe had feared? Was this why he had asked Hopewell to keep his eyes and ears open?

Hopewell did not move from his hiding place till the eastern sky began just slightly to grey with the first approach of dawn. Only then did he slip quietly, and unchallenged down the ladders, back to the sailors' quarters.

Eight

Unfortunately, Hopewell was not able to speak to the Captain alone, not that day, and not the next day. As they sailed along the south coast of England, towards the west and Cornwall, Captain Wolfe did not emerge from his cabin at all. By contrast, Davy Jones never seemed to be far away. And Hopewell was kept far too busy to even consider sneaking up to the foredeck and the Captain's cabin, even if he could have done so without catching Davy's eagle eye.

Hopewell had soon learnt how hard work was on board ship, and how no one, as Wolfe had warned, could escape it. As a jack of all trades, Hopewell had to do whatever was asked of him: scrubbing and washing decks; helping with rigging; helping down in the gun deck. Mostly, however, his chores consisted of galley duties with Kit Sly, helping out the cook, William Gotham. That was the hardest work of all. It was very hot down in the galley, because the brick oven was lit. Because the sea was calm and flat, hot meals could be prepared. In stormy or unstable weather, however, everything was eaten cold, because of the risk of fire.

But it wasn't just the heat in the galley that made

Hopewell sweat. He had heard that ships' cooks had the reputation of being difficult folk, and William Gotham certainly lived up to that reputation. He was unpredictable and heavy-handed, and woe betide any foolish boy who made a mistake with a sauce, or dropped a ladle, or simply looked sideways at him.

Fortunately for Hopewell, his special standing with the Captain stood him in some good stead with Gotham. The cook was not exactly friendly towards him, but at least he did not lay a hand on him. But Kit Sly bore the brunt of the cook's bad temper, he, and the ship's cat that hugged the boy's heels, a cat that was no longer quite so thin, but sleeking out with the good diet of ship's mice. Kit did not seem to worry too much about the kicks and blows directed at him, and indeed seemed sometimes to court disaster by his cheeky manner. But though Hopewell did not much like Kit, he had a natural aversion to bullies. He longed sometimes to punch Gotham on the nose, but of course did not do so. He knew that even Wolfe was unlikely to protect him if he tried anything like that. Besides, Kit seemed able to take care of himself. Hopewell simply tried to ignore Gotham's evil temper, and hoped that Wolfe would remember him soon and move him from galley duties. Yet he knew enough by now to realize that would be the first mate's job, not the Captain's; and if Davy did not care about Kit being maltreated, why should he care about Hopewell's finer feelings?

He had watched Davy carefully, whenever he caught sight of the first mate; but had noticed nothing untoward, and had heard nothing more. It had definitely not been

Kit's voice addressing Davy, that night on the foredeck. But Hopewell was still no closer to finding out who it might be. He had tried to listen to the other men's voices, but to listen to twenty or so separate voices is not an easy task. Still, even if Kit Sly was not involved in that, it was more or less certain that he could not be trusted. Nobody could be trusted, in these circumstances, only Captain Wolfe himself. And he was inaccessible these days, whilst the first mate was everywhere and anywhere, it seemed.

Hopewell knew by now that the first mate was a truly powerful man on this ship, even amongst a crew of men who seemed neither gentle nor biddable. Indeed, Hopewell thought he had never seen a more desperate cast of ruffians, not even in the thieves' alleyways in London – and none of them, apart from Kit, showed the slightest interest in him. He didn't mind that – it was better to be ignored by men like that. But they followed Davy's orders willingly enough, which must show he was a force to be reckoned with. He might not be the ship's master, but it seemed that Davy Jones was in day-to-day charge of the running of the *Golden Dragon*.

Somehow, he must elude Davy Jones' surveillance and speak in private to Captain Wolfe. He was fairly sure the first mate would do nothing until they were well into the open sea, well away from any possibility of help. That would not happen for a while yet. The ship would put in at a couple of ports on the way out to the wild western seas beyond Ireland, and it was unlikely Davy would make a move before then. There would be too much likelihood of getting caught if they were still within reach of civilization.

And at least he wasn't sick any more. Hopewell felt that he had his sea legs, and could scurry about the ship with the best of them. Even Master Gotham, as miserly with compliments as he was prodigal with temper, told him, after Hopewell came back from a foray into the animals' quarters with a good clutch of unbroken eggs, that he might make a sailor yet. Hopewell took this to be a great compliment, coming from the surly cook.

That same day, they stopped in briefly at Truro, in Cornwall, to pick up barrels of fresh water, fish, ale and more supplies for the voyage. They had now been three days and three nights at sea, and Hopewell was beginning to forget he'd ever lived any other way. He had a strange pang as he looked at the harbour from the deck of the ship, but he was not yet ready to go back to land. In any event, what was there for him there? And he could not just leave Captain Wolfe to the mercy of Davy Jones' murderous intentions. He had caught sight of Wolfe today, disembarking briefly at Truro; but he had been kept too busy to get anywhere near the Captain. He was beginning to wonder how he was ever going to do so.

That afternoon, as they were getting the galley fires ready, he felt emboldened enough by Gotham's seeming growing friendliness to ask him, 'Master Gotham, have you sailed before with Captain Wolfe?'

'Oh yes,' said Gotham, 'we all have, we all, except for you, and Kit Sly, and that dratted cat,' he added, aiming a kick at it. 'But it were a long time ago, boy, when we sailed for England's glory.'

'Where has Captain Wolfe lived, since then?'

'A bit everywhere, like . . . I think he was in France, and in Venice too, for quite a while . . . there's call there for brave and bold seamen, working for good lords . . .'

'And what of Davy Jones?'

'Davy Jones? He was in Venice too, I think and also in—' He shut his mouth, suddenly, and Hopewell, looking to see what was the matter, saw Davy Jones emerging from the gloom.

'Gotham,' said he, without preliminary, his flat dark eyes unreadable, 'the Captain asks you to make him stargazy pie, seeing as we loaded on good fresh fish in Cornwall, and we're going to need good stargazin' soon.'

'Yes, Davy,' said Gotham, his smile a little weak, 'I'll do just that, never you fear.'

'Master Jones,' said Hopewell, hesitantly, taking his chance, 'I was wondering if the Captain wanted to—'

'The Captain is very busy, Hopewell,' said Davy, looking at him with the dead gaze of a snake. 'You'd do best to leave him alone. That is my advice.'

'Yes, sir,' said Hopewell, meekly, but seething with fury inside. Next port of call was Cork, in Ireland. It would be the last port they stopped at. At Cork he'd try to speak to Wolfe.

Davy left, and though Hopewell tried to re-engage Gotham in conversation, the cook was morose now, and did not want to speak any more. He yelled at Kit Sly instead for cutting carrots badly, cuffed at him for dropping an egg, and generally behaved like a bear with a sore head. Kit Sly, however, took no notice, and indeed even winked at Hopewell, who did not wink back.

That night, after their work was finished, Kit sought to chat with Hopewell. If Hopewell had been more observant, he might have noticed that the other boy was looking distinctly jumpy, even excited. But he did not notice, only that Kit was being a nuisance, trying to talk to him of this and that, when he, Hopewell, was wondering about Davy Jones and how best to get around him. Wild thoughts surged through his mind. What if – what if, in fact, Jones was keeping Captain Wolfe a prisoner in his own cabin? What if he'd already killed him? But no, surely not. That would be stupid, and Davy Jones was anything but stupid, he thought. Anything but . . .

'Hopewell,' said Kit at last, sighing, 'you do not listen to a word I say.'

Hopewell snapped, 'I am busy, Kit. Busy!'

'Busy, just like Captain Wolfe?'

'The Devil finds work for idle hands to do,' said Hopewell, tartly, moving away. Kit muttered after him, 'And for busy ones too, Hopewell,' but Hopewell didn't listen.

Nine

Two days later, on a fine morning, under a sky full of flying mares' tails, they reached Cork. Although they had intended to stop there for a few days at least, there was a good south-westerly blowing, which would augur well for their voyage into the western sea towards the site of the Lost Island, and so they would only be stopping long enough to take on board more water barrels and supplies. So Davy Jones handed out some wages to each man, including Hopewell, and told them that they had an hour or two to spare, to make themselves scarce, but to be back before midday.

It was perfectly clear that he would not stand for Hopewell to stay on board. Surely, Hopewell thought forlornly, as he trooped meekly off the *Golden Dragon*, Captain Wolfe would also disembark and then he'd be able to talk to him? Brushing off Kit Sly's invitation to come and have a jug of something together, Hopewell hung around the ship for as long as he dared; which wasn't very long, given Jones' suspicious glares at him.

So eventually Hopewell wandered away from the quay with a sense of foreboding. Would Jones strike now, while all the other sailors were away? Surely not, because you needed a crew to sail the ship: unless, that is, he had already lined up some Irish cut-throats to take their place? Remembering the O' Neil's gallowglasses, Hopewell thought with a faint shiver that these would not be men who needed much encouragement to be pirates. But even if England was not fully in control of Ireland, and the chiefs had jurisdiction over much of it, they still owed allegiance to the Queen, and the Queen's law, at least to some extent. Besides, if it became known that English ships' captains could be killed in Cork, and their ships taken over with impunity, then no one would want to put in there. A port made its living from ships coming in, after all. No; now he was sure Jones was waiting for something else, some signal perhaps, some special time . . .

The port area of Cork was a district of mean little hovels and taverns, much as you found in the same kind of place in London. His fellow sailors had lost no time in finding the traditional drunken pastimes of sailors in port, and he could hear the sounds of merriment spilling out into the street. He looked in at the doors of one or two of them, and at the second one, caught sight of Kit Sly drinking with William Gotham and several others of the crew at a rickety table. Heavens, thought Hopewell, with irritation, the silly fellow's even brought the dratted cat with him there! Just then, Kit raised his head and saw Hopewell, and made eager motions for him to join them; but Hopewell shook his head, superbly. No! He did not fancy some sour tavern, reeking of old wine and full of long-toothed bawds; no, he would find something altogether more suited to his new station in life, as future heir to a large fortune. The manner made the man, wasn't that what all the ancients had said? Even with only the few miserable coins he had been given as wages, he was not going to put himself at the level of the pinched-faced cabin boy, with his cropped head and ingratiating smile. And so he walked firmly away from the bawdy-houses and taverns, hoping to come to a more salubrious place.

However, it soon became depressingly clear to him that the town was not equipped to provide a visiting stranger with a gentlemanly experience. Away from the port, and further into the maze of alleyways, it was a place where Hopewell felt not only a stranger, but also an unwelcome one. Men with faces that looked as if they had been cut out of stone with quicksilver-sharp knives, stared challengingly at him; bright-eyed women washed glances over him that were full of a mocking indifference; children threw stones at him, a wizened beggar on a street corner spat on the ground as he went past. And all around him, there was a babble of that strange, barbarous tongue that was Erse, or Irish, and the hodge-podge of English and Erse that they called gallimaufry. Hopewell felt the stinging insult of it rise in him like bile from his martyred stomach. How dare these barking natives not speak the Queen's tongue, that might let strangers know if they meant well or ill!

Seething with indignation, he decided he'd had quite enough of exploring Cork, and began to make his way back to the quays. But, alas! In his haste, he had forgotten to note where he was going, as alley merged into alley, and he realized he was quite mazed, he began to panic.

Time was getting on; he must get back to the port before midday or the ship would sail without him and Jones accomplish his plan of killing Hopewell's benefactor, Captain Wolfe, not to speak of grabbing the fortune that was at least partly Hopewell's.

If the people around him had looked unwelcoming before, now, to the confused Hopewell, they looked positively malevolent. Knife features became cruel and inscrutable; bright eyes seemed alight with the wild joy of anticipated savagery; stone-throwing children seemed to edge closer, and that barbarous babble became filled with a menacing roar. He was trapped here, a vulnerable English stranger, and these people would think nothing of killing him, he thought. He began to run, thinking he could hear behind him the sounds of doglike pursuit, like the sound of a hunt on the trail of a fox, or a stag. He would be run down, here in the stone forest of Cork . . . Once, he looked over his shoulder, and saw, indeed, that he was being followed; a pack of children, thin, peaky faces glowing with wild glee. It made him run faster, the breath screaming in his throat, his muscles on fire with effort.

All at once, he heard, floating from somewhere nearby, a sound that made the hair rise on the back of his neck. It was a voice; a thrillingly beautiful voice, singing a strange, gorgeous song quite unlike even the lovely ones Hopewell had heard in London. And somehow something in the music told him he must reach the voice, and he would be safe within its bounds. He looked over his shoulder; and saw that the pursuing children had slowed, that they, too, were listening, stilled. A sobbing relief filled him, and he followed the voice, but the children followed him, quietly now, as if they were following their leader.

In this way, they came to a place where a silent circle of people gathered around; and pushing through them went Hopewell, to set eyes on the singer. She was a young woman, and though ragged and barefoot, had the carriage and beauty of a queen, with a meltingly beautiful face, long hair as black as a night at sea, with flowers like stars wound in amongst it. But most beautiful of all was that sweet, thrillingly low and rich voice that made shivers and sparks travel up and down Hopewell's spine, seeming to melt his flesh, his blood, his bones, so that he was all yearning, all longing to hear, to see, and do nothing else. He forgot his new-found cynicism about women; he forgot his fortune, his fears, his hopes, Captain Wolfe, the *Golden Dragon*, Cork itself. Lost to the world, to time, to himself, to everything but pure, piercing delight, he stood there, watching her, and listening, as if he were at the beginning and end of the world. It seemed to him that somewhere deep inside of him, he had known this song all along, though it was strange to him; and that somehow, the singer's face was familiar to him, though it was the face of a stranger. And all around him, the crowd pressed, no longer unfriendly, but with a longing that seemed just like his own.

The singer stopped singing. She beckoned, with two fingers outstretched, and Hopewell found himself propelled forward. He was all a-tremble now, his flesh and blood and bone resettling in shaking pain on his spirit. She looked deep into him; and he seemed to see his dreaming soul reflected there in her eyes.

'You seek the Lost Island, my dear . . .'

He did not wonder at understanding her. He said, simply, 'It is not I who seek it, but my Captain. Do you know it, Lady?'

'All know it who seek it,' she answered, softly.

'Do you mean that I . . .'

'Watch for the White Ship,' she broke in, looking him full in the eyes, 'watch for the White Ship. But beware . . . beware . . .'

'Beware what?' he said, urgently, as her voice seemed to fade, her eyes to cloud. But she did not answer him. Instead, she leant forward, and her eyes flashed with a sudden green passion; and Hopewell felt a sharp pain on his forehead, a pain greater than any he had felt before, and he knew no more.

A throbbing ache, a voice shouting in his ear, a reek of wine: and Hopewell lifted his head and saw that he was in unfamiliar surroundings. Around him were familiar faces, however; and he saw that they were some of the sailors from the *Golden Dragon*, including William Gotham and Kit Sly, grinning at him. He raised his head a little further, though it hurt fiendishly, and saw that Davy Jones was regarding him with a sardonic air.

'You're not the first one can't hold his grog, boy,' was all he said; and Hopewell peered at him, painfully beginning to be aware that singer, song, beauty, were all gone, and that he was in a mean little tavern with his shipmates.

Lightning-livid thoughts fried and criss-crossed in his poor brain; why was he here, when he'd been *there*, before? He groaned as it all came back to him; he had looked in at a tavern boy, seen his shipmates, but walked on. He had wandered the streets; there had been people; he'd been pursued; and then, there was the singer, and the song. So why . . .

'You'll have a bruise on your head the size of a pigeon's eye, friend,' said Davy Jones, 'the force you hit the table with, indeed. Did you not ever taste wine, back in London?'

'It were whisky, he were given, though,' said William Gotham, grinning.

'Whisky, eh? Money's all gone, then,' said the first mate.

Hopewell stared at him, trying to force his ragged thoughts into some patchy semblance of order. 'I did not have any such as you say,' he muttered. 'I went a-walking the streets . . .'

There was a burst of derisive laughter at this. But he continued, doggedly, 'I went a-walking, and there were many Erse there, and . . .'

'A strange thing indeed, to find Erse in their own land, lad,' said Gotham, winking at the rest of the company.

'No, that's not all; I was pursued by them, but at last was saved by a woman . . . a singer . . . a beautiful one . . .'

Another burst of laughter. 'We all have those visions, lad,' said another man, kindly, 'when we swim down to the bottom of a whisky cup! You've been here all along, boy, with us.'

Everyone around him nodded, even Kit, who said, with a harsh gurgle of laughter, and an ugly, knowing look, 'I even signed for you to come in with us, so I did!'

'But I didn't come in, I walked away!' Hopewell glared at the boy. 'You know I didn't; I walked away! And I saw her, I did, I did; and she said . . .' He trailed off as he caught Davy Jones' steady, unreadable glance. But there was a tremor in his soul, a terror, almost, at what had happened. He was sure, he was positive, that he had walked the streets, and seen the singer. It had happened. It *was* real; and not some whisky dream. He remembered pushing open the door, the cabin boy beckoning to him, shaking his head, and then going out into the street . . . It was real, for sure. But somehow, he'd been brought here, afterwards. Why? He had no idea, and no idea either of why the other sailors would be lying. Then revelation dawned on him. Perhaps . . . perhaps it was because they were all in on Davy Jones' plan, and if it was reported to Captain Wolfe that he, Hopewell, was a fantasist who did not even know reality from a drunken dream, then how could he be trusted to tell the truth about anything? Thus, how would the privateer believe him if he told him of a mutiny? He must try and get to Captain Wolfe first, and tell him all that had happened. But would Davy Jones allow that to happen?

Ten

Of course he did not. They put off from Cork early
that afternoon, blown by the favourable wind that
made the little ship fairly scoot along. But still Captain
Wolfe did not emerge, and still Jones kept appearing
at Hopewell's side, just when Hopewell thought he
might have a chance. Still, at least, thought the boy, he
did not appear to have said anything to Wolfe about
Hopewell's strange adventure in Cork, but busied
himself on deck with the preparations for setting out
again.

The Captain made only a brief appearance that
night, to talk with the steersman, then retreated almost
immediately. Hopewell lay amongst the snoring sailors
that night, his head still throbbing uncomfortably, but
his thoughts much clearer, thinking of all that had
happened, one part of him still longing for the singer,
longing for the song, but unable to recapture either; the
other worrying over what would happen to Captain
Wolfe. The midsummer moon, Captain Wolfe had said;
the Lost Island is found when the midsummer moon is
on the western sea. And full moon would be in only a
couple of nights or so . . . But maybe the first mate still

needed the Captain's knowledge of where exactly they must head for? The old philosopher who knew about the Lost Island had been Wolfe's friend, and not Davy's; and so perhaps the villainous first mate knew he needed the old privateer, up to a point.

But as Hopewell thought and fretted and planned, the part of him that had been troubled by the strange experience he had had in Cork slipped further below his consciousness, so that when he awoke the next morning, after a singularly unrefreshing sleep, he was almost ready to admit to himself that he had indeed been in a kind of dream. He could almost see himself coming into the tavern at Kit Sly's invitation, sitting at the table with the other men, and spending the bits of money he had, and the little time, on getting as drunk as a lord. Certainly, thinking of it now, he could not remember the tune of the song, or hear the singer's voice, in anything other than the elusive, frustratingly evanescent fashion of a half remembered dream.

That day, and the next, the air was bright and clear, the sea sparkling with a thousand lights, and the ship ran before the good wind like a deer runs before the bow. Though they saw not one other ship in the whole of that vast and heaving sea, the sailors seemed all of a sudden less surly, as if the visit to Cork had put new heart in them all. Even morose William Gotham smiled once or twice. Only Davy Jones looked every bit as unpleasant and scowling as ever. But Hopewell took as little notice of him as he could. His own spirits had, he realized, been raised by his strange adventure in Cork, though he was not sure why. And for the first time, he actually began to talk properly with Kit, and found to his surprise that the boy was not such an unpleasant companion after all. Well, especially since Kit let him talk about things that interested him, and was flatteringly intent when Hopewell described richly embroidered details of his life, in which adventure and excitement featured very plainly.

But even these pleasant interludes did not quite negate the thing that most puzzled and hurt Hopewell. And that was the fact that Wolfe never even bothered to come and see him, or call him to his side, or have anything whatsoever to do with him. It was very odd, this cold shouldering, especially given the Captain's original friendliness, and his claim that Hopewell was of supreme importance. Why had he not told him exactly what that was? Why was he keeping himself apart? Why, oh why did he not see what Davy Jones was up to?

Then, at last, came the second evening after Cork, and the event that Hopewell had been praying for all these days and nights. Captain Wolfe sent for him, in the person of Davy Jones, who was quite clearly unsettled by his commission. Hopewell did his best not to look too triumphant, but he could not help a small smile stealing over his face at the thought of the wicked man's discomfiture. At last, he would be able to speak his mind . . . Perhaps Davy had already got to the Captain, and so Wolfe might not believe him. But at least he would be able to talk to him.

But when they arrived in the cabin, he thought at first that it would be as before, with Jones watching him like a hawk. For they both went in together, and Jones shut the door. The Captain was standing in his cabin, hands behind his back, seemingly absorbed in contemplation of the picture on the wall. His table was bare of papers now, with only the candlestick standing on it.

Wolfe did not turn when Davy and Hopewell came in; nor did he turn when Davy said, in a plainly reluctant voice, 'Here he is, Dick.'

'Good,' said Wolfe, without turning around. 'Leave him with me.'

'Dick . . .' The first mate was clearly disturbed; his eyes darted from the Captain's back to Hopewell's face, and back again. 'Would it not be better if . . .'

'No,' said Wolfe.

'But perhaps if I . . .'

'Davy.' Captain Wolfe turned around. 'How long were we shipmates?'

The first mate looked at him in silence for an instant. Then, slowly, he said, 'More years than I care to remember.'

'Did I not always deal fairly with you, then, Davy?'

Davy's expression softened. 'Always.'

'Well, then, have I ever given you cause to distrust me? Do you think I would abandon my friends once I came within reach of real riches? Answer me honestly, Davy.'

A strange expression came over the first mate's ugly face. Hopewell watched breathlessly, and somewhat indignantly, thinking of the treacherous conversation he'd overheard on deck. 'No, Dick, no to both questions.'

'Why, then, do you hesitate when I ask you this?' The Captain's grey-brown eyes held the flat dark eyes of the Welshman in a kind of fascinated intensity, and Hopewell saw the first mate's expression change yet again. Davy looked away, and said, in a low, quiet voice, 'I do not know, Dick. I truly do not know.'

Wolfe came to him and put a hand on his shoulder. 'My dear friend, and companion in what has too often been struggle and misfortune, we are almost at the edge of the greatest fortune that will ever come our way. We will become great again, you and I. The old days of the *Golden Dragon* will come again, that I promise you. Is this not the time to screw our courage to the sticking-point? Surely you cannot hesitate in this?'

Davy Jones stared into Richard Wolfe's eyes for what seemed to the waiting Hopewell like an age, then the first mate dropped his gaze, shook his head, and left.

As soon as he had closed the door behind him, Hopewell gabbled, 'Sir . . . oh, Master, glad it is I can speak to you at last! I've been wanting to speak to you for so long!'

'Is that so?' For an instant, Wolfe seemed lost in a dream; then, abruptly, he shook himself and turned to Hopewell.

'Well, then, my young sprog, I'm all ears. What is it you want to tell me?'

And so, at last, Hopewell was able to recount to him all that had befallen, the night when he had been so seasick. Though he also told Wolfe some of what had happened in Cork, he did not tell all the course of his vision, or dream, for he was afraid of being laughed at: only that Jones had played a trick on him to make it seem as though he were a fantasist or habitual liar, and thus discredit him in Wolfe's eyes.

The Captain listened with a still, set face, his eyes still in his pale features, and did not interrupt at all. When at last Hopewell had finished, with a lame, 'And so, sir, you see just what a bad man Davy Jones might be,' Wolfe gave a deep sigh, and sinking down into his chair, rested his arms on the table, deep in thought. Or sorrow. Or both. For a long time he sat thus, and Hopewell did not dare to interrupt his reverie, but watched the unmoving privateer. Then just when Hopewell thought he would never speak again, he raised his head and said, 'Why have you told me this, Hopewell?'

'*Why*, sir?'

The Captain's eyes flashed dangerously. Hopewell stammered, 'Er . . . Captain, I thought you said to er . . . to keep my eyes and ears open, and I . . .' He gulped, could not finish. In all his worrying and wondering, he had not stopped to think what would happen if the Captain did not believe him.

Wolfe's voice was tight and hostile. 'You told me you thought Davy Jones misliked you, Hopewell. Is this your idea of revenge?'

Uncontrollable tears pricked at Hopewell's eyes. He blinked them away fiercely, and stood straight and defiant. 'No, Captain. It is the truth I am telling you. Unvarnished, unembroidered, naked, simple truth.'

Captain Wolfe stared at him. Then, slowly, he nodded. But his face stayed set and hard. 'If, then, it is the truth, Hopewell, what are you going to do about it?'

Eleven

'What am *I* going to do about it?' Hopewell repeated, rather wildly. 'Sir, I thought that you would . . .'

The privateer laid both hands on Hopewell's shoulders, making the youth look up into his face. 'Hopewell, I told you when I first met you that you were of supreme importance in this enterprise. Do you remember that?'

How *could* he have forgotten? Hopewell nodded, unable to look away.

Wolfe's eyes looked deep into him. 'And now the time has come, and you alone can decide the next course of events and whether we will find the Lost Island. Are you willing to do so?'

Hopewell's throat was thick with emotion. He could not keep his eyes off Wolfe's face. But he managed to stammer, 'Sir, if I could know how . . . why . . .'

The privateer dropped his arms and swung away from Hopewell to stare at the painting again. In a muffled voice, he said, 'The old philosopher I knew — he told me that the only way to open the path to the Lost Island would be to force the hand of the Lord of Alchemists. And that would only be done if a boy such as yourself guided events, because innocence and its bright courage alone may open the path to us. And you are a true innocent.'

'Sir!' Hopewell could not help his movement of dismayed protest.

Wolfe turned around, slowly, and smiled. It was a very sad smile. 'You think it an insult, don't you, Hopewell? But I can assure you it is not. Experience lies too heavily on most souls – including mine. Innocence is what makes the world afresh, each time. And that is the lesson of the Lord of Alchemists, and the reason why he hides the Lost Island from our ken.'

'But, sir, you told me that the old philosopher had devised formulae and such to plot and find the Lost Island, at midsummer moon in this year on the western sea, and that we were going there to make our fortunes . . .'

Wolfe rubbed at his face. 'Yes. That is so.'

Hopewell smiled, eagerly. 'So you already have the means, sir. We are going towards the midsummer moon, just as your friend said; we will be there very soon, surely. Perhaps even tonight, for is it not the night of the full moon? When that time comes, the way to the Lost Island will be revealed, there, somewhere on the western sea.'

'Do you truly think so?' said Wolfe, slowly. Hopewell, with a weird mixture of pride and anxiety warring in his chest, nodded. The privateer sighed, deeply.

'Ah, Hopewell! I fear too much, these days. It is because of growing old.'

'Oh, no, Captain Wolfe, never! All I have seen of you tells me that your heart has not grown old! You will find the Lost Island, sir, I am sure, and make your fortune. And mine too, I hope,' he added, with a quick smile.

Wolfe laughed at that, and ruffled Hopewell's hair. 'You do me good, boy,' he said.

Hopewell's heart swelled with pleasure. But he did not forget what he had originally come to tell Wolfe. 'Sir . . . er, forgive me, Master, what are we to do about . . .'

'You can call me sir, if it pleases you, dear Hopewell,' said Wolfe. 'What are we to do about Davy Jones and his pretty plots, then, think you? Get him to walk the plank? Pitch him into the sea? Boil him up in the galley? Tie him to the mizzen mast? Drop him in the bilge?'

There was a strange hilarity to him now, which Hopewell found slightly disturbing, but not enough to disconcert him. He began, eagerly, 'Sir, if I had been able to speak to you before we reached Cork, we could have left him there. But now . . .'

'Now he threatens everything,' said Wolfe, harshly. 'I do not believe all the men are with him in this, only a few. That boy he hired, Kit Sly; he is involved, thinks I. Did you recognize the other's voice?'

'No, sir,' said Hopewell honestly. 'It *could* have been Kit . . . but it did not sound as shrill as him.'

'It doesn't matter. What matters is that there are others involved. But Davy is their guiding light. Without him, they would collapse quickly. Now, see you, Hopewell, Davy has been my shipmate for many years, and I know him well. I suspected that there was something wrong with him, because he is not usually as surly as he is now, and not so jumpy neither. But I had bethought myself it must be some money worry he had, on land; I know that he has had dealings with usurers and shady money men, in the past. Davy is a close and secret man, though he is also one of rare and bloody courage, and such a man, if he goes wrong, may do far more desperate deeds than those of piddling vice or virtue, Hopewell. Once, I would have trusted him with my life. But no more.'

Here, his expression saddened again. 'It is a terrible knowledge, Hopewell, that sits on my soul now, for I fear there is only one recourse against betrayal and mutiny, but I would wish beyond all reckoning that I did not have to use it against one who was once a dear friend.'

Hopewell's legs trembled. He said, in a voice as shaky as his limbs, 'But sir, he already suspects you know something of his true feelings . . . If you move against him openly, he may kill you. Sir, you cannot challenge him, for there is no telling what he might *do*.'

Wolfe's eyes bored into him. 'Do you see, Hopewell, why I asked you what you were going to do? You understand better than I do myself what must be done.'

'You honour me too greatly, sir,' whispered Hopewell, feeling sick to the stomach. It was one thing to dream of honour and glory and daring deeds of battle; it was quite another to think of the reality of taking on a hardened sailor more than twice his age. Wolfe saw his agitation, and smiled wearily.

'Do not think I will ask you to challenge him to a duel, or even to slip a knife in his ribs,' he said.

'Oh, but, sir, I am ready to do whatever must be done,' said Hopewell, white to the lips. There was a part of him that screamed in terrified astonishment at what his mouth was saying; and another that rejoiced fiercely in the prospect of destroying a wicked man, and those two parts warred with yet another, that wished it were back as a groundling at the Globe, watching a drama open-mouthed, but able to go home safely afterwards.

'Are you sure, Hopewell? Are you quite, quite sure?' Wolfe's forehead was beaded with sweat, his mouth worked spasmodically, his eyes were full of unshed tears. Hopewell thought, with a kind of detachment, that the Captain looked ill. Ill, and very old. A sort of pity stirred in Hopewell, all the more painful for being unexpected, and quite unwanted. Was the legendary privateer just another man fallen on hard times? Was the shabbiness of the *Golden Dragon* a truer indication of the state of his standing than the fine, scented richness of his clothes? What if – oh, worm of a thought – what if the whole tale of the Lost Island were nothing but that – a tale?

'I am sure, sir,' he said, at last, with a huge effort.

Wolfe took a deep breath, and crossed to the chest. 'Then I will show you what the philosopher left for me,' he said, and reaching into the chest, lifted out a bundle wrapped in oilskins. 'I have studied this hard and long,' he said, but just then he was interrupted by a thunderous knocking on the door, and the shrill, excited voice of Kit Sly, crying, 'Captain! Captain! Master Jones says to come and tell you, there's a wondrous white ship on the horizon, sir! And she's flyin' the flag of Spain!'

Thrusting the parcel under his arm, Wolfe strode to the door and opened it so suddenly that the galley boy practically fell into the room. The privateer grabbed him by the doublet, and hauled him up. 'What is that you say, boy?'

'A ship, a ship sailing under Spanish colours! Master Jones, says, Captain,' the boy gabbled, 'he says that the ship, though she's a small, light caravel, she's as fine-looking as the big galleon you captured in the Carib Sea, sir!'

Instantly, Hopewell saw the age and sadness drop from Wolfe's face like a mask. 'A Spanish ship! Alone out in this empty sea!'

'Master Jones says she looks like she's carrying a fair cargo, sir. Maybe she thought to evade pursuit, going this way.'

'I'll wager she did!' Wolfe's eyes sparkled. 'A gift from the gods, then! Are the guns ready?'

'Master Jones says they are, sir. He says she should come within range very soon.' The galley boy smirked. 'She looks too fine and light to have many big guns, sir.'

'Don't be sure of that, Kit. These Spanish ships are usually well protected, even when we're not technically at war with them. But we'd best take the flag down, to be sure. We don't want them knowing too early who they have to deal with.'

He's forgotten the other things we were talking about, thought Hopewell, half admiringly, half despairingly. What if — the thought struck him suddenly — what if this were a trick on the part of Davy Jones, who knew his erstwhile friend well enough to know what would appeal to his old privateer's heart, starved of booty and glamour?

But it was useless to even try and reason with Wolfe, who had already left the cabin in Kit's wake. Hopewell followed at a run, head spinning. It was not until they were nearly halfway up to the fo'c'sle deck that the memory suddenly struck him; the realization of just where he had heard about a white ship before. The vision, or strange journey, in Cork; the beautiful singer, telling him to watch for the white ship. The white ship . . . the white ship.

And yet he had not told anyone about that part of the dream.

Twelve

There was a great deal of expectant activity on the ship now. Davy Jones, a spyglass to his eye, was watching the western horizon from the main deck, while sailors were readying guns on the poop deck, the long-range falcon guns in the fo'c'sle and the stern, and down below in the gun deck, the big minion guns. When Wolfe arrived, Kit and Hopewell in tow, the first mate wordlessly handed the instrument to his captain. As he did so, he caught Hopewell's eye, and the boy could not help colouring under the first mate's flat scrutiny. But Jones said nothing to Hopewell, and instead spoke to Wolfe. There was a tremor of excitement in his voice.

'She's a splendid thing, isn't she, Dick?'

'She is indeed. Splendid. And all alone.'

'The guns are ready. We can just wait till she gets near.'

'We're not at war with Spain at present, Davy, remember.'

'I remember, Dick. But is Spain at war with us?'

'Will not Spain always be at war with us?' Wolfe laughed. No trace of dismay or sense of betrayal in this talk, thought Hopewell; only the comfortable banter of old comrades-in-arms. It was bewildering; but a relief, too. He had done his duty, telling Wolfe. Now, if he were to be spared having to back up his words with actions he would rather not have to carry out, all to the good. Perhaps, if they boarded the ship, then Davy might be killed in the battle. Or he might have his greed sidetracked, somehow. In any case, there was a breathing space, for Hopewell. But . . . what of the woman and her strange words about the white ship?

The white ship was fast becoming more than a dot on the horizon, visible only to the telescope. Now, though dusk was fast gathering, its luminescent beauty was visible to the naked eye, and Hopewell, like everyone else on board, stared awestruck at it. It looked to be indeed a small, light caravel, skimming like a swan over the sparkling sea, with sails as white as snow, and timbers scrubbed so clean they also appeared white. As Kit had said, it flew the royal flag of Spain, but as it came closer, they saw that it also sported a most unusual, painted figurehead: a great, white swan, with golden eyes. Like just such a magnificent bird the white ship flew towards them, riding the waves with effortless grace, like a beautiful bird that does not know it is coming within the purlieu of ruthless hunters.

The men on the deck watched it come in silence; the excited chatter of earlier replaced by a grim, spellbound watchfulness. Hopewell himself stared at the glorious thing with a wildly beating heart, wishing that the white ship would somehow escape its fate, and yet, in another way, fiercely relishing the prospect of capturing such a magnificent object. As the white ship came closer, figures began to be distinguished on the decks, figures rather extravagantly clothed in pure-white livery. The sailors on the white ship had obviously just realized that they could not see a flag flying on the *Golden Dragon*; and that would ever have sent alarm bells ringing on any ship. They were to be seen running hither and thither, and pulling up what looked to be great silver guns into position. On the *Golden Dragon*, that activity had long since been readied; all that was needed, and waiting, was the order to fire.

When would Captain Wolfe give the order? Closer the other ship came, and closer, and still he said nothing. Was he, after all, going to let her go past unharmed? The tension of waiting on the *Golden Dragon* seemed itself like a tangible thing. The strange summer dusk would continue for a few hours more, and so visibility would still be good for a while yet; but surely it was not a good thing to allow the other ship to come too close and able to fire into them? All at once, though, the other ship appeared to turn, and begin to tack away in the opposite direction.

'She's wearing! She's wearing! We'll lose her!' shouted Davy. And now Captain Wolfe, suddenly springing into action, flung the telescope at Davy, and straightening to his full, not inconsiderable height, he cupped his hands to his mouth, and called out, in tones that rang out across the sea: 'Stranger! Stay and deliver!'

The words echoed across the silver sea, and seemed to bounce on the great white ship. And a voice came calling back from its deck, the voice of one of the white-clad sailors, calling back in heavily accented English, 'We come in peace! Let us continue on our way!'

Wolfe's smile was like a sword-feint on his face. He called back, 'There is no peace that cannot be broken. Stand and deli—'

'Sir, sir!' Hopewell clutched at Wolfe's sleeve. A strange urgency gripped at him. 'Sir, No! let her pass!'

Wolfe shook him off. A third time, he called out, 'Stranger! Stop, or we will fire! If you run before us, we will hunt you down! For what is it you have to hide? Stop, and we will show you mercy! We are the *Golden Dragon!*'

Suddenly, there was a roar and a whoosh, from the other ship; but if the Spaniard had tried to hit them, she had failed miserably, for it was quite clear the *Golden Dragon* had not been hit, though not far from where she was, the sea boiled and heaved. Wolfe laughed. 'Trading men should not try to live like soldiers!' he called out; and in the next instant, 'Davy, give the order to fire, all the guns, straight at the Spaniard!'

And so it was on. The *Golden Dragon*, fast and nippy, hunted the white ship relentlessly, firing at her as she limped away from them like a broken-winged swan. The air was filled with roars and explosions and smoke, a pounding of shot that nearly deafened Hopewell, screams and yells. After that first broadside, the white ship did not try to fire back at them, but ran before them towards the horizon, a poor prey trying hard to get away. Yet, under a cannonade that would have torn a lesser ship to shreds, still the white ship kept going, with a determination that was almost the desperate courage of a living thing.

On board the *Golden Dragon*, it was bedlam, with men running, shouting, yelling, the deafening roar of the guns, the acrid smell of powder, the wild scent of hunting excitement. Like the others, Hopewell was kept busy, and did not have time to reflect on much of anything beyond the momentary tasks. He had never felt this mixture of fear and glee before, this sense that anything was possible, this fear that a most terrible thing was happening, that the greatest, most beautiful thing in the world was running helpless before them, and that soon her spoils would be shared amongst them all like the spoils of the hunt. He did not know whether to cheer, or to pity; to scream, to cry, or to laugh; and so full of wild emotion was he that he could scarcely see anyone else, not even Wolfe, clearly, though once, he caught sight of Kit, huddling in a corner, hands over his ears, the cat flat on the boards by his side, and smiled, pityingly; then found himself touching the boy on the shoulder to give him a comforting squeeze.

Then, just at the limit of the fiery horizon, on the steadily darkening sea, the white ship suddenly stopped. And as the *Golden Dragon*, with the full force of her headlong course, came bearing down on her, the beautiful swan ship turned – and came straight at them, its huge silver guns blazing like the most livid lightning storm. Faster and faster she came, with supernatural strength and speed and power, and now it was the turn of the *Golden Dragon* to be the hunted. Wolfe screamed orders for the gunners to fire, again and again, but it seemed to make no difference at all. Cannonball after cannonball fell on the white ship's deck, and still she kept coming, her sails in shreds, her timbers scored and pock-marked, but whole still, and hideously relentless. And as she came, it seemed to the terrified, screaming men on the *Golden Dragon* that the white ship grew bigger and bigger, and darker and darker, metamorphosing before their very eyes, rising up out of the sea, and into the sky like a massive storm cloud, a cloud of frightening purple-backed, roaring intensity, bearing down on the suddenly frail *Golden Dragon* with the irresistible malevolence of vengeful nature breaking her bonds. As the cloud bore down on them, so the sea began to boil and steam around the ship, and waves of mountainous size and volcanic fury rose around them. The ship reared, then plunged into the maelstrom, its timbers shrieking and rending, terrified sailors clinging to anything they could grab. Once more, the ship tried to raise herself up, but then, with a terrible rending sound, the mast came crashing down: and in that instant of utter terror, Hopewell caught a glimpse of the wild-eyed first mate grappling with the captain on the madly pitching deck. But he had no time to see more, for in the next instant, he was swept bodily off the ship, into the raging black sea.

Part Two

The Island

Thirteen

Down, down, down into the sea he went, and up, up, up again, tossed like an insect in the maelstrom of the tempest. Not only could he not see or speak, he could barely breathe; it was as if a vast hand held him in a crushing power, squeezing his ribs, his head, his lungs, forcing him towards some vast cavernous mouth, where all would be extinguished for ever in the bottomless belly of darkness. In the lair of the monster that was ocean, it was his gallant, frail animal body, servant usually, that desperately fought the unequal struggle, fought an instinctive battle for life, seemingly not guided by its normal master, his drowning, airy spirit. Limbs struck up; heart pumped violently; muscles ached with the mad effort of the fight, pounding breath burst through lungs and into lips; hands and arms clawed and grabbed; and suddenly, as if the monster ocean had tired of the piddling creature's irritating struggles, Hopewell shot up through the waves, ejected from the belly of darkness like a burped-up morsel. As he did so, his flailing arms found something solid to hang on to; and then his poor battered body clung to it, without thought, clung and clung, while the breath whistled ghastly in his throat, seeming to tear the delicate tissues there, and his head swam with darkness. For a long while, he could do no more than float quietly in the quiet moonlit sea, his head resting to one side, his hands clasping the thing that was supporting him – a plank from the murdered *Golden Dragon*. The tempest that had come on so suddenly had just as suddenly ceased, it seemed – or was that only a trick of time? Whilst his faithful body fought the sea, had time not stopped too? He did not know; could not think, yet, as his spirit crept meekly back, finding a lovely home again in the bruised body that had never given up.

At length – at great length – Hopewell found he could lift his head up. And the sight he saw then made him gasp with terror and dismay; for he was all alone, or so it seemed, in the middle of the great sea, quiet now as a pond after its volcanic treachery. The full moon had risen in the east, and its light fell softly all around him, showing him the pitiful remains of the dead ship: broken timbers, a sodden sail, floating barrels occasionally clinking together with a sound all the more dreadful because it was so homely. In the distance, he could see a line of the poor wooden remains, floating up and down on the swell of the waves. Not a sound or sight of other human life; it was as if the whole of the *Dragon*'s company had been swallowed up by the ghastly ocean, devoured bones and blood and all. Trembling, Hopewell closed his eyes. Had he survived the tempest only to be lost for ever on an endless sea? Would it not have been kinder for him to die at once than to be slowly tormented by the pangs of thirst and hunger and terrible, lonely fear, his body slowly, ironically dessicated by the watery endlessness around him, so that he would become no more than a vile, pallid thing? Sobbing aloud, he cried out to God or Fortune or whoever might listen to him to end it quickly, not to make him rot away in body and spirit, slowly, slowly, relentlessly as on the rack!

The tears on his face were warm; and as they trickled slowly into his mouth, the salt of them seemed like a microcosm of the salt of the sea. Suddenly furious with fate, he beat at the water with a puny fist, screaming defiance at the sky. The water splashed up all around him; and drops landed on his swollen tongue. Once again, faithful body knew before airy master, and he drank greedily, his parched throat responding, opening like a flower, before his stunned mind registered an incontestable, astounding fact: this water was not salty, not bitter, like the salt of tears, like Ocean should be. It was sweet, it was cool, it was clear. It was fresh water; and he a sailor floating in a freshwater – sea, floating in it . . .

From tears to laughter, from laughter to fear: Hopewell's peal of joy rang out over the silent moonlit silver scene, before being stopped by the knowledge that nowhere, in all the world he knew of, was there a sea whose waters were sweet and not salt. He trembled. Could it be . . . was it that he . . . he was already dead, that his spirit had already escaped the bounds of earth, and sent him to this place? But if he was dead, if this was death, then surely it was not so to be feared . . . and yet, yet, he was all alone, all alone. No angels came walking softly over the waves to greet him, no loving Lord called him to His side, no Mother Mary clasped him in her arms. If this was the afterworld, then it could not be Heaven. And it surely was not Hell. He remembered his mother whispering that in the old days, people had spoken of another place, a kind of place neither Heaven nor Hell, but one of suffering, and loneliness. Purgatory, the place where souls went which were not yet good enough, or purified enough, for Heaven, yet not bad enough for Hell.

His father had said this was a wicked and wrong notion of the monks; but his mother, not quite as certain in her Puritan ideas, and who perhaps secretly regretted some of the old things, had whispered to Hopewell that she was not at all sure, for how could one be sure of God's kingdom? Hopewell had been much struck by the thought, momentarily; then had put it from his mind, and not thought of it again. Now, it returned in full force, as he floated in trouble of mind on this silent, sweet, unnatural sea, borne on its invisible currents and swells. But could it, after all, be Purgatory, if he could see around him evidence of the wreck; if the very thing he was resting on had been torn from the ship's side? He worried at it for a while: but could find no answer to it in any of the corners of his mind.

The strange thing was that the further Hopewell floated, the more he was carried on this sea, the more the most recent events of his life seemed to become almost effaced, while the early parts of it were clear as day. So the Lost Island, Wolfe, Davy Jones, even back to London and Annie and all the rest of it, seemed far back in the distance, like dreams, whilst the farm in

Worcestershire, the smell of the ploughed fields, the warm breath of his father's pair of horses, the satisfying feel of the eggs he'd had to gather as a child from under the stern of trim, ship-like, indignant hens: all these seemed to be in the air around him. He remembered other things too; how his mother had insisted he go to petty school, and thence to grammar school for a year, though his father thought it was not necessary, and Hopewell himself had groaned at the thought of more instruction. His grammar-school master had been a dry old pedant, with no sense of humour, whom Hopewell and his friends had unmercifully tormented with silly tricks. But he had at least taught Hopewell the rudiments of Latin, and the beginnings of logic: not enough to read the ancients fluently, but enough to sound impressive in front of the wheelwright, later, when his father decided there'd been enough of this pettifogging foolishness and the boy must earn his living . . .

Hopewell could just see his father, standing there, solidly planted on his sturdy feet, looking just like an allegory of Yeomanry, solid and serious as one of his own solemn sheep, for his was not the firebrand version of Puritanism, but that of a man who mistrusts all wonders but loves good works. His mother, too, he thought of; large, soft-eyed and gentle as a milking cow she was, but with sudden flashes of steely determination that even his father knew better than to try and defeat. His brothers, too; they were quite a lot older than him, men already when Hopewell was but a small boy, large and solemn and respectable as their father. No sisters, though he knew his mother would dearly have loved a little girl. She'd had to make do with Hopewell, her youngest, and, he knew now, most cherished. But wanton, wanton! He groaned aloud. How often had he bothered to write to his poor mother, or thank his father, truly in his heart, and not just at the edge of his lips, for all they had given him? Now, he'd never be able to tell them.

He put his hand over his heart, tears of self-pity and love for his parents, mixed, falling unchecked down his cheeks. As he did so, he felt something sharp in his doublet.

Frowning, he pulled it out of the folds, and exclaimed out loud: for it was the bit of mirror the beggar had given him, back on the quayside in London. He gazed into it for an instant, seeing his red-rimmed, blue eyes, his sodden hair which looked black rather than fair now, because of the weight of water in it; his slack and trembling mouth. Then with a muttered exclamation, he threw it from him. What good was it, here? But as the piece of glass landed on the water, a strange thing happened. In the instant between the silver shard piercing the fluid silver of the sea, and it vanishing under the waves, the rays of the moon seemed to catch at the bit of glass, and throw back a reflection that was for all the world like a bright track, a pathway on the sea. And as Hopewell's glance was drawn along that shining path to its end, he saw, as if scales had dropped from his eyes, that the distant line of brown which he'd taken to be some more remains of the shipwreck, broken timbers bobbing in the sea, was in fact, and incontestably, a line of coastline. He gave a great shout of joy then, and relief, and delight; and mind and body now entirely working together, as one, he began paddling furiously towards that most beautiful sight.

Fourteen

It seemed that his whole progress was charmed now, as if the sea itself, after nearly swallowing him whole, wished now only to speed him on his way to salvation. In a very short time, the line of coast resolved itself into gently sloping, fertile-looking land running down to a horseshoe-shaped bay, and though Hopewell could not of course see the whole extent of that land, he thought it must be some kind of large island. The Lost Island, he thought happily, paddling along the last few minutes, the Lost Island of the philosopher, discovered in the path of the midsummer moon! And he, who unlike his father but like his mother, never wondered at wonders, but took them for what they were, and naturally, that they should be given to him as well. For was he not Hopewell Shakespeare?

He reached the warm shallows and stood up, the water lapping softly around his waist. Yes, it was a beautiful country he had made landing on: a rich and soft-looking country, grassland beyond the beach, dotted with trees of good size, as well as, further on, smaller clumps of things which he rather thought might be flocks of some grazing animal, most likely sheep. In the far distance, he could see the gleam of something that looked like a building of some kind, though he could not quite distinguish *what* kind. He would go there, and find the Lord of Alchemists and ask him what he must do to make his fortune. For a moment, then, he thought sadly of Captain Wolfe, and wished that he could have come to his journey's end here too; but at least he, Hopewell, would try and accomplish what the old privateer had wanted to do. It would be, at least, the most fitting monument to his memory.

Once on land, he shook himself like a dog, noting with delight how the air here seemed scented and balmy as a summer's day, with none of the chill of night at all. Under his feet, the silvery sand was pleasantly warm, and all at once, he felt as if he had come to a place that could be home: not like the farm he had grown up on, but some other kind of home, a dream one of the soul. Yet this *was* no dream; it was real enough, and the nightmare of the tempest slid quietly from his mind. Not even the sea's whisper and hiss on the sands and pebbles of the beach could trouble him any more, for he had been borne safely on it to this place.

Now he was safe, he must walk to the building he could see in the distance, and ask for the kindness and hospitality of its master. Just then, a picture of how he must appear struck him: he could really have done with that looking-glass, now, he thought, with a laugh that owed as much to a sudden lightness of heart as to a wry recognition of the absurdity of the thought itself. He must look like a rogue or sturdy beggar type: he had lost his shoes somewhere in the sea, and his clothes were wet through, and would likely shrink as they dried. He ran his fingers comb-like through his disordered hair, and wrung out the first of the water from his sleeves. It would have to do; and doubtless the Lord of Alchemists would easily be able to conjure up new raiment for him, just like that! And food, too . . . ah! His stomach rumbled with the dream of the delights which he hoped would await him on this blessed, this enchanted, this lost-and-found island. With a light step, he turned his back on the sea, and began walking up the slope towards the pasturelands, gleaming white under the moon.

It was much further than he had realized at first, but not the length, and not the tiredness, worried Hopewell at all, for this land was so gentle to walk in, its air so sweet, that it was like being borne still in the water, but without any of that element's wetness or instability. The moon set, and soon only the starlight guided his steps; but those heavenly bodies, here in the skies over Lost Island, seemed not so much bigger and brighter as somehow more themselves than they had been back in the English skies. It was a puzzle, right enough, but not one to break your head with; one to be grateful for.

He passed amongst the clumps of trees, and came to a singing little stream over which was a ford. Under the starlight, the stream bed's pebbles sparkled in the water like so much gold and silver and precious jewels. Halfway over the ford, Hopewell bent down to look at these more closely, and as his fingers sifted through the clear water to pick up the pebbles, it seemed to him that his very skin was sparkling in that water, as if it were coated with a fine mesh of gold. Laughing in delight, he grasped at a handful of pebbles, but started back in surprise when they slid between his fingers like slippery little fish. Indeed, the pebbles appeared to have grown tails and darted away to hide amongst the waterweed, further down the stream.

Hopewell shook his head and finished crossing the stream. 'I have seen a great wonder,' he said to himself; 'now I know I am in the land where all alchemy begins! A very great magician indeed must be the master of this place!'

Towards dawn, he came to a place where the flocks were grazing. The animals stopped eating as he approached, and raised their heads to look at him. Hopewell called to them softly, as he had used to call his father's flocks, 'Whist, whist, whist, my fine ladies, my fine sproglets, here, here, here, to me, to me!' And then they were all around him, nibbling at his fingers, breathing softly on his hands, their sweet animal smell rising up like childhood all around him. He saw that in amongst the white, white sheep were some black as night, and just as beautiful, and quite a few, too, that he recognized as not being sheep at all, but goats; and shook his head at that. 'What can your master be thinking of, putting sheep and goats together? Methinks I will have to give him some advice of husbandry, that I will, eh, my fine fellows?' And with that he went on, with a whole curious troop of kids and lambs at his heels, walking briskly into the first rays of the rising sun. Most of them did not stay long, but skipped away on other light-headed errands, so that soon only one exceedingly bright-eyed little goat, with a coat as long and silken as a lady's shawl, still trotted beside him. Hopewell turned and looked at it sternly. 'On your way, kidlet,' he told the little goat, 'go, see your friends and kin. For I go to see the master of this place.'

The kid looked at him with bright dark eyes that seemed almost human in their intelligence, and bleated, once, softly, for all the world like it was pleading with Hopewell. 'No, no,' said Hopewell, trying hard to be even more stern. 'What will the Lord of Alchemists think of me, if I come to his palace with a little goat trotting at my heels? Best go back to the others, my little friend.'

The kid did not budge, but bleated again, even more pleadingly. Hopewell threw up his arms, and looked around, furtively, to make sure no one was watching him being bested by a *goat*, for sweet Heaven's sake! 'As well try and persuade a stone to speak as try and force a goat to do what it does not want,' he said to the kid, resignedly, and trudged on, closely followed by the bounding, lively little animal.

As the sun rose higher and higher in the sky, and the birds of morning woke up, making the air around them resound with song, Hopewell came closer and closer to the building, and saw it in plain view. Perhaps that should not be *plain* view, for there was nothing plain about it, not at all. If the countryside around it was just like the farmland of Hopewell's childhood, so what he saw now was more like something harking back to the wonders of the ancients, but with true, modern refinement as well. It was a round building of most pleasing proportions, built in some pale, yet glowing, golden stone, with many windows at the top, and pillars at the bottom, with steps leading up to the great carved wooden front door. There was a very fine balcony circling the windows as well, so that the whole mansion had the appearance and shape of two buildings joined together: a drum waisted by a circle, and a dome for a roof, covered with sparkling, white tiles that were as glittering as salt in the sunshine. It was this glitter which Hopewell had seen from as far away as the beach.

Around the building was a garden walled by a semi-circular, golden stone wall, so that it was not completely enclosed, and in this garden a fountain played, and all kinds of flowers and herbs and fruit grew in a sweet and extraordinary profusion, yet with each thing carefully in its place. The whole effect, though gorgeous, was oddly familiar to Hopewell, who, after thinking about it for some little while, decided at last that it looked exactly like the Italy he had seen represented at the Globe many a time, for one of Will Shakespeare's Italian plays. This was a setting fit for *Much Ado About Nothing*, for instance: he could just imagine the reluctant lovers, Beatrice and Benedick, sparring with each other in the gardens; or, leaning on the balustrade, there would be Juliet, calling out to her Romeo. It was as if the painted stage setting had come to life. And so it was amazing but not altogether strange to him, and therefore he was not afraid, only excited.

He looked around him for a sign of human life, whether of master or servant; but there was no one. He walked up to the great wooden door of the domed mansion, but it was shut fast, and no one answered his repeated and thunderous knocks. There was only the little goat sticking still to his heels, and he turned to look at it, a frown creasing his brow. 'Now where is everyone, kidlet? I would like to present my greetings to your master: do you know where he is?'

At that moment, out of the corner of his eye, he caught a flicker of movement at one side of the building: what looked like a flash of red: a skirt, perhaps, or cloak? He ran towards the place, the little goat galloping after him. But by the time he reached it, whoever it was had vanished. He stood irresolutely there for an instant, scratching his head. 'Well, well, I suppose I had better . . .' The goat tugged at his sleeve. 'Stop that, kidlet, stop that, I'm trying to think!'

'Mehhhh,' shrilled the goat. 'Mehhhh!' it said again, pulling at him. Hopewell glared at it. 'Stop that,' he said, and tried to pull his sleeve away from the little creature's mouth. But the cloth, weakened by exposure in the sea, tore right across. Hopewell was hopping mad. 'You pesky little varmint! You addle-pated fleabag! You little seed of mischief-maker! Now look what you've done! I'll look just like a beggar now when I . . .'

'You looked just like a beggar before,' came a light voice, suddenly, behind him, and Hopewell spun on his heel to find – no one, and nothing. 'Just like a beggar,' said the voice, again, mockingly, and Hopewell, turning around again to face in the other direction, suddenly thought the voice was familiar. But still he could see no one. Yet the mocking voice echoed all around him, trilling with laughter irrepressible as a fountain, 'Naught but a beggar, indeed, indeed, indeed!'

Poor Hopewell! He spun on his heels once, twice, three times, whilst the little goat regarded him with puzzlement and the mocking laughter echoed all around him. Finally, he'd had enough.

'Are you afraid of beggars, then, that you do not show yourself?' Defiantly, red-faced, he glared all around, thinking that at last he'd had the final word, for the garden was silent a moment; but then the voice said, just as lightly, 'Afraid of beggars who cannot even ask what it is they need? Rather be afraid to be a beggar who cannot even accomplish his task,' and now Hopewell, following the sound of the voice more closely, from sheer frustrated rage, lifted his head: and saw that a girl was standing on the balcony of the building, a young girl, younger than himself by about five years or so, barefoot, dressed in a bright red gown, with skin of a dark olive colour, black eyes, and braided hair the golden-brown colour of ripe hazelnut shells. There was nothing familiar about her. She was a complete stranger.

'So, you manage to find your eyes at last!' said the girl, and Hopewell, miffed at being thus tricked by a little gypsy-looking slip of a thing, looked sulky and said nothing. But the goat bounded and frisked, and gave every appearance of delight, so that Hopewell, uncertain as to her status in this place, thought he had better play it cautiously. He would have to treat her more courteously than she had treated him, anyway.

'Lady,' he said with an effort, 'will you tell me if I have come to the place where dwells the Lord of Alchemists?'

The girl tossed her head. 'I am not called Lady,' she declared. 'My name is Flora, and that's my goat you have there, my friend, Caprice.'

A better name for the goat's mistress, Hopewell thought.

'Lady Flora, then . . .'

'Flora, Flora, Flora,' chanted the girl, twirling on her balcony. 'Have you lost your ears as well?'

'Flora, then,' snapped Hopewell, very crossly indeed. 'Have I come to the place of the—'

'You don't need to repeat it,' interrupted Flora, 'I know perfectly well what you said the first time.'

'Well, is it?' said Hopewell, completely losing his patience.

'Why, yes. If that is what you choose to call our home, then so be it,' said Flora, and bowed. Hopewell gnashed his teeth, but managed to say, 'Will you take me to your lord, if you please . . . er, Flora?'

'My lord?' said Flora.

Hopewell was struck by a sudden thought. 'Your father, perhaps?' he hazarded cautiously. 'Your father, the Lord of Alchemists.'

'Ah, I see. That's what you want.' Flora grinned, and Hopewell scowled. But her next words quite wiped crossness from his mind.

'You're not the first sea-bedraggled beggar to ask that today. The world is beating a path to our door, it would seem.'

'Who else came here?' shouted Hopewell. 'Please, Flora, tell me: did anyone else come to you from the sea? From the tempest-tossed murdered ship called the

Golden Dragon? Please tell me: are any of my comrades alive?'

'Full fathom five,' sang Flora, 'full fathom five, down they dive, up again, all those desperate men, through the wild wild shouting sea, come to pester me!'

'Please, Flora: was there a Captain Wolfe amongst them? A tall, well-favoured man, with a splendid beard?'

'There may have been,' said Flora, 'and then again, there may not. But how will you know, unless you come in?'

'Come in?' echoed Hopewell. 'But the door is—'

At that moment, with a booming clang, the big door of the mansion opened wide. As it did so, Caprice tweaked at Hopewell's sleeve with an urgency that he no longer wanted to deny, and taking the steps two at a time, he raced after her into the marvellous mansion of the Lord of Alchemists.

Fifteen

Hopewell found himself at the beginning of a long corridor, its sky-blue ceiling most sweetly vaulted, and the creamy walls covered in the most fantastically intricate paintings he had ever seen, so that he had to pause every so often to look at them. On the walls were fauns and satyrs capering in a sunlit wood, and dryads, and nymphs, and all kinds of woodland beings of that kind, dancing with shepherds, and milkmaids, and even beribboned goats and sheep. But the pretty scenes didn't end on the walls. The floor, of a rich, glowing wood, was inlaid with squares of mother-of-pearl and ebony to form yet more pictures. These were of the sea – there were mermaids, Neptune with his trident, shell-like ships and dolphins. Glancing up to the ceiling, Hopewell could distinguish little cherubs and cupids and other airy things, frolicking in the blue sky.

'It's like the world,' he said, solemnly, to Caprice; and the little goat waggled her ears. 'You see, kidlet, here are three of the four elements, earth, air and water; now where can fire be, I wonder?'

Caprice hadn't stopped to listen to the rest of his discourse; she had already trotted down the end of the corridor, where an arched doorway led through into – what? Hopewell forgot about his cleverness in understanding so quickly the scheme of this first of the Alchemist's rooms, and galloped after her. 'Wait! Wait!'

Here, in a room that seemed to Hopewell vast as a castle hall, though much more convenient, was the fourth element – fire. An enormous, unnecessary example of the element burnt with a quantity of scarlet and gold flame in a massive fireplace, elegantly contained by a vast carved marble mantelpiece. But it was much more – and less – than it appeared at first: for both fire and fireplace were, in fact, what is known as *trompe-l'oeil*, or cheat-eye, in good plain English, and painted on, not real. Even the marble of the great mantelpiece, Hopewell found when he approached it, was a trickery, though so skilfully done as to be completely convincing. But even this wonder paled before the next sight to meet his eyes: for on a great long table, at one side of the room, was set a feast to water the mouth of any living thing, much more so a youth who had not eaten for a whole night and a morning. Roast and boiled meats, platters of vegetables, flummeries and jellies, honey cakes and gingerbread: nothing was lacking, no, and not even the drink, set out in clear bottles the very colour and limpidity of dew.

Apart from the laden table, and the painted fire, and a red-curtained alcove down one end of the room, there was nothing there; and, certainly, no one, except for Hopewell and the goat. It was not good manners, he knew, to begin on a meal before your host even greeted you; but oh, everything was so quiet, and, ah, the food looked so inviting, and his stomach grumbled so piteously! He looked at Caprice, and the kid looked back at him, more solemnly than before. No; he could not . . . he must not . . . He must look for the master of the house; oh, where, oh where was that imp of a Flora? Had she gone to fetch her father? It looked like – his glance straying back to the table, and back – it looked like they were expecting a great company, to eat all this most marvellous feast. They surely could not begrudge him just a little . . .

'Ow!' he hissed, as the goat's sharp little teeth nipped his wandering hand. He drew it back, and glared. 'Mistress Caprice,' he said, 'you take too many liberties, methinks!' Head held high, one hand rubbing at the still stinging spot where the little goat had bitten him, Hopewell stalked off in high dudgeon towards the curtained alcove. He swished aside the curtain, still in a huff; and discovered there a large chest, and, laid out on it, a complete suit of clothes such as he would have given his eye-teeth for, back in London. Fine hose; a doublet of green and blue, combined, such as would suit his colouring admirably, with large crystal and jet buttons, most cunningly inlaid with swans' heads; a dark blue cloak; soft leather shoes, intricately worked; a velvet cap in the same dark blue, with a large peacock's feather in it, secured by a pearl-headed pin. 'My stars,' said Hopewell, kneeling down beside the chest, 'a body might think these clothes had been tailored just for me!' For indeed, they seemed to be exactly his size, even to the shoes.

He looked at Caprice; the goat looked back at him, blinked, and sat down as goats sit down, on their sides, with a permissive air of infinite patience, as if to say: Go on, then, do what you must do, I'll wait. Hopewell's heart skipped a beat. With this rig on, he'd be a sight, sure, to see!

Quickly, he pulled off the sea–stiff clothes he'd come in, and after a moment's thought, shoved them into the chest on top of whatever else was in there. Now, he tried the other things on. As he'd thought, they fitted perfectly – snug as a second skin. There was a polished metal mirror in one corner, and he looked happily at the reflection of himself it threw back. 'Well, Caprice,' he said, twirling around to catch sight of his back view, as well, 'methinks I could walk in the procession of the Queen herself, today, if she were well enough to have processions these days!'

Caprice looked at him, and seemed to nod, if a goat can be said to nod. 'Come, kidlet,' said Hopewell, gaily, making for a door set in the back of the alcove, 'we must press on, and find the master of this house, to thank him for this, and also to remind him of the feast in the other room!'

Beyond the door was another painted corridor, longer and narrower than the other, which ran round in a kind of twist towards a set of marble stairs. Hopewell saw that this corridor had a design on it of growing green things, vines and tendrils curving all over, and flowers the colours of the rainbow sprinkled on them. Running down this corridor, he almost felt as though he were an insect, running around in the bottom of a patch of meadow, grasses and herbs and flowers brooding over him, like trees do to men. For some reason, this made him think of Flora. It would be just like her, he decided, if she was waiting to ambush him somewhere in this painted jungle . . . But he reached the stairs without mishap, and bounded up them two at a time, closely followed by Caprice, whose neat little black hooves made thin, but piercing, clattering sounds on the stairs as they went up.

Very soon, they came to a mezzanine floor, which had not been apparent from the outside, and which seemed almost to float, as if suspended whole from the ceiling on invisible wires. There was a row of little steps leading up to this floor; and both Hopewell and Caprice went up them without hesitation. But here Hopewell stopped in his tracks; for sitting with his back to them, writing industriously at a large square table in the middle of the mezzanine room, was a figure of great potency. Dressed all in rich black velvet robes, with a black velvet skullcap whence escaped strands of pure white hair reaching to the collar of the robes, the figure seemed to be a man a little below the average in height, if not in weight.

In front of the man, on the table, and quite visible to Hopewell where he stood in awestruck silence, were many accoutrements of the magician's profession: a large globe of the world, a glittering, silver skull, crystal vials in which gurgled some fugitive, elemental substances, glass plates covered with plant specimens, and powders in different colours. Against one wall was a neatly made curtained box bed, and near it, covering nearly the whole of the rest of the three walls of that room, was an enormous floor-to-ceiling bookcase, stuffed full of books in deep colours of worked leather. Hopewell's eyes opened even wider at this, if that were possible. That there should be so many books in the whole, entire world, let alone in one room, almost beggared his imagination. He had quite forgotten about Flora and the annoyance she had caused him, before; he had forgotten about wanting to see Wolfe; forgotten even about how hungry he was, and how fine he looked in his new clothes; forgotten everything but that he was in the presence of the greatest magician in the world, the Lord of Alchemists himself.

Caprice had stayed quietly by his side for quite a while, as if aware that he must be given time to take it all in; now, she gave a little tug at Hopewell's sleeve. The youth hardly noticed, so absorbed was he in contemplation of the man who must be the Lord of Alchemists; so the little goat tossed her head, and trotted forward briskly, bleating loudly. The man waved a hand. 'Caprice, Caprice,' Hopewell heard him murmur, 'once again, have I not told you to come in quietly, when I am in the midst of study?'

Hopewell was scandalized, if a little gratified, as well, to see that the little goat was no respecter of persons, for she gave a smart little nip at the man's sleeve, as if to say, Look, look, look! It worked: the old man spun around, and Hopewell saw a scholarly, wrinkled face, with sparkling brown eyes magnified by round nose-spectacles, a face set off splendidly by thick white whiskers, the beard of which reached almost to the man's breast.

'Bless my soul!' said the old man, scratching rather distractedly behind Caprice's ears and staring at Hopewell. 'Who are you?'

Hopewell came forward eagerly but shyly, nonetheless. When he was almost in front of the magician, he gave a deep bow, sweeping off his cap, just as he had seen actors playing courtiers do on stage at the Globe.

'Lord of Alchemists, and Master of the Lost Island, I present my greetings from a far-distant shore,' he said, solemnly. 'I am Hopewell Shakespeare, scion of the Shakespeare family, of great renown.'

'Is that so?' said the man, rather faintly. 'I cannot say I have heard tell of it before. But then,' he added, kindly, 'I have been much absorbed in my study and research these many years.'

'Oh, yes, sir,' said Hopewell, fervently. 'That, one can plainly see.'

The old man smiled. 'It is good to see a young one who appreciates learning,' he observed. 'Well, my lad, as you have given me your name, I will give you mine. I am Doctor Prosper Bonaventure, master in philosophy, astrology, alchemy, fortune telling and clerking, late of Paris, Prague, Venice, and many other places. And now of the Lost Island, or *Perdita*, as I have called it in my research, from the Latin and the French and no doubt the Spanish, is that not so?'

Thus appealed to, Hopewell stammered, 'Oh, yes, sir, that is . . . indeed . . . I do not know . . .'

'Never mind,' said Dr Bonaventure in fatherly tones, 'you will remember the name, I'll be bound. But, my dear boy,' he went on, with a little smile, 'why do you stare at me so, with such roundness of eyes?'

'Oh sir,' breathed Hopewell, 'it is just that I am so glad, and so honoured, to meet the greatest magician in the world, the Lord of Alchemists, and seeing that he is not some great and terrible sorcerer, as I had imagined, but a man most kind and jolly-looking.' Remembering what Wolfe had said, he rushed on, 'But so extraordinary, too. You must have seen so many things, sir, in your long, long life. Yet you look very youthful, sir, for one who must be more than a thousand years old! But then, as you no doubt have invented the Elixir of Youth, that is not surprising, is it? I thank you, sir, for allowing me to come ashore on your Lost Island . . . on Perdy . . . Perda . . .'

'Perdita,' said the old man, patiently. 'Yes, I do admit that I *am* well preserved, for one of my years,' said Dr Bonaventure, with a pleased gleam behind his spectacles.

'But, I must tell you now, Hopewell,' he went on, rather reluctantly, 'that I am not – ahem, unfortunately – the Lord of Alchemists. I am, my child, still a student indeed when it comes to the greatest art of all, though I have been a year and more on this blessed island.'

'You are not the Lord of Alchemists, sir?' Hopewell was crestfallen. Bonaventure spread his hands in rueful acknowledgement. 'No, I am not, lad, but let me tell you this – I too am waiting for the Lord of Alchemists, who I know resides here. He has been absent on a long voyage, but will return in good time.'

'Did Flora tell you this, sir? Is she the daughter of the Lord of Alchemists?'

'I believe so, Hopewell. She is a most . . . flighty and unique little creature, that I know, and quite able to support herself in her father's absences, on account of the bountifulness of his island.'

'Did she tell you when the Lord of Alchemists would return, sir?'

'No. But I think it must be soon.'

'Did you get here, sir – did you get here like me?'

'Like you, Hopewell?' Dr Bonaventure looked roguishly at him. 'How was that, my dear?'

'Well . . . it's a long story, sir, but I came here through shipwreck, I suppose.'

The old man nodded incuriously. 'Yes, many come that way, I think. But as to me – do you know, I am not at all sure how it happened? One moment, Hopewell, I was in my house in Venice, eating a plate of beans; the next, I open my eyes and find myself here.'

Hopewell gaped at him. 'Strange indeed, sir!'

'Strange indeed,' said Dr Bonaventure complacently, 'but then, my life has been full of strange things. That is what happens when you are a deep thinker on all sorts of matters, my child,' he added kindly, to the awestruck Hopewell. 'I will have much to write about, won't I, when the Lord of Alchemists returns, and I can go home.'

'Home, sir?' Hopewell glanced around him. 'But surely . . .'

'Yes, it is a most marvellous place,' said Bonaventure, following his glance, 'and I have done much wonderful study and research here. But now I long to show the world of men all the glorious things I have learnt here, and become known as the greatest benefactor mankind has ever known. The things I have learnt and discovered, Hopewell,' he went on, tapping at his papers, 'would end all human striving and effort, and by doing so, end all misery. I am writing a herbal, Hopewell, to cure all ills; and a star chart, to guide sailors unerringly, wherever they may be; and a philosophy of life, so that all may follow the perfect way to live. And so I wish to sacrifice myself, sacrifice the peace and contentment I have learnt here, in order to do my stern duty – to pass on the knowledge of the Lost Island to all my suffering fellows in the world. That is the only fortune I wish to pass on, the only one worth having.'

'Oh, *sir*!' said Hopewell, clasping his hands together, very moved by this splendid speech.

Bonaventure looked at him benignly. 'I would help you, too, Hopewell,' he said magisterially, 'help you achieve your heart's desire, your own fortune.'

'Oh, sir!' said Hopewell again. 'Then you must indeed be getting close to the knowledge and power of the Lord of Alchemists.'

'Hush!' said Bonaventure, putting a finger to his lips. 'One should not speak thus of the master of this place, you know, Hopewell, or there is no telling what he might do . . .'

'But he must be a *good* enchanter,' said Hopewell, eyes widening, 'or else, why would this place be so beautiful and smiling?'

'I am not sure it is thus for everyone who lands on it,' said Bonaventure, 'though I have not enquired too closely into this, indeed.' He leant towards Hopewell and whispered, 'The island, I am convinced, deals with those who land on it according to their deserts. There is more to this place than meets the eye, young man. Keep your wits about you, I should.'

Hopewell stared at him, then nodded, meaningfully, man to man. Well! If Dr Bonaventure was not the Lord of Alchemists, then he might be a friend, and a teacher, perhaps, even. Perhaps Hopewell, too, could become absorbed in study and research and return, older, wiser and with just such a splendid beard as the good doctor's, in triumph to the world as a benefactor of mankind . . . Yes, that would be a nice thing to aspire to; a fortune far richer and fitting than a mere handful of gold.

'Sir,' he said, shyly, 'would you make me your student? I am a quick study, I promise you. I know already some Latin, and can passably decipher Greek,' he hurried on, 'and know a great deal about Illyria, and Verona, and other such far off and wondrous places, and also I know about strange happenings, and desperate love, and some of the philosophy of the stars, given as I go for my education most often to the Globe, where such things are explored . . .'

'The Globe?' said Dr Bonaventure. 'It must be a new school of philosophy, for I have not heard tell of it. But you look a willing boy, Hopewell, and I find that more and more do I need an assistant to keep notes for me and wash out vials and find new specimens on the island for me to study – for indeed, the place is bursting with new kinds of plants, with all kinds of properties, properties I have not yet quite discovered. Flora is not steady enough, no, not indeed, for such a task. If such an assistant could also help me to trial out these properties, then that would be even better. You see, Hopewell, a great and famous philosopher such as myself cannot experiment on himself, for the results of such experiments would be useless to the common range of mankind, whose constitution is somewhat different. Do you understand, Hopewell?'

'I think so,' said Hopewell, frowning a little, for something about what the doctor was saying troubled him slightly. Was he intending that he, Hopewell Shakespeare, was of the common range of mankind? He was swiftly reassured on this point by Dr Bonaventure, who catching sight of Hopewell's expression, said, hastily, 'A student of mine is of course different to the common herd of mankind; and his dedication to the exact science we will discover together will, of course, be as important in the betterment of mankind as his master and teacher's.'

This was a better thing to hear, by far; and Hopewell smiled with great satisfaction, owning that he would, indeed, like to become Dr Bonaventure's assistant. He was about to explain his decision in greater detail when Caprice gave a high, merry bleat. The door down one end of the room opened, and in came Flora, closely followed by – Kit Sly and Davy Jones!

Sixteen

For a moment, Hopewell could only stare. The galley boy and the first mate, dressed, like Hopewell, in fine new clothes, looked rather different to the way they had done back on the *Golden Dragon*. Davy Jones, soberly dressed in dark greens and black, looked every inch the respectable gentleman, despite the beginnings of a salt-and-pepper stubble on his chin, whilst Kit Sly, rigged out splendidly in red-brown and yellow, his hair beginning to regrow sooty and wild on his inexpertly shaven head, had somehow a softer and younger look to him. Both of them started when they saw Hopewell, and cast a quick glance at each other: a glance that filled the youth with indignation, for it reminded him instantly of the last scene he had witnessed on board the *Golden Dragon*, just before the ship had gone down, broken up by what he knew now quite clearly to be the supernatural power of the White Ship. He had seen Jones flinging himself on the master of the *Dragon*, grappling with him, no doubt to make sure he would not survive the shipwreck.

'Murderers!' he shouted, springing towards them. 'Murderers! What did you do with Captain Wolfe!'

The two looked at each other again. 'What we did, Hopewell?' said Davy Jones in his soft Welsh voice. 'Why, nothing, lad.'

'Nothing,' echoed Kit Sly, with a sideways grin.

'Lies, lies,' shouted Hopewell, greatly excited. 'Sir,' he went on, turning back to the astounded Dr Bonaventure, 'these men are criminals, villains of the deepest hue! They plotted mutiny and murder against their own captain, and in the last desperate moments of our ship, made sure poor Master Wolfe would not survive. They must be held fast, sir, and tried for their wickedness.'

Bonaventure looked back at him, and shrugged helplessly. 'I am sorry, lad,' he said at last, 'but I am not the master of this island, and cannot dispose as I should like. We will have to wait for his return to see what decision the Lord of Alchemists may make as to their fate. Meanwhile, they are here; the Lost Island has not rejected their coming, Hopewell. But who knows what is in store?' Hopewell saw that there was a twinkled meaning, deep in the philosopher's eyes: Remember what I told you, said the twinkle, the island deals with those who make landing on it according to their deserts . . .

'Who knows what is in store, indeed?' Davy Jones had the impudence to echo. 'Now, listen, lad, I know you think the worst of me, and Kit; but you are mistaken, gravely mistaken. And now you and I and Kit are here on this island, the only survivors of the poor *Golden Dragon*; instead of fighting each other, we should make common cause. Besides,' and here his glance slid towards the good doctor – 'I see that this is a place where good manners and learning and beauty are the law; and it ill behoves us to disturb its peace and tranquillity with shouting and waving of arms.' He gave a smarmy smile, and Hopewell was annoyed and amazed to see that the old philosopher responded with a smile of his own.

'You are right, sir,' said Dr Bonaventure, calmly. 'This is not a place to carry on old feuds, no, not at all.'

Hopewell felt choked with indignation, as all the pairs of eyes were turned on him in reproof. It was worse even when Davy Jones held out one calloused hand to him. 'Shake, boy,' he said, and this time his smile was not smarmy, but triumphant. 'Forget old injuries and suspicions, eh? Start afresh, in a brave new world?'

'What of Captain Wolfe?' said Hopewell, 'poor Captain Wolfe, who cannot start afresh, who wanted so to reach this place . . .' Suddenly, tears filled his eyes, and he could not continue. But Davy Jones said, quietly, 'Dick Wolfe was once my greatest friend, Hopewell: but he is gone, and it does his memory no honour to remember him as he was at the last. It was because of his sad change that the *Golden Dragon* was lost, and all those men's lives, Hopewell.'

It was too much for Hopewell, who would have flung himself there and then on the Welshman and scratched his eyes out, if it had not been for Flora, who deftly caught his arm in a grip that was surprisingly strong. 'Enough, enough,' she said.

'Flora is right,' said Bonaventure, looking earnestly at Hopewell. 'All that is in the past. You are here, on the Lost Island, and here, those who wish to be allowed to remain must put all bitterness behind them.'

'Yes,' said Flora, 'or they get nothing to eat. Isn't that so, Kit, Kitty, Kitty-cat, Kit,' she continued, dancing around the silent Kit Sly in such a teasing manner that Hopewell almost sympathized with him. 'Look at me, I'm a naughty mouse, Kit, Kitty-cat, show me your claws, come out of hiding, Kitty-cat,' went on Flora, dancing around; and Caprice danced with her, whilst the bemused Sly turned round and round, trying both to keep an eye on the girl and the goat, and look nonchalant at the same time: a patent impossibility.

'Where *is* your cat, Sly?' Hopewell said, not unkindly. Kit's eyes widened, but before he could speak, Davy broke in, saying, 'The cat used up its ninth life, I'm afraid, Hopewell. Isn't that so, Kit?'

Kit nodded, dumbly. But Flora laughed again, so that Hopewell found he could spare a little indignation on Kit's behalf, in the face of her casual cruelty.

'If we must share this island, then I suppose we must share it in peace,' he snapped. 'All of us.'

'Good, good,' said Dr Bonaventure, rubbing his hands, 'now you are all, as it were, guests on the Lost Island, and must keep to its laws and rules. Isn't that so, Flora, my dear? Wouldn't your father have it this way?' he added, trying to distract the girl from her irritating game.

But Flora took no notice. With a peal of laughter, she draped an arm around Kit Sly's thin shoulders. 'Come with me, my friend,' she said, 'we'll beat them to the table, so we will, Kitty-cat; and then, you and I can play together. You'd like that, wouldn't you, Kitty?'

Hopewell almost felt sorry for Kit Sly at that moment; for the boy's green eyes grew round with a kind of fright, and he cast a helpless glance at Davy Jones. But, proving the old adage of there being no honour amongst thieves, the older man took no notice at all, allowing the girl to drag the boy away, with not a single expression of any kind of concern. Instead, he turned to the old philosopher, with a smarmy smile and a solicitous glance.

'Sir – may I perhaps assist you down the stairs?'

'Very kind, very kind,' said Dr Bonaventure, hoisting himself out of his chair and pointing towards a carved stick near the bookcase. Whilst Hopewell hovered, ineffectually, unwilling to leave the field totally in possession of the abominable Welshman, Jones went to fetch the stick, and brought it back to its owner.

'It is a most marvellous library you have, sir,' he remarked. 'I do not think I have seen a finer – not even, perhaps in the palace of the Doge, in Venice.'

'Ah! You know Venice!' The good doctor was positively beaming.

'I do indeed.'

Liar, thought Hopewell. Smarmy liar.

'I spent many years in Venice, Master . . . er . . .'

'Master Jones. Davy Jones.'

'Ah! A good Welsh name indeed! How long were you in Venice, Master Jones?'

'Quite some time,' said Jones, with a mysterious smile.

'Ah, that is wonderful! We will have much to discuss then. I am glad to have found a companion of the mind, Master Jones. This island is a lovely place to live, but it is hard sustaining an intellectual conversation with Flora, or Caprice, you understand,' he added, with a hearty laugh.

'That I do understand, indeed, Dr Bonaventure,' said Davy Jones.

Hopewell was dismayed by this turn of events. The good doctor was far too guileless and unworldly, he thought, and needed saving from the consequences of his folly. Determined to regain Dr Bonaventure's attention, he said, eagerly, 'Sir, when will I be able to begin work as your assistant?' Bonaventure turned a rather impatient face to him. 'When, Hopewell?'

'Hopewell is an eager learner, a quick study, sir, who will soon understand all there is to do – and much else that there is not to do,' said Davy Jones, raising a wry eyebrow. Hopewell flushed angrily, and was about to retort with something suitably cutting, when Flora's clear, teasing voice floated up from downstairs. 'If you're not down in two blinks, you'll get nothing, nothing at all!'

'She means it,' said Bonaventure, hastily shuffling towards the stairs. 'We had best hurry, my friends, or there will indeed be nothing left. Flora already has some of the powers of her father; and I'm afraid she uses them in a most capricious manner.'

Seventeen

The food was every bit as good as it had looked, laid out on the table. No servants attended them at all; indeed, in all his time here, Hopewell had not seen a single servitor or attendant, but that did not surprise him. What was the good of an enchanted island, after all, if you had to have gossipy cooks and cleaners and drabs and scullion maids like everywhere else? Nature herself served the Lord of Alchemists, it appeared; and so the Lost Island floated in that Golden Age when no one had to toil or spin or reap or sow, but only eat and drink and be merry, without effort or suffering. Of course, Dr Bonaventure worked at his study, but Hopewell thought that was a form of scholar's merriment, every bit as entertaining for minds such as the old man's as romancing and playgoing might be for others like himself. Remembering what Flora had said, in her teasing way, about feuders getting nothing to eat, Hopewell found that his hunger was too honest and pressing a guide to allow him to brood for too long over the misfortune of being on the Lost Island with his two least favourite people. Indeed, at one point, he surprised himself by exchanging looks, and even bare words with Kit Sly, in a way not entirely hostile.

After all, he thought, the boy was just the pawn of the older man; it was Davy Jones who was the wicked mover in the events on the *Golden Dragon*, and it was Davy Jones who must pay eventually for what he had done to Captain Wolfe.

Meanwhile, though, the Welshman seemed to have the good doctor wrapped around his little finger. Bonaventure paid little enough attention to anyone else whilst at table, but though Hopewell tried hard to at least eavesdrop on some of their conversation, Flora's high spirits prevented him from hearing much at all. When the meal ended, the old philosopher and the former sailor went off together upstairs, still talking, and Hopewell, uninvited to that particular conclave, had perforce to follow in Flora's and Caprice's wake, with Kit, as they raced out into the garden. Perhaps reinvigorated by the food, relaxing in the atmosphere of the island, Kit seemed suddenly of a light heart, and merry, and jumped around as if he were discovering a childhood he had never had. Indeed, moment by moment, the boy's pinched face seemed to be filling out, his eyes becoming less mean and darting, his lips less set, his hair shining in the sunlight, and soon, he even began to laugh, his laughter of a surprisingly light and silvery tone. It was as if he were turning into a different person in front of their eyes, like a butterfly emerging from an ugly chrysalis.

But this transformation did not necessarily cheer or amaze Hopewell, particularly. Annoyed at being relegated to the category of unimportant ones by Dr Bonaventure's dismaying preference for the company of Davy Jones, he showed his ill humour by stalking manfully at some distance behind the playful three, who chased each other around the fountain, and ran races up and down the paths, shrieking all the while. But it soon grew impossible to maintain his dignified imperturbility; for Flora, then Caprice, then Kit, shyly at first then more and more boldly, began using him in their games. First of all, Flora turned him into the unwitting safety-point for some kind of mad chasing game; golden-brown braids bouncing on her shoulders, bright, black eyes dancing, she darted up to him and tipped him on one shoulder, then the other, all the time shouting, 'Home! Home! I'm home! You can't touch me!' He'd barely recovered from the annoyance of that when Caprice, choosing a moment when his back was turned, butted him smartly on the behind, sending him stumbling in the most undignified manner.

'Oh, poor Hopewell,' said Flora, in a hypocritical voice, 'naughty Caprice, to do such a thing . . .' and she made as if to help him up, to pat him down, with clucking noises of tut-tutting, and a kind of almost loverlike concern which made Hopewell's skin crawl with embarrassment. But the whole thing was all made much worse by a bright-eyed Kit, softly singing a tune Hopewell knew only too well:

'It was a lover and his lass,
With a hey, and a ho, and a hey nonny-no!'

It was too much for a crimson Hopewell. Kit couldn't have known the meaning of that song to him, but he remembered all too well his own singing of it just before his bewildering last encounter with Annie, back in London. With a frustrated roar, he launched himself at Kit, who easily skipped out of the way, and made a silly face at him from a distance. 'Oh, what could it be that ails thee?' he cried out, in a falsetto tone, and Flora clapped her hands and laughed.

'The fool's worm of self-importance ails him,' she said, 'and will not let him be, but dances a dull step in his belly!'

'Why, then, methinks we should teach the worm some new steps, then,' replied Kit.

'Methinks we should,' chimed in Flora, laughing, 'you have fine notions, my Kitty-cat!'

'Think you the worm should be taught the galliard, then?' said Kit, moving towards Hopewell in a way he found positively alarming, especially with Flora moving in on him from the opposite direction, and Caprice, head tossing, bleating loudly, from yet another. Leaving behind any shred of dignity, Hopewell took to his heels, and fled like the wind down the garden path, as if all the hobgoblins of the world were after him. He ran and ran and ran, the breath whistling in his throat, hearing the sound of their laughing pursuit behind him, desperately determined that he would not fall into their thievish, prickling, irritating, disturbing clutches, for anything on earth. He had no idea what they might do to him, but suspected it might not be at all to his liking.

★ ★ ★

Finally, he reached a place where three paths met. He looked wildly around, then took the third path, which led directly to a small clump of apple trees, clustered around a lovely, clear little pond. Quickly, he shinned up one of the biggest trees, whose leafy branches would hide him from his pursuers' sight. He crawled into the thick of the leaves, and held his breath, waiting. Pretty soon, he heard the sound of their running steps, then a pause. Hopewell's heart rattled in his chest as he strained his ears to listen to what they were saying.

'I think he went this way.' That was Flora.

'No, this way.' Kit.

'He must have gone up that path; look, there's a door out into the meadow, and it's open. The other one leads to a maze; and no one who does not know its secret can get out of it. Let's go, then, Kit. We'll catch him soon enough, and tickle him till he cries for mercy!'

Peals of laughter, then they were gone, the running footsteps moving rapidly away, then nothing. Silence fell again, and slowly, Hopewell recovered. His legs, he found, were shaking, his hands trembling, there was a nausea in his throat. Yet his pursuers were only two children and a goat. He did not need to be afraid of them, he thought. Somehow, though, it was not quite fear, but something close to it, that had lent him wings, and showed him the right place to hide. Well, now, it was safe, they would exhaust themselves running in the meadows and come back too tired to play whatever trick it was they had been intending to play on him. They would soon forget; they would soon find some other plaything, and meanwhile, he would go back to Dr Bonaventure and make sure that he would be otherwise employed when next they tried to make a monkey of him.

He climbed down more slowly than he had climbed up, and looking at the invitingly clear water of the pond, suddenly found that he was very thirsty. He would have a quick drink, and then go back to the mansion and speak firmly to the philosopher.

He knelt on the soft grass before the little pond, and cupping his hands, drank. It was just as sweet and pleasant as it looked, and he drank a little more, and was just about to drink for the third time, when all at once, he drew away with a startled cry. There was the reflection of another face in the water, a grave, beautiful, emerald-eyed young woman's face, framed in midnight-black hair, regarding him with a steady, intensely disturbing expression. A face he recognized with a piercing sweetness of the heart: the singer in Cork.

'Lady, you are here . . . oh, who are you?' he whispered, and the face smiled at him, and a finger, small, fine, and rounded came up to its lips. So clear was the reflection, so beautiful, so alluring, that Hopewell had a sudden conviction that if he reached down into the water, he would be able to touch the downy skin, stroke the wonderful hair. Trembling, he tried to suit action to thought; but of course, as soon as his fingers broke the surface of the water, the reflection vanished, and he was left bereft.

'Where are you?' he called, when the reflection did not appear again. He thought, if that was truly a reflection, and not just an alchemist's trick, then the original must be somewhere. And he was sure that this was no trick; his heart could not be persuaded otherwise. Where might she be? He looked at the water, then directly up into the branches of the tree nearest the one he'd been hiding in himself. If she was anywhere, she'd be there, he thought, in the leafy mass directly above the water. Then, as he was looking, leaves rustled, softly, leaves that had been moved by no wind. In two steps, and quite forgetting about his pursuers, Hopewell was peering up into the leafy mass. 'Lady,' he called, with a soft catch in his throat, 'Lady, please give me word if you are there?'

No sound, not even the rustle. I could climb up, Hopewell thought, and look properly. She's probably up there, hidden in shadow and leaf. But something new in his heart, some awakening modesty, some deep-seated lover's fear, stopped him from doing what his heedless nature would once have done without a second thought. So he just stood under the tree for a moment, hoping she might show herself of her own accord. Finally, remembering words he'd heard in some long-ago romance, 'Oh, fair unknown, will you not make yourself known to your humble admirer?'

'Humble admirer indeed,' came Flora's teasing voice, almost in his ear, making him jump wildly.

'What on earth are you doing, Hopewell?' A panting, laughing Kit was just behind Flora, on Caprice's heels. They seemed, as he had hoped, to have lost interest in tickling him, or chasing him, or any other childish nonsense, but he was sure it would not take long for them to start up again.

'Just looking at this tree,' he said, hastily. Hopewell

had flushed scarlet, but nothing on earth or out of it would have induced him to betray his secret, for he remembered all too well the galley boy's reaction to his story, back in Cork. He'd make mock of this, as he had of that; and provide even more fuel for Flora's foolishness. So he put on a considering look, and made as if he had a husbandman's interest in the quality of the fruit that hung from the tree's branches.

'These apples look as if they might get the blight,' he said, solemnly.

'Oh, do they? Pray tell me, Hopewell, how may we remedy this sad state of affairs?' Flora had her head on one side, as if engrossed in his opinion.

Hopewell was immediately suspicious, and a little embarrassed. 'You are the daughter of the Lord of Alchemists,' he muttered rather ungraciously. 'You are bound to know more than I of such matters.'

'It's not every day, though, that we get such a learned visitor to our shores,' said Flora, with a reverent air, though she spoilt the effect by winking at Kit, who looked as if he might burst with the laughter bubbling inside him.

'If you don't want to listen, why then, why not say so, directly?' huffed Hopewell, and stalked off again up the path back towards the garden, his backbone tingling, for he was hoping that the three rascals would not come in full cry after him.

Eighteen

They didn't; and so he reached the mansion without further incident, and passed swiftly through the first long painted corridor, into the hall where the feast had been set, into the little alcove room, through the meadow corridor, up the stairs to the mezzanine. 'Dr Bonaventure!' he called out gaily, as he ran up the steps, 'I have come to tell you that . . .'

But the room was empty. Neither the philosopher nor Davy Jones were to be seen. Hopewell hesitated a moment, wondering what to do, and where to go. He had no intention of going out into the garden again; perhaps the pair were up on the top floor, in that balcony room he hadn't seen yet. He was about to set off again when his eye was caught by the sight of Dr Bonaventure's piles of notes and papers, still on the table. Perhaps it might be a good idea to cast his eyes quickly over them, and so be able to impress the good doctor later with a true disciple's knowledge? He was sure the old scholar was easily vulnerable by way of his vanity, and had a fear that now that Bonaventure had met Davy Jones, he might ask *him* to become his assistant. And then he, Hopewell, would be left to the tender mercies of those three imps out there.

He sat down at the table, enjoying the sensation of the soft cushion under his bottom. Sitting there, at the philosopher's own desk, he could hardly contain a wriggle of pleasure, imagining himself as the famous scholar of the future, giving learned lectures to attentive audiences. He sat up straight, adjusted imaginary spectacles with one hand, the other stroking at a magnificent, illusory beard.

'Now, then, you boys, attend,' he said, sternly enough to his invisible audience, just as his own grammar-school master had done, 'attend, and you will learn some great wisdoms to store by in your small heads.' No, no, that was not quite the right note to strike; he would not be some poor mazed schoolmaster having to deal with unruly, walnut-brained boys; he would be at a university, dressed in flowing robes, and laying down the law to rich men's sons, and clever students up from the provinces. 'Attend, masters,' he rasped, 'today's lesson will be . . .' He looked down quickly at the closest papers to him, his eye lighting on a scrawled note in the margin, 'about the subject of metamorphosis, and how the flowers of the *Millefloria Bonaventura*, may indeed be the key to it . . .' He looked up, bemused. 'What is this I read, however? Metamorphosis? Why, by the little Latin I have, that does mean changing of the shape indeed. Is this the kind of experiment Dr Bonaventure means me to undertake? Let us see what else there is, in his notes.' He read on, but found nothing half as interesting, or startling, as that note in the margin. Most of it was an ordinary herbal such as the one Mistress Page owned, as

147

her only book. Dull descriptions of salad herbs and decoctions of flowers were of no moment to him whatsoever. He thrust aside that lot of manuscript, and leafed through the next one, the one on the stars Dr Bonaventure had also told him he was working on. Again, nothing very exciting, from his point of view, though he picked up a few names here and there which he might drop into the conversation one day: Ursa Major, Ursa Minor, Orion, Canis Major, Cygnus . . . Under the star book was the one on the philosophy of life, and this was the dullest of all, covered in crabbed notes, scrawls, and crossings-out that made it fiendishly difficult to read. With a great effort, he managed to decipher some:

> *'If it be but certain that innocency be at the base of non wisdom, then be it bound to say that experience be at the bottom of wisdom; therefore, if one seeks for the top of wisdom, not its bottom, one would seek for the middle ground between innocency and experience, which hath not yet a name but is mere potential, and that potential unknown to . . .'*

Forsooth! It made his head ache. What words these scholars used! He was not at all certain he'd understood even the bottom of that, let alone the top or middle. He was about to give up on the whole thing when he suddenly noticed that there was another lot of papers lying under the philosophy of life ones: papers done up in an oilskin package which he recognized at once. He had last seen this package under Captain Wolfe's arm, on board the *Golden Dragon*! He was sure the Captain had not let go of the precious thing, for it was the relic of his dead friend who had discovered that there was a pathway to the Lost Island, and that a fortune awaited those who found it . . .

Surely its presence here proved beyond doubt that Davy Jones had indeed murdered the master of the ship, for Hopewell was sure that even in the rage of the storm, Wolfe would not have let go of it, and would rather have gone down to the bottom of the ocean than allow Jones possession of it. Hopewell pulled the package towards him, and unwrapping the oilskin, looked at the papers thus revealed. Yes, they were the same, the very same that he had looked at in Wolfe's cabin, he was sure of that, though of course he still could not read the vast majority of the words that crowded their pages. What was Dr Bonaventure going to do with them? Why had Davy Jones given it to him? Could it be that once again, the duplicitous Welshman was going to inveigle another in his schemes?

Hopewell did not want to stay there too long, just in case he was discovered, so after swiftly putting everything in order, with the oilskin package securely under the other books, he left the room and made his way back into the gardens. Keeping a wary lookout for Kit and Flora and Caprice, he paced up and down near the fountain, his head so full of thoughts that he felt as if it might burst with the heat of his brain. In the end, he decided that the answers lay in three directions. Firstly, that the fortune that was to be had, somewhere on this island – Davy Jones was determined to have it, by whatever means he could. Already, through the manuscript's secrets, he had somehow contrived to land unscathed on the island, when men better than him had perished. It would only be a matter of time before he plumbed all the secrets of the manuscript. Secondly, he must still need the interpretation of a learned man like Dr Bonaventure to understand the other philosopher's full thesis. He could easily achieve that by flattering the abounding vanity of the old man − for Hopewell saw that defect clearly now, in light of Bonaventure's desertion of him. Thirdly, that Dr Bonaventure was merely a means to an end, and once Jones got what he wanted, then the old philosopher would be in the way. He had been ruthless with Wolfe, who was supposed to be his friend; just what would he do to that poor, fond, kindly man with his gleaming spectacles and his pretty air of self-regard? Hopewell did not want to think further on it, but sighed, deeply. This meant that once again, he, Hopewell, stood by way of being a friend in need to a man about to be betrayed most foully. This time, though, he would not allow Jones to deflect him from his course.

His chance came sooner than he had expected, for that very night, after a meal as copious, and mysteriously appeared, as the midday one had been, Flora brought out a vast chessboard from somewhere, and proposed a game. Dr Bonaventure blinked, and excused himself, and said he was too tired for such things, and must really put his old bones to bed; so Hopewell, seizing the chance before Davy Jones could forestall him, jumped up and offered to escort the old man to his room.

'That is very kind of you, boy, kind indeed,' said Dr Bonaventure, and leaning heavily on Hopewell's arm, he took up his stick with his other hand, and proceeded at a snail's pace out of the hall and into the corridor. Hopewell sensed several pairs of curious eyes on his back, but no one tried to stop him. Indeed, they were already beginning to argue over pawns and positions as he and the old man left the room.

When he was sure they could not be overheard, Hopewell bent down to the philosopher's ear and whispered, 'Dr Bonaventure, there is something I must tell you. Davy Jones is not a man to be trusted.'

Dr Bonaventure stopped for an instant and looked at Hopewell, his brown eyes shrewd. 'My dear boy, I think you have told me all about that, wouldn't you say? You accused him of being a murderer, and a mutineer, and Heaven knows what else, did you not, this morning?'

Hopewell did not allow himself to be dismayed. 'Sir, he is all those things – but more, too. He is after the fortune that is hidden on the Lost Island.'

This time, Bonaventure smiled. 'My dear Hopewell, if that is all! We are all seeking after Fortune, who is to be found somewhere on sweet Perdita. But it is no use seeking her; she will find you, when she is ready. Master Jones will learn that too, if indeed he does not know it already.'

'But sir . . .' Hopewell bit back the words that had been about to rise to his lips. If he told the doctor that he had seen the oilskin package, which after all had been hidden out of sight under the other papers, then he would also have to admit to the fact that he had been snooping and prying amongst the philosopher's private things. It was not an easy decision to make; but he made it, and decided thus to keep his mouth shut, for the moment.

When they reached Dr Bonaventure's room, Hopewell turned down the bed for him, put the stick away, fetched the old man's nightshirt from a storage chest, and was about to leave him to his bedtime preparations, when Bonaventure said, 'Wait, Hopewell. Will you read to me, perhaps, tonight? It is a long time since I have heard a young voice reading aloud: Flora simply will not sit still long enough. And tonight I am too unsteady in my mind to go to sleep as quickly as I usually would.'

'Sir, that I would do gladly. Which book is it you would like me to read?'

'Choose, Hopewell. Anything that takes your fancy. There is a great deal there.'

There was indeed. At the bookcase, Hopewell stood in indecision for quite a while, whilst behind him, Dr Bonaventure made his preparations for bed. Most of the books appeared to be learned tomes of one kind or another, but here and there were other things: a book of chronicles, and another of poetry. He did not recognize any of the titles, however; none of them seemed to be of the fashionable kind that was sold in London. Then his eye fell on one word: *Metamorphoses*.

'Yes, that's a good one,' called Dr Bonaventure from across the room. Even without his spectacles, he seemed to know exactly what book Hopewell had under his hand. But then, perhaps he knew the position of each book by heart, they being his only friends for a long time. 'Ovid, yes, that's right,' he went on, as Hopewell extracted the book and turned back to him. Tucked under the bedclothes, a nightcap on his head, the old man looked surprisingly small and frail, though his voice was as firm as ever. 'Do you know about him, my dear boy?'

'He was a Roman poet, sir,' said Hopewell, who had certainly heard the name of Ovid in brief moments of attention at school. A brief panic seized him; would the book be in Latin? He opened it, quickly, and saw with relief that he could read it easily, for it was in English translation.

'He was a genius,' said Dr Bonaventure, not noticing Hopewell's flurry, 'a man *with* a genius, rather, you understand. And his was a genius for mischief. It caused him great grief as a man, as it causes us much wonder, for it gave him the enmity of the Emperor, yet gave us these marvellous stories of his.'

'Yes, that is sad and ironical indeed,' said Hopewell, wisely nodding his head, as if he remembered the whole thing.

'Sad and ironical, yes, those are the right words to use, Hopewell,' said Dr Bonaventure, and Hopewell felt a glow of pleasure at the praise. He pulled up a chair next to the bed, and opened the book.

'Begin at the beginning,' said Dr Bonaventure, and closed his eyes. 'I like to hear of the creation of Creation.'

And so Hopewell began at the beginning, a little shakily at first, but with a gradually steadying voice, telling Ovid's story of the creation of Heaven and earth and the seas from Chaos, and the Golden Age, and then ill deeds of some of the first men, and how the gods were angry, and how some of the wicked men, like Lycaon, murderer many times over, had been transformed into wild beasts as a result. If only such a fate could fall on Davy Jones, Hopewell thought, as he read of the wolf Lycaon being hunted down. He read and read, till it seemed his throat would seize up and his tongue drop off; but every time he tried to stop, Dr Bonaventure's eyes would flick open, and the old man testily murmur, 'Continue, continue, I am not asleep yet.'

It was not until Hopewell was well into the second part of the book that a loud snore came from the direction of the bed. Looking up warily, Hopewell saw that the old philosopher had definitely fallen asleep, his nightcap askew, his mouth wide open. Quietly, Hopewell got up, tiptoed over to the bookcase and replaced the book in its place, then left the room, just as quietly.

Nineteen

Flora would not let any of the remaining three go to bed until she had comprehensively defeated each of them in a game of chess. Despite her age and frivolous manner, she was a fierce, even deadly, player, given to cries of savage triumph when the last of her opponent's pieces was swept off the board. Kit had already been vanquished by the time Hopewell came back down from reading to Dr Bonaventure, but Davy Jones had obviously put up a gallant struggle. That struggle continued painfully on, but finally he too had to admit defeat, and then it was Hopewell's turn. Flora did not have much sport trouncing him, however, for he lost sight of the game for moments at a time, unable to fight against his drooping eyelids. He had the indistinct impression, in fact, that Flora was unnecessarily postponing the inevitable by deliberately restricting her game, and tried to rise to the challenge. But his weary body would not let him.

At long last, Flora crowed, 'Checkmate!' and Hopewell would, if he could have opened his mouth long enough, have cheered. As it was, he merely made a vague gesture signifying he accepted his defeat. It must have been well past midnight. All he wanted was to stretch out on a bed and go to sleep. Flora's next words almost made him wake up, though, for she said, briskly sweeping up the chess pieces into a drawstring bag, 'Now, it's time for you all to go to bed. You've kept me up long enough!'

Only Davy Jones laughed at her effrontery; and that quickly broken off, as he caught Flora's fish-eyed stare. Calling to Caprice, she gathered together the rest of the chess game, and got up. Seeing that the others were making no move, she went on, 'What are you waiting for?'

They all scrambled up. 'But, Flora,' stammered Kit, speaking for them all, 'we do not know where we ought to . . .'

What kind of hostess was she, anyway? Her father would not be happy with her when he returned, Hopewell thought, mightily disgruntled. Abandoning his guests in this high-handed manner . . .

'Do you need to be told everything?' Flora was already at the door, with Caprice beside her. Then, as if relenting, she turned, and with a big smile, added, 'You'll know them when you see them,' and was gone.

'Of all the annoying . . . !' Hopewell was beside himself with crossness, and even Kit was looking uncertain. But Davy Jones smiled, shook his head, and said, 'Come, you two, this is the island. You don't expect things to work the same as you're used to, do you? Let's go upstairs, and see what we can find. If all else fails, we can always bunk down in a corner somewhere. That's no great sorrow, is it; there's more space than on a ship, anyhow!'

Hopewell did not like to admit that Davy's words sounded reasonable, but they did. Still, of what use was reason in this bewildering place? But he could not think of any smart retort, so followed Davy and Kit willingly enough, up the corridor, bypassing the mezzanine, where Dr Bonaventure still snored peacefully, to follow the marble staircase up to the top floor.

This proved to be a great circular space, with a great domed pearly coloured ceiling, and walls painted in deep shades of blue and gold, with windows set into them at intervals, and three large, coloured pictures on three of the wall panels, the last being blank. No sign of any rooms; just the space, the pictures, the windows, which in their ornateness themselves looked almost like framed pictures, only containing darkness, though, at this time of night.

Hopewell sank on to the floor, overcome with disappointment and tiredness. Even Davy looked rather nonplussed. 'Well,' he said, 'we'll have to go back downstairs, then.' But Kit was moving around the space, peering curiously at the windows, and then at the pictures. Suddenly, he gave an exclamation.

'I've got it! Come here, quick!'

The excitement in his voice was such that it made Hopewell spring to his feet, and Davy Jones hurry to Kit's side.

'Look,' said Kit, with a strange tremor in his voice, pointing to the picture in front of him. It was an amazingly realistic portrayal of a walled garden, with roses and other flowers in full bloom, and fruit trees in bright leaf, and a sundial in the middle, an ideal garden such as a high-born lady might sit in and embroider, or read, in the sun. A door was set into the wall, and it was towards this that Kit now leant. Astonished, they saw him reach for the latch of the door; and even more astonished, heard it click; then the door in the wall opened, and Kit stepped through the space, smiled at them over his shoulder, and disappeared.

Hopewell and Davy stared at each other for a moment; then with a cry of delight, Davy went to the next picture. He beckoned Hopewell over. 'Look, boy, look! It's the Doge's palace!'

Hopewell had never seen the Venetian ruler's palace, of course, but, looking at the so-real painting before him, he thought he could almost hear the sounds of the great city floating towards him. The painting was of a vast palace surmounting a bank of the Venetian canal, with a myriad windows and doors looking over the water. There was a gondola or two plying their way past the palace, and busy figures bustling about.

But if Hopewell was impressed by the realism of the picture, the former first mate's face was transfigured, so that the ugliness had almost vanished. Turning to Hopewell, with a curious, remote smile, he murmured, almost as if talking to someone quite other, 'It was the best time of my life, you know, the best . . .' And then, reaching into the picture, unerringly he found a door in the lower level, and pushed against it. It opened; and for an instant, before he slipped through the opening, Hopewell thought he caught a glimpse of someone waiting in the shadows beyond: just a glimpse of the shine of long, golden hair. Then the door was shut firmly in his face, and he was left behind, alone, looking at a most marvellously executed picture of Venice.

He reached forward then and tried the door through which Davy had gone, for he rather fancied spending the night in Venice. But his fingers touched only the painted surface. He tried other doors in the palace, with the same result. He went back to Kit's picture, and tried the door in the garden wall. To no avail.

What of the third picture, then? He stood looking at it for a long time, as a strange, unexpected feeling of profound homesickness swam up from his deepest self and into his consciousness. For the painting was of a theatre; no, not just any theatre, but the Globe itself: there were the wooden balconies, there the dirt-floored O where the groundlings stood, there the stage, the stage door leading beyond it . . . There was no one in the theatre; it was perfectly quiet, and empty, and dark. Yet there was an air of tension about it, somehow, an air of expectancy. The Globe was just waiting to be reanimated by the human magic of the playwright and the actors and the audience; just waiting.

With a fiercely beating heart, Hopewell reached for the door at the back of the stage, and felt it open under his hands, and then he stepped through.

And there she was, in the shadows behind the stage. At first, he could catch only a glimpse of her, his green-eyed lady, her midnight hair tucked up under some kind of hood, but then she turned fully to him, and laughed as she saw the expression on his face. For she was dressed most scandalously, not in young women's dress, as was proper, nor even in the ragged clothes he had seen on her in Cork, but in the attire of a male courtier – or rather, he realized with a shock – the costume of an *actor* playing a courtier. Yet she was most definitely and positively a woman – a young woman his age – from the tip of her shining black hair, to the soles of her dainty feet, and all points in between. He was horrified.

'You cannot do this, Lady,' he cried out, 'it is not allowed, not fitting, and women must not go on the stage.'

Her green eyes flashed merrily. 'And how will you stop me, then, sweet friend?'

So bold was she, that his breath was taken away.

She laughed again then, and went to the door that led to the stage. 'No!' he managed to cry out, 'if you do that, you will disappear, again, as you did in the garden, and in Cork!'

Her hand was on the door's latch as she turned and answered, 'But there is the Globe outside, the whole world, Hopewell, dear! Do you truly want to stay inside this small space here, this shadow of a shadow, when all awaits, outside this door?'

'No,' he said, leaping for the latch before she could open it. 'I do not know if what you say is true, but I am afraid you will only vanish if you go through there. Please, Lady, stay awhile and speak with me. Will you not tell me: are you of mortal kin, or a fairy?'

She turned away from the door with a curious smile. 'Mortal as you, Hopewell dear.'

'A great lady of this place, then. Yet Flora does not speak of you. Are you her elder sister, perhaps?'

'No,' she said. 'I am not. No great lady, either, of this place or any.'

He heaved a secret sigh of relief at that, for what great lady would look twice at a mere wheelwright's apprentice, even one who was going to make his fortune? 'You must be a shipwrecked lander like us then, too. But when did you come? Were you on the White Ship, perhaps? Why did you make no sign to me then? And where do you hide yourself the rest of the time? I have not seen a trace of any other's habitation, here, so you must live secretly . . . But then,' he went on, thoughtfully, 'I have not explored the whole island. Will you not tell me where is your home?'

'So many questions,' she said, smiling; and then her face was suddenly serious again. 'You spoke of secrets,' she went on, 'so ponder on this one. If it is true that the proud and lovely lily, festering, smells far worse than any weed, then the sweetest scent can come from a secretly blossoming flower that is passed over by the ignorant, thinking her to be a weed.'

Hopewell's weariness had dropped off him like a leaden cloak now, and he felt as light as a feather. 'Am I then to be thought of as ignorant, and thus passed over?'

'That is up to you,' said the girl, with an enchanting smile that tilted the corners of her lips. 'It depends on whether you are brave enough to remember me, and to not deny me.'

Hopewell gazed and gazed at her, as if he could not look away, which indeed he could not. 'Oh, Lady! The more I think on it, the more I cannot believe you are not a fairy. . .'

'I told you I was mortal like yourself,' said the girl, 'and so I am. Yet there is indeed enchantment here; for we meet each other in the night world in a place that is full of meaning for both of us. You see, on this island, Hopewell, it is only in the night world that we can see the truth, the essence. But even that is better than in the world we come from: for there, truth is nearly *always* hidden.'

Hopewell's breath caught in his throat. 'Will you tell me your name, then? You seem to know mine, and surely if we are to meet each other truly as you say, we must be able to call on each other . . . heart to heart.'

'My name?' said the girl, with another curious smile. 'I call myself Marguerite.'

'Marguerite? That is a French name,' said Hopewell, rather thrilled by the revelation. He struggled to remember the little French he had heard, from the Huguenot merchants Master Page sometimes dealt with. 'Je parlay pas bocoop Fransay,' he struggled through at last, 'may je vooz aime, Marguerite, vooz et tray jolie, je voodray vooz . . . er . . . donnaye un . . . un . . . un . . . oh, blow this French, a kiss, yes,' he finished, fervently.

Marguerite threw back her head and laughed frankly.

Hopewell, dashed, blushed scarlet, to the roots of his hair.

'I know 'tis a poor French I speak,' he mumbled, 'but 'tis all I have. And indeed you speak the English well enough. I just wanted to . . .'

'Hopewell,' said Marguerite, in a most solemn voice, though her eyes danced and sparkled, 'it was not your

French I laughed at, for indeed I understood that as a gift, a courtesy to me, but . . .'

'My request, then,' said Hopewell, still bright red. 'It was forward and foolish of me. Forgive me.'

'What is a kiss?' said Marguerite, and Hopewell, startled, was about to enlighten her, when she went on, softly, in a voice that made her words sing almost like a song:

'What is a kiss? Mere acquaintance of lips,
Or meeting of soulmates, aching for more?
How is a kiss? Delicate sips,
Or hot-blooded, full-throated roar?
Why is a kiss? For lust or for love,
For remembrance, for healing, for sorrow?
Where is a kiss? Not in Heaven above,
But on earth, with no thought for the morrow.
Whose is a kiss? A many-branched thing:
For a lover, a parent, a child, a dear friend:
A queen's hand, a saint's relic, a bishop's ring:
For all of these, a kiss is a sweet thing to send.'

'That is a lovely verse,' said Hopewell, when she paused, 'a lovely one, and I have not heard it before. Will you not tell me, Mistress Marguerite, what . . .'

She put a finger to her lips. 'I have not finished,' she said, severely. 'Here are the last lines.'

'But what of the kiss that we give to our foes?
The lips of the Judas make, of the sweet wine, aloes.'

'I do not like these last lines,' said Hopewell, after a moment. 'They do not go with the rest of the right pretty verse. It is not good to mix the dark with the light.'

'It is mixed so all the time,' said Marguerite, her green eyes steady now. 'It is mixed all the time, in our lives, Hopewell, just as the motley is mixed with the purple, as the good with the bad. You were shocked when you saw me dressed in my actor's weeds,' she went on, 'and yet, are we not all actors on this stage of life, are we not all in disguise, in different stages of metamorphosis? Such is my costume. And as such you see me, in the night world.'

'You could have told me that, in words,' said Hopewell, sternly, 'and I would have understood, night world or not. But the costume is not necessary to prove such a thing. It is indelicate, for one thing.'

'Well, then,' said the girl, rather sadly, 'if you truly think that is so, then perhaps we cannot yet see each other truly, even in the night world . . .'

'No, no, no!' cried Hopewell, in a panic; 'don't think badly of me, Lady, I did not mean it that way. Of course you must do as you think fit – but, see you, I would so love to see you dressed in women's things. I have seen too many men on the voyage, and then on the island, which I have to share with men again, and prickly, little Flora, whose womanhood is not even in bud yet. If indeed we are to meet only in this night world – will you not allow me to look for clothes for you, in the storage chests of the Lord of Alchemists, splendid clothes, fit for a queen, for surely I will find them . . . and bring them to you, tomorrow night?'

'That might be indelicate indeed,' said the girl,

with an expression midway between sternness and amusement. 'But hark, Hopewell – it grows light, and we must now each go back to our own place . . .'

'No, not yet, surely,' said Hopewell. 'There has hardly been any time that has passed; we have only been speaking together for a few minutes; it cannot be morning!'

But the door was slowly opening; and the girl, ducking his outstretched arm, slipped under it, and thus through the doorway, and disappeared. Hopewell leapt after her; but the door slammed in his face. Just before it did so, though, he had a glimpse of her hurrying away, not through the Globe as he'd thought, or even the circular room, but on some green-shaded path. But the door was closed before he could do more than catch that glimpse, and though he banged and hammered at it, it did not open.

Twenty

'No! No!' Hopewell shouted. 'Please! Open up! Open up!'

'Open up?' It was the laughing voice of Kit Sly. 'You'd best open your *eyes*, indeed, Hopewell. It's already well into morning.'

Hopewell sat up with a jerk that nearly dislocated his neck. For a instant, he thought he'd truly gone quite mad. Where was he? There was no sign of the Globe, the space at the back of the stage, or even the circular room. He rubbed at his eyes, and looked around him. He was in a small, but cosy-looking room, lying in a high, comfortable, curtained bed, which he certainly never remembered getting into; there was a tall piece of furniture in one corner, a storage chest in another, and a window with a windowseat in yet another. And there was Kit Sly, standing there grinning down at him. When he saw Hopewell's eyes were fully open, he said, 'Thought you were going to sleep for ever, friend. Best get down to breakfast,' and went to open the window, so that fresh, scented, morning air came floating softly through.

Hopewell stared around him again. He groaned, and

put his head in his hands. 'Are you going to tell me I dreamt it all, again?' he whispered. 'But I drank nothing, last night.'

Kit turned and looked at him. 'Did I say anything about dreaming, or drinking?' he observed, gently. And at the expression in his face, Hopewell understood that something very similar must have happened to the other boy, and remembered the door in the walled garden, and how Kit had slipped through. He said, 'Oh, Kit, what did *you* see, in the night world?'

'Wondrous things,' said Kit, with a strange look on his thin little face. His eyes, green as Marguerite's, but with none of her shine and sparkle and subtlety, were filled with memory stronger than dream. Hopewell understood that he did not want to speak about what had happened to him, in that garden, and in what might have lain beyond; and he found that he, too, did not want to speak of the emerald-eyed girl, for there was a strange modesty in him that wanted to keep it for himself.

'I do not remember going to bed at all,' he said at last, frankly.

'Neither do I,' said Kit, 'but, mind you, I was nearly asleep on my feet anyway, what with Flora's tricks!'

They looked at each other, and laughed, and for the first time Hopewell felt a real sense of comradeship, even friendship, for the skinny little galley boy with his half-starved angularity turning slowly to a more filled-out look.

'She is a little pest,' Hopewell said, 'and a most persistent one.'

'She is, indeed,' said Kit, 'but I think we try to thwart her at our peril.'

'You could be right, at that,' agreed Hopewell. What did he really mind about Flora and her pestiferous tricks when he had the night world to look forward to? After all, Kit had also experienced something like it, so it must be real, and not a dream.

'We'd best be downstairs,' said Kit now. 'Dr Bonaventure and Master Jones are already there, and Flora, too, of course. She threatens to give our food to Caprice, if we do not hurry!'

'She is indeed a true little pest,' grumbled Hopewell, but he jumped out of bed anyway, scrambled into his clothes and raced off after Kit. As he ran, a thought came to him: though Marguerite had not told him where she lived in the everyday world, if that was what the daylight island could be called, she had not denied the fact she lived *somewhere* on the island. In a secret place . . . a secret place . . . he would find that place! He would go looking for her; the island could not be all that big, and he had so far only seen a very small section of it. Today, he would strike out in one direction; tomorrow, in another; and so on, until he had covered the island, and found her, and they could be together both in the day and the night . . . But he did not want anyone else to know what he was doing. How could he organize it without being followed, and pestered? He needed some excuse. Of course! He would appoint himself Dr Bonaventure's assistant, whether the old man wanted him to or not.

Flattering him would do the trick anyway, he was

sure. For there was a confidence in Hopewell now, a bubbling joy that knew that all obstacles were as nothing to the man with a mission!

Everyone seemed to have that look about them this morning, though, if you discounted Flora, who looked much the same as usual, and kept feeding pieces of fruit to her goat. The table groaned with fruit of all kinds, and sweetmeats, and small ale, and all kinds of good things, but Hopewell hardly noticed what he was eating, so intent was he on his plan. He had quite forgotten the oilskin package of papers he had seen the day before, and even if a stray thought about it did enter his mind, he dismissed it, for after all, what could he do? Dr Bonaventure was right. Whatever had happened on the *Golden Dragon*, Captain Wolfe was dead, and Davy Jones was alive, but they were all on this island, and there was precious little chance of them leaving it with a fortune. Or leaving it at all. Who cared, really, if it meant that Marguerite would stay here too? The homesickness that had assailed him the night before seemed to have disappeared.

'Hopewell, attend!' came Flora's imperious voice, almost in his ear, it seemed.

Startled, Hopewell glared at her. She tossed her head. 'I asked you a question, Hopewell; did you sleep well?'

The innocuous question, from her, was so unexpected that he gaped. She grinned. 'Do you want me to repeat it a third time? Your dreams have sent you deaf, Hopewell. They must have been good.'

He blushed, and she laughed. He stammered, 'Yes, thank you, Mistress Flora, I slept very well.'

'Your father has made a most restful and wonderful palace of dreams, Flora,' broke in Davy Jones. 'Is it any wonder all of us have slept the best sleep we have ever had in our lives?' He turned to Dr Bonaventure. 'But you, sir, I expect, have grown habituated to the night world of the Lost Island.'

'Not at all, not at all,' said the old man, heartily. 'Why, I visit it every night, and thereby gain more knowledge and understanding! The Lord of Alchemists has indeed created a place of great wonders here, Master Jones; and the more you know it, the more you'll marvel.'

'Tcha,' said Flora, with a snort, but Dr Bonaventure paid her no attention. 'Now tell me, Master Jones: was Venice the same as when I was there?'

Hopewell listened with a certain amount of interest: for Venice, of course, must be where Davy Jones had gone to, in his night journey. He must already have been speaking of it to the old man . . . Hopewell remembered the glimpse of long golden hair in the doorway, and thought that strange as it seemed, the Welshman might himself have a secret love, locked somewhere in his heart's memory this morning.

'I do not know quite when you were there, sir,' said Davy Jones, with an inward smile, 'but I can assure you it looks as beautiful, and dangerous, as ever. The women are still bold and frank; the men soft and subtle; and each of them are still deadly.'

'Er – quite,' said Dr Bonaventure, with a slightly dismayed expression. 'It is indeed a most striking place.

I was employed, you know, by one of the Doge's special favourites, a most intelligent and percipient young man.'

'He must have been, of course,' said Jones, still with that inward smile, 'to have been your patron.'

'Quite, quite,' said Dr Bonaventure, happily. With a sigh, he went on, 'And I wish to Heaven I had understood quite how true that was, for I made the greatest mistake of my life in Venice, you know.'

'It is easy enough to make a mistake in Venice,' said Jones. 'It is a city of masks. How to tell what is under them?'

'That is most true,' said Dr Bonaventure. 'I trusted to my judgement, and it proved untrustworthy. Ah well! One learns, one learns. And it was only thus that I reached the Lost Island.'

'Is that so? I should like to hear that story, sir, when you have the time to tell it to me,' said Jones. There was a curious, almost tense stillness about him now, that quite belied his smarmy words. But Dr Bonaventure did not notice. 'Of course, of course,' he said. 'When you wish to.' If there was a slight bitterness in the tone, nobody remarked on it.

'Perhaps today?' Yes, Davy Jones was certainly interested, thought Hopewell, a little puzzled. But the old philosopher's next words quite wiped any questions from his mind, for Dr Bonaventure frowned a little and said, 'Well, today I was going to go looking for a specimen which I . . .'

'Dr Bonaventure, Dr Bonaventure,' cut in Hopewell, excitedly, 'do not bother yourself with that! I will go looking for it for you! You only have to tell me, sir, what I should look for, and I will find it, I am sure.'

Dr Bonaventure looked at him, lips pursed. 'I don't know if I . . .' he began, but rather to Hopewell's surprise, Flora came to the rescue. 'Why not?' she shrugged. 'You know you don't like clambering over rocks and haring over hills, Dr Bonaventure. Stay here with Master Jones, and speak of philosophy, and Venice and such things. I am sure it will be a much more pleasant day for you.'

'Yes, so it will be,' admitted the philosopher, 'but Hopewell is not used to the—'

'He will *get* used to it,' said Flora, firmly. As she spoke, a terrible thought struck Hopewell. Could it be that the girl was thinking of coming along with him? Goat, and Kit and all? The thought filled him with horror, so that he gabbled, 'I am sure I will find it easily, and all on my own.'

'Who wants to come with you?' said Flora, haughtily. 'Kit and Caprice and I will have a much better time on our own, won't we?'

Caprice bleated enthusiastically, but Kit looked a little apprehensive, as well he might, thought Hopewell, overjoyed he was going to be left alone. Proudly, he said, 'I have quite good eyes, and am quick on my feet, and I promise I will be back long before dark.'

'You see, Dr Bonaventure,' said Davy Jones, with a wry look, 'your specimen will be in good hands.'

'Hmm,' said Dr Bonaventure, looking decidedly wry himself.

'I will go straightaway,' said Hopewell, rising rather

precipitately from his seat. 'That way, I can be sure of finding it quickly.'

It was Kit who said, with a barely suppressed grin, 'Find what, Hopewell?' and Hopewell sat down again with a bump. Sheepishly, he mumbled, 'Sorry. I should have waited.'

'You should, you should indeed,' said Dr Bonaventure, bustling to his own feet with a broad smile, 'but never mind! I like your spirit, Hopewell. Come with me, and I will show you a sketch of the plant I want you to find for me.'

And so, he led the way back to his room, whilst four pairs of momentarily curious eyes watched them go. But as they left the room, Hopewell heard the conversation resume easily behind him, and breathed a sigh of excited relief. Any disquiet he felt, deep inside, about Flora's real intentions, he kept firmly suppressed. He'd had plenty of experience in the past at eluding others, and thought that he would easily be able to lose them, even should they follow him. After all, he'd even managed to hide from Flora before . . .

They had reached the study by now, and Dr Bonaventure was shuffling amongst his papers. Finally he brought out a piece of much creased paper, and pointed out a sketch to Hopewell.

'See? It is the *Millefloria Bonaventura*, a plant which I have sketched from what Flora has described to me, but which I have yet to find.'

'Ah, *Millefloria Bonaventura*,' said Hopewell, before he could stop himself. What had he read about it in his secret perusal of Dr Bonaventure's papers? Oh yes, metamorphosis. It was associated with *metamorphosis*.

'Do you know it?' said Dr Bonaventure, most surprised. Hopewell shook his head, vigorously, not wanting to admit to his earlier curiosity.

'I merely wanted to remark on the splendour of the name, sir, so fitting and euphonious,' he said, in a disgustingly buttery voice. But Dr Bonaventure, as Hopewell had earlier remarked, liked flattery, and saw nothing strange in it. Comfortably, he nodded. 'Thank you, Hopewell. I am pleased it sounds well to your ears. Now, then, to find the plant. It grows in . . .'

'The woods?' said Hopewell, eagerly, remembering the green path where Marguerite had vanished from view. Dr Bonaventure frowned just a little. 'No, Hopewell. It grows in cracks amongst rocks, that I know, from what Flora has told me; but as to where, she would not tell me. My own studies and deductions, however, have led me to conclude that it probably grows in rocks on the shore of the island; and there are most rocks on its eastern shore. Take the sketch with you, Hopewell, and study it carefully, for I have been told that *Millefloria* can be hard to find: it is easy for the ignorant to bypass it, for it is a secret little plant, and I believe looks like nothing so much as a paltry weed, when it is first spotted. But it has this extraordinary property: it blossoms into the most beautiful, most scented, most magical thing, later . . . Why, whatever's the matter, Hopewell? Are you unwell, man?'

For Hopewell had gone quite pale, then red, then pale again. Had those not been the very kinds of words

174

Marguerite had used? Was this not the most glorious omen that he would succeed in finding her? Hastily, he sought to reassure Dr Bonaventure that he was feeling quite well, and that it was just excitement at being honoured by Dr Bonaventure's entrusting this task to him that had made him lose countenance for a moment. Dr Bonaventure was satisfied by that; and with a friendly tap on the shoulder, he gave Hopewell the sketch, and said, 'Thank you, my lad. You are being most helpful; more helpful than you might ever know.'

Little chance of that, thought Hopewell, with a sudden flash of inward joy; who's helping whom here, is not quite clear yet! And so, with a bright heart, and a light step, he bid farewell of the old philosopher and set off.

Twenty-One

'Hey nonny no,' sang Hopewell softly as he walked briskly away from the mansion, in the direction indicated to him by Dr Bonaventure. Such a beautiful day it was, he thought to himself as he bounced along merrily, and the sun seemed to shine more warmly because of the sunshine in his heart. Nobody had followed him: he had checked once or twice by ducking behind a tree and waiting a few seconds before emerging again. No goat came bounding after him, no shrill little voice mocked him. He was alone, quite alone, but with his memory of Marguerite like a great glow in his chest.

By and by, he remembered that in his rush to get away, he had forgotten to bring any food with him. But what did it matter, in a place where golden fruit hung on every tree and the water was clear and pure as molten crystal? Suiting the action to the thought, he broke off a couple of fruit from one of the apple trees he passed, and munched deep into the sweet, snowy flesh. This might be what the Garden of Eden had looked like, he thought, and had a momentary qualm: was it not an apple tree that Adam and Eve had eaten from, defying God? But no one had prohibited the eating of the fruit here, he reassured himself in the next moment, and he finished the apples with gusto, and threw the cores away. Next, he drank some water from a little rockspring, and refreshed his face, too, just for the pleasure of the coolness on his face, the elusive scent of it. Marguerite said it was in the night world of the Lost Island that we see truth and essence, he thought as he walked along, but even in its daylight mien, the island has purer, more essentially beautiful traits than any place in his own world, far away.

Where was England? he wondered next, as he made his way through a little wood carpeted with bluebells and primroses, like a Worcestershire wood in the spring. Could you say it was at one point of the compass from here, or was he truly off the map? Again, that little tremor; if ever he wanted to leave – which he did not, not at present – how could he do so? But then, he reassured himself again, when the Lord of Alchemists returned, he would ask him. If he needed that answer, he would ask that question. All would be well.

Now he came out of the wood and into an open space of heathery hill, where he could see a few dots that soon resolved themselves into sheep. Like the other flock had done when he first arrived, these ovine gossips came at the gallop to come and stare at him, their yellow, guileless eyes full of curiosity. Hopewell smiled to see them. 'Whist, whist, friends,' he said, as they crowded around him, 'give me room, give me room!' They stared at him still, and bleated mournfully, and jostled him to one side, as if trying to get him to change his path. 'I declare,' said Hopewell, 'I declare you don't want me to go that way. Why not, friends? Ah, if only you could speak!' He waited hopefully; so full of magic was the air here that surely even a wish uttered like that would come true . . .

But the sheep remained sheep, and dumb in human speech, though they bleated most insistently, and kept pushing at him. At length, he gave in, and, surrounded by his woolly guides, the youngest closest to him, he struck off up the hill and off the path he had been following, which led to the shore. Perhaps, he thought, with a sudden delight, perhaps they know what I want, and are leading me towards Marguerite, towards her lonely house, here in the heather. So convinced grew he of this explanation that he began to get clammy, itchy palms at the thought. Oh, was he ready? What would he say? Would he be struck dumb at sight of her?

The sheep took no account of his turmoil, but pushed him on, bleating all the while. Suddenly, the leader stopped; and all the young ewes and rams around Hopewell stopped too, and Hopewell, deep in his dreams of just what he *would* say, fell over them. He picked himself up, and glared at his companions. 'Now listen, lads and lasses,' he began, waggling a finger at them, 'you must really . . .'

But whatever he had been going to say died on his lips; for just then, the whole flock moved away from Hopewell, standing to one side of him, and he had a clear view of just what they'd brought him to see.

On the heather lay a slaughtered sheep, its throat torn out, the blood already congealed into a dark mass, its sides ripped and torn, so that the bones showed redly through the mangled flesh. Flies were already gathered around its eyes and nose; but when Hopewell, struck by a strange kind of horror, bent down to touch the dead flanks, he found they were still warm to the touch. It had not long been dead; perhaps only that morning, perhaps only that hour. Hopewell swallowed. It was not the fact the sheep was dead that moved him – for after all, he was a country boy, well used to the slaughtering of the animals he cared for – but the fact that it had been killed with such savagery, in such a place. The sheep had not been killed to be eaten, for although it was so mutilated, there was no sign that whatever had killed it had feasted on it; it had been killed just like that, for no apparent reason. It seemed like such a terrible violation of the beauty and peace of the Lost Island, that death could have visited it so harshly, that the iron smell of blood should hang on an air that should by rights only carry scented breezes.

His next thought was sharper, more frightening: *what* had done this thing? Nothing he had seen so far of the island went any way towards explaining this. But then, as he had told Marguerite, he had not explored the whole island. What did he *really* know of it? For all he knew, there might be any number of wild beasts hiding here. The thought was not a comforting one. Turning his back on the poor slaughtered animal, he looked wildly around him. The other sheep stood at a distance, unwilling or unable to approach their murdered comrade. Fat lot of good they would be if some ravening thing came leaping at him out of the shadows, he thought. He patted his side, in the vain hope that his gesture might somehow cause a sword to appear there. When it didn't, he sat down on his haunches again, downwind of the smell of blood, trying to think. Why had the sheep brought him here? Did they want him to report on what he'd seen to the others? Was it a kind of warning? Dumb they might be, in human terms, but in this place, even the dumb animals showed their essential selves more clearly than in the world Hopewell was used to. He looked at the flock again, and read all at once a kind of sad waiting in the many pairs of yellow eyes turned on him, a sadness that made him swallow again.

'Whist, whist, friends,' he said, getting up slowly, and coming towards them, 'it is an evil thing has done this, and no mistake. I will pick some heather and flowers and lay them over your comrade. The island will take him back into its heart, my friends, I am sure of that.' And he saw no incongruity at all in the words he was saying, and who he was saying them to, and nor did he do so when, his arms full of heather, he laid it gently over the body of the dead sheep. The others stood around him, quietly, watching. Soon, the iron smell of blood was overtaken by the sweet spicy scent of the heather, and the red bones and raw flesh covered with the tough branches of the plant, not so much hiding the piteousness of it, as transforming it.

When the dead sheep was quite covered, the leader – the biggest ewe – gently nudged him out of the way, and standing solemnly in front of the now flower-strewn place of death, she bleated once, long and low, and deep, and all the other sheep answered likewise, unmistakably farewelling their luckless companion. Then the leader turned, looked at Hopewell; and with a toss of her head, moved away slowly, up the hill, the rest of the flock following after her, parting before Hopewell, but not jostling him any longer. It was quite clear they had achieved what they had wanted to do, and they saw no further need to remain.

The young man stood looking after them for quite a while after they had disappeared over the brow of the hill. Then he looked down at the dead sheep: and saw, with a start of astonishment, that both the mangled remains and the heather that had been laid over them had vanished, leaving a green, bare space on the hill. Bare, that is, except for one thing, in the middle: a little plant with a white daisy-like flower, proudly lifting its head to the sky. Hopewell stared at it; then bending down, in a dream, he gently touched the little flower, and the touch of his finger released a fragrance quite elusive, yet so evocative that it made his head reel. He had seen and smelt flowers like this one before . . . wound in Marguerite's midnight hair. His heart thumped. Oh, what did it mean? What did it mean?

At his feet, the little flower closed up, as if his touch had something of the approach of night in it. He got up again, and thought deeply. Had the whole thing then been a kind of shadow game? A kind of mazed sign, a deliberate riddle? But no, the dead sheep had been real enough, and the smell of blood. He had not imagined those; no, not the sheep either, and the strange way in which they had behaved. Something real had killed that poor creature; something which still, presumably, lurked out there . . . perhaps even interrupted in its killing, and

181

now waiting for other prey. The fact that the dead sheep had become metamorphosed into the lovely white flower was no guarantee against the reality of the killer. The metamorphosis had happened because this was the Lost Island, realm of the Lord of Alchemists, greatest of all magicians; but presumably even the greatest of all magicians could not conquer death, or stop the intrusion of evil into his ideal state. What, then, was the nature of the being which had killed so savagely? Was it merely a wild beast ... or something more? No one had mentioned such a creature to him – but would not Dr Bonaventure and Flora, at least, know of its existence, if it was a creature of the island? If they did – why had they not warned him? And if they didn't know – what did it mean?

So Hopewell argued with himself, and trembled and thrilled, both, to the questions and the possible answers that ran riot in his brain. He was not sure whether he should immediately return to the mansion, and tell of what he had seen, or keep going on his journey to the shoreline to see if he could find *Millefloria* – and Marguerite. That she was somewhere on this island, that he wanted above all to find her, he was sure. That now he knew there was also some kind of danger here, some savage thing lurking, did not change his mind in that, though he was scared, as well. He took a deep breath, and decided. He would press on; for after all, why should it be any safer to return pell-mell the way he had come? The beast could be lying in waiting for him anywhere; if he allowed its presence to dictate his every move, then he would be diminished, somehow, he knew.

'I am Hopewell Shakespeare!' he called out, suddenly, to the silent hillside. 'I am not afraid of anything!' Absurd it was, he knew; for he was afraid, dreadfully afraid, of a lot of things. But it was important, nevertheless, for a reason he was not quite sure of, to hear those words ringing out, to hear his own name impressed on the landscape.

Twenty-Two

Down the hill he went, towards the shore which soon he saw quite plainly. The hill levelled into a grassy sward, and then a sandy stretch of beach, forming a little cove, with a reef of rocks at one end. The sea – vast, shimmering, with long, lazy waves – hissed and slunk at the shore, its wild smell filling him with a kind of answering wild restlessness. Hopewell stood looking at it for a moment, staring at its great emptiness, and imagining what he would do if a ship suddenly appeared there, on the horizon. Wave; attract attention; call the world back to him? No! He would do nothing, for he would never leave this island without Marguerite – whatever happened, he vowed that. And so, he turned towards the rocks, remembering Dr Bonaventure's words, about *Millefloria*'s habits.

The rocks formed a kind of great broken bed, with the closest to the sea being harsh and spiky, but the ones further away pock-marked with little crevasses filled with clear, quiet water. Charmed by their peaceful beauty, Hopewell found himself staring into all these little rock pools as if he were gazing into a mirror, or the pool under the apple trees in the mansion garden, hoping perhaps that the reflection of Marguerite's face might swim up to him from the sandy bottom. But all that swam up were funny little fish with goggle eyes; whilst tiny, transparent crabs scuttled away, and sea urchins and starfish crouched down at the bottom, pretending to be fixtures and not the mobile animals they really were. The farm-bred, London-veneered Hopewell had never really seen such things before, and he lost sight of his plan, and even his longing, for minutes at a time as he grabbed with mischievous fingers at the little denizens of these rock worlds, laughing to himself as they fled from his hands. 'Ha, ha, ha,' he said, aloud, 'I'll wager you're thinking some monstrous giant is after you, eh, little folks?' He had no intention of hurting them at all, just in giving them a hurry-up, seeing the funny little things scuttle, the solemn shellfish lose their dignity in their panic, the little fish, that had been swimming so heedlessly up till then, flip and dart in their attempts to escape. He dabbled his hands in the water, making waves that must seem like a great storm to the little creatures of these tiny worlds. Then, tiring of that, he sat back on his haunches and just watched them regaining their poise and their boldness, a funny inward smile lighting him from top to toe. At last, he got up, and walked on over the rocks, keeping an eye out for *Millefloria*, but seeing not a single specimen of the plant Dr Bonaventure had sketched.

Round the corner, he came to the next beach. This had quite a different atmosphere to the last little cove, for the hills sloped steeply directly above it, forming a broken, white cliff. At three or four places on this cliff, yawned the openings of what looked like caves. Hopewell looked curiously at them. Caves . . . there was one not far from his father's farm, a limestone cave like these, which was called the Hermit's Home. Some legends said that the last king of the English, Harold, had sheltered there one night . . . Hopewell had oftentimes gone there as a child, to hide from the wrath of his father. It had been quite big and roomy, big enough for him to think of setting it up as some kind of permanent home. Hopewell smiled to himself. Such were the dreams of children! But his smile left him as a sudden thought struck him. He gave a low whistle. Of course!

He scrambled over the cliff, going carefully as the stone was quite friable and liable to crumble under too-heavy steps. It was quite easy to climb, however, with plenty of handholds, and he had soon managed to heave himself up to the level of the first cave.

'Marguerite?' he called out softly, at the cave-mouth, trying to peer into the gloom beyond. No answer; but as his eyes became accustomed to the dimness, he saw that this one was quite shallow, anyway, and seemed to be quite innocent of any kind of occupation. He pushed on to the next cave, which, again, proved a disappointment; and likewise the third. But the fourth, highest cave was quite different. At first sight of its interior, Hopewell gasped. For the whole place, far from being gloomy, sparkled with a hundred, no, a thousand, gleams of light. Rather than being a mere limestone cave, it seemed to be made of crystals and diamonds. They sparkled from the ceiling and the floor and the walls, in their natural yet unearthly, pristine yet strange beauty, like the great pillars and sculptured decorations of the palace of some ancient, mountain king. In the centre of the cave was what looked like a high-backed chair, made not of wood but of a solid slab of part snowy-white, part crystal-clear gemstone, and one of the most beautiful things Hopewell had ever seen. All was quiet and still; but such a throne, such a natural palace, must have a queen fit for it. Hopewell could not resist it; he walked into the cave and stood for a moment lost in admiration at the frozen beauty within. Then, with a sigh, he shook himself, and looked around for signs of who might be living there, without seeing anything in particular. But behind the great chair, hidden from view of anyone just casually looking in, was a passage: a long, dimly lit, sandy-floored passage which disappeared off into the distance. Hopewell stared down into it, thinking that there must be other rooms beyond. Should he go in, further into the heart of the cliff? Whilst he was trying to decide, his glance fell on something small and white at the foot of one of the rocky walls of the passage, quite close to the entrance. Hopewell recognized it at once: the same kind of white daisy that he had seen on the hill, and in Marguerite's hair . . . It was withered, and rather crumpled, but nevertheless the same. He did not need to think twice about it: stooping to pick up the little flower as he went past, he set off happily down the passage.

It went on and on for quite a while, and seemed to be going down into the heart of the cliff, rather like a flight of stairs going down into the bowels of some castle. But it was quite a broad passage, and so Hopewell did not feel concerned, though his pulse did beat a little fast. In his hand, he held the little crushed daisy, and its scent seemed to permeate the air around him, chasing away any notion of damp and depth and the close feeling of being, to all intents and purposes, under the earth.

At last, the passage opened out into a circular space, rather like a rock-walled hall. Hopewell gasped, and took a step back; for it seemed to him as if he had stepped into a vast, frozen menagerie of strange, terrifying beasts. From the walls innumerable pairs of savage eyes glared at him, and creatures were arrested in the very act, it seemed, of springing on him. Hump-backed creatures like vast beetle-browed cattle; boars with massive tusks; monstrous stags with wildly rolling eyes; bears so huge that their heads nearly touched the ceiling; wolves of such size that their jaws could easily have contained the whole of Hopewell's arm, from shoulder to fingertips; lions with teeth that looked more like rapiers: all of these rendered so lifelike in their full-blooded power and terror and glamour, that it seemed a mere click of the fingers would restore them to full function. Hopewell devoutly wished this would not happen; he clasped his hands together to make sure he would not do so inadvertently, and stared around him, not wanting to go forward or back.

After a while, the eerie silence of that place began to get on his nerves. By rights, it should have been full of blood-curdling cries and roars and growls, a kind of vastly amplified version of the sounds you could hear coming from the wild animals imprisoned in the Queen's menagerie at the Tower of London, whose cries could often be heard floating over the Thames. Of course, in many ways, Hopewell was rather glad that the painted animals on the walls of the cave did *not* make any kind of sound, for the opposite would not have augured too well for his continued survival. But such is the contradictory quality of human nature that the very lack of that dangerous cacophony made the hairs on the back of his neck stand up. He really did not want to stay here any longer, he thought; and began backing away, back towards the passage, eyes firmly on the whole of that spellbound zoo, keeping them well in sight.

Then all at once, a sound: so small that at first he thought he'd imagined it. He backed away faster, then froze like one of the creatures on the wall as the sound came again, clearer this time, though still it was but a whisper. What was it? He listened intently, and it came again. This time he heard it quite clearly. Not a growl, not a roar, not a howl or snort or anything remotely belonging to anything beast-like; but a human voice. A human whisper, drenched in sorrow, crying, seemingly right under his feet, 'Cruel . . . ah, so cruel, to leave me here, alone . . .'

Hopewell's whole being flooded with a wave of heat, though the hairs on the back of his neck stood up stiffly as if coated with ice. For a long moment he could do nothing at all. For the voice was one he recognized. And it was not Marguerite's; nor any girl's or woman's voice. It was a man's voice. A man's voice he had last heard shouting orders on the *Golden Dragon*!

In the next instant, it seemed as if the air in the cave shattered into a thousand shards, as Hopewell suddenly regained control of his faculties, and charged around the room, shouting, bellowing, 'Captain Wolfe! Captain Wolfe! Where in Heaven's name are you, sir? Captain Wolfe! It's me, Hopewell Shakespeare! Sir, please answer me – where are you?' Silence, for a heartbeat; then Wolfe's voice came again, this time less sorrowful, but instead with a point of excitement in it, 'Hopewell? Is that really you? Really you, and not some mocking shade?'

'No sir, it's really me, really me, I vow!' Hopewell looked wildly around. Where *was* the privateer? He could see no place in which he might be. The passage had ended in this room; there was nothing beyond it. Remembering the circular room in the Alchemist's mansion, he thought that perhaps things might work in the same way here, and raced around the room, scraping the walls with his fingers as he did so. But nothing clicked open, nothing slid apart: the rock walls remained rock walls, and his fingers were only bruised by contact with them, no more.

'Hopewell?' Wolfe's voice sounded a little sharper. 'Are you there? What are you doing?'

Yes. Definitely, the voice was coming from somewhere under his feet. 'Sir,' said Hopewell in a trembling voice, 'I'm still here, but I do not know where *you* are. Will you please . . .'

'Under the big wolf,' said the privateer, with a kind of dry chuckle. 'Look at the floor under the big wolf, Hopewell. Directly under his paws, there's a trapdoor.

It's closed. There's a ring on top that serves as a handle. Just pull up the ring, and the trapdoor will swing open, and I'll be able to get out.'

And Hopewell, going to where the Captain had indicated, found to his astonishment that it was just as he had said. Directly under the painted paws of the big wolf, was a trapdoor, painted to reassemble the rest of the rocky floor, enough to satisfy anything but the most searching of glances. The ring was there, too, and all he had to do was heave on it – for it was quite heavy – and the trapdoor swung open. Hopewell peered down into the hole below. It was quite dark in there, and at first he could see nothing, so that he got a real shock when one of Captain Wolfe's hands suddenly appeared at the opening, then the rest of the man himself. Hopewell gave another gasp. For the privateer, who had been still so splendid on the *Golden Dragon*, despite having come down somewhat in the world, who had looked still reasonably young, now resembled an old, old man. He was dressed in the rotting rags of his ancient finery; his beard and hair had grown long and wild and grey and matted, with no hint of black in them at all; he had a pronounced stoop. Only the grey-brown eyes were the same: wild, direct and commanding, they fixed on Hopewell with the same power as before. The shrunken lips curved into a smile. 'Pleased to see you, Hopewell. Help me up, boy,' said Richard Wolfe.

Twenty-Three

At last, after mighty struggles on Hopewell's part, the privateer stood on the floor of the cave, swaying a little, taking deep, ragged breaths. Hopewell supported him for a little while, till the older man regained his balance. Pity and affection swelled in his heart. Who had imprisoned Richard Wolfe? And why? Why did he look so old? These questions burned in him, but for the moment, he did not wish to ask them.

Wolfe got his breath back. Without saying a word, he hugged Hopewell tightly, kissed him on his right cheek, and then released him. 'Thank you, Hopewell,' he said, at last. 'Without you rescuing me, I would have been in the darkness for ever. I am in your debt.'

'Oh, sir, no,' Hopewell protested, colouring. 'Anyone would do what I have done. It is nothing.'

Wolfe smiled briefly, bitterly. 'You misjudge yourself and others, Hopewell,' he said. Now he looked at Hopewell as if seeing him for the first time. 'But, lad, you look mighty fine these days. You, I perceive, have found your fortune.'

'Sir . . .' stammered Hopewell, as the full extent of the gulf between his own undoubted good fortune and the torment of the privateer, struck him. 'Sir . . . I merely landed on the Lost Island, and have been welcomed by the Lord of Alchemists . . . that is,' he added hastily, 'by his daughter, Flora, an annoying little chit, but not an ungenerous one. And I—'

Wolfe interrupted him, none too gently. 'How long have you been here, Hopewell?'

Hopewell stared at Wolfe. 'Sir . . . only a day and a night, and then this day. Wondrous times, too.'

Something flared in the man's eyes. 'Ah!' He was silent a little while, then went on, 'I fear for me it has been rather different, Hopewell. But come – I do not think I can bear to stay underground any more. Let us go up into the light.'

'Yes, of course, sir,' stammered Hopewell, trembling at the strangeness of the fact that such a short time could have so aged the privateer. He took Wolfe's arm and together the two of them walked slowly up the passage, into the crystal room which Wolfe did not even glance at, and finally up the rest of the cliff, going slowly, finally to stand on top of it, on the heathery hill. Here, Wolfe halted an instant, looking out to sea, intently, as if looking for a sail. Then, shaking his head, sadly, he motioned to Hopewell that he wanted to keep going.

By and by, Hopewell hazarded a few words. 'Captain Wolfe, this is indeed the Lost Island we were looking for. I have been staying in the marvellous mansion of the Lord of Alchemists. Why, then, have you not . . .' He found he couldn't finish his sentence, but Wolfe finished it for him.

'Why have I not found my fortune, as you seem to

have found something fortunate indeed? This is, as you say, the Lost Island, and by rights, with the help of my poor dead friend, I should now be enjoying the fruits of my labour. But I am not, Hopewell, and do you know why? Why, lad, betrayal – betrayal, pure and simple, from the part of a man more wild and wicked at heart than even the bloodiest beast.'

'Sir?' Hopewell's scalp prickled.

Wolfe stopped, so suddenly that Hopewell nearly fell over him. His voice filled with rage, he said, 'You see me here, boy, as a broken man, an old man, for though you say you have only been a day and a night and a day on this enchanted island, to me it has seemed as ten years. I have been tormented day and night by the shade of a wicked man who tortured my mind even more than my body; rats have gnawed at my flesh, the cruel breath of the predator blown on my face. And all this because the man I once esteemed as my greatest friend – nay, dearer even than a brother – has repaid me by duplicity and treachery. I survived the wreck of the *Golden Dragon*, Hopewell, by God's mercy, as did you, and those undeserving others; but when I lay insensible on the beach, my erstwhile friend stole from me the book my philosopher had given me, took it from me because whilst, despite all, I would have shared with him the fortune that was due to me – yes, shared it, in honour of our long and great previous friendship, and not in fear – because he was too greedy to think of sharing it with me. He wanted it all; and so he stole the book, and had me dragged into the dungeon where you found me, and only visited me to taunt me, and demand from me the last remaining secret I held. You see, Hopewell, the Lost Island was to be my grave, but not yet. For there were still secrets I held deep within me, and so I must be kept alive, and tortured into giving them up. Yet I have not, to this day, this hour, told him what he wanted.'

'Sir,' said Hopewell, horrified beyond telling, 'was the wicked man Davy Jones?'

'Aye, Hopewell, lad. It was.' Wolfe's sharp eyes rested on Hopewell. 'You look most agitated about it, lad.'

'Oh sir!' Hopewell burst out. 'That is because indeed Davy Jones – and Kit Sly, though I do not think him as wicked as his master – they, indeed, sir, are on the Lost Island, too, in the mansion of the Alchemist, and in the confidences of . . . Sir!' he broke off, excitedly, 'Davy Jones indeed has the package of papers – the papers the old philosopher had written, and I think he—'

'You have seen them, boy?' Wolfe grasped rather painfully at Hopewell's arm. 'Has he understood them yet?'

'Indeed, I have seen them, sir, but as to him understanding them, sir, I do not know. He was showing them to—'

'We *must* stop him understanding them! You must get them for me before it's too late!'

'I . . . I will try, sir.' He'd have to get into Dr Bonaventure's study, unobserved, somehow. But he would. He would!

'Now listen, Hopewell. You and I will go to a place somewhere not far from the mansion, where I will not be seen. Is there such a place?'

'There is a grove, sir, a little grove of apple trees, where

195

a man may hide easily,' said Hopewell, remembering his own hiding place, and then, with a little skip of the heart, the face he had seen in the pool. It was a good place that one, and a kind one for the distressed privateer. 'It is in the furthest, quietest corner of the gardens, and there is water there, and plenty of fruit to eat. I will make sure no one will come near, sir.' Yes, it was best that way, he thought. After the failure of his last attempt to tell Dr Bonaventure the truth about Davy Jones, he did not think the philosopher would listen to him, and as to Flora, she was of too uncertain a nature to be fully trusted. It was probably better to wait, until the master of the place returned, and all wrongs could be righted. Best leave Davy Jones in ignorance of the turn of events.

Wolfe smiled. 'Good. Now, Hopewell, I want you to bring me some clothes, food, wine, a blanket, and a good sharp knife – oh, to cut my hair and beard,' he added, with a slight bitterness, seeing Hopewell's expression. 'I will not spill blood, not yet, not here, anyhow.'

'Sir, the Lord of Alchemists will soon return,' gabbled Hopewell, 'and he will judge Davy Jones as he deserves. That was what Dr—'

'The Lord of Alchemists will soon return?' said Wolfe, sharply. 'Is he not there, then?'

'No, he is away on a voyage. His daughter Flora is our hostess. Such as she is,' Hopewell added with a smile.

'I see.' Wolfe's eyes narrowed. He took Hopewell's arm again. 'We must go, now, without delay.' Seeing that his brusqueness surprised the boy, he added, 'I have been too long helpless, lad. But I vow my heart already feels many years lighter.'

Hopewell had been feeling rather miffed, it was true, but was mollified by Wolfe's words. Poor Captain Wolfe, who had been so wickedly and shamefully treated! It would be good when the Lord of Alchemists returned, and would make his true judgement on them all.

As they went along, Wolfe talked but little, sunk in his own thoughts, and so Hopewell was fairly silent too, turning over and over in his mind all the extraordinary events that had happened that day, and what they might mean. It was not that he had forgotten Marguerite – for how could he, when she inhabited the deepest, most glowing reaches of his heart? But he knew that though he had so far failed to find her place, the place where she hid during the day, he would soon see her in the night world. Meanwhile, there was the amazing and piteous coming back to life of Captain Wolfe; and the treachery and duplicity of Davy Jones; and the knowledge that somewhere, on those hills, roamed a creature that had savagely killed a sheep, for no apparent reason other than the lust to kill. Darkness mixed with light, he thought suddenly, remembering Marguerite's words; and he hoped with all his heart that the darkness would not overcome the light.

It took a long while for them to reach the outskirts of the Alchemist's garden, for Wolfe must of necessity walk somewhat slower than Hopewell, and take frequent rests. When at last they came within sight of the walls, the sun was already beginning to set in the west. Leaving Wolfe to shelter behind a tree, Hopewell went to check that nobody was about in the gardens. Finding that all was quiet, he went back to Wolfe and took him to the grove, settling him in comfortably under the trees at the very back of the grove, well hidden from sight.

'Now go, right away and bring those things I asked for. Don't forget about the knife.' Wolfe settled into the soft grass with a visible wince. But just as Hopewell turned to go away, the old privateer hissed, 'Don't forget the papers, Hopewell. All of them, remember. I need them all!'

'Yes, sir. I will try to . . .' Hopewell began, but the Captain, obviously overcome by weariness, had closed his eyes, as if ready to go to sleep, and Hopewell did not want to press any point with him. He would try, at any rate. If he could not get the papers today, he would get them tomorrow. Meanwhile, he must find things for Captain Wolfe, without anyone seeing him. He could only hope that they were all busy elsewhere.

When he came into the mansion, he could hear sounds of merriment coming from upstairs, and the running thump of feet, with the clattering of little hoofs mixed in as well. Good, he thought, quietly slipping into the curtained alcove where he'd found his own fine clothes. He opened the storage chest. His sea-bedraggled clothes were still in there, scrunched in a corner where he had flung them, but by far the greatest space was taken up by a great brocaded blanket, and a bundle, done up in linen. Opening the bundle, he saw a set of good dark clothes, much like the ones Wolfe had been wearing, but in much better shape than his original ones. Good. These would do. Tiptoeing out with his great bundle, he went into the dining hall and saw that though the table had not yet been laid for the evening meal, there were the remains of some earlier meal there – a heap of cakes and a jug of wine – and a sharp fruit knife. Grabbing a large napkin off the table, he threw the cakes and knife in it, knotted it up at the corners, and with the clothes bundled under one arm, the cakes and knife balanced precariously on top, and carrying the jug in the other hand, he slipped out again, not bothering to close the front door, but going as quickly as he could, back to the grove.

Wolfe was still, apparently, asleep, so Hopewell deposited everything near him, and fled back to the mansion, closing the door behind him just as a laughing, red-faced Kit came panting down the corridor towards him, with Flora and Caprice in hot pursuit. They stopped when they saw him. 'Well, well, the wanderer returns, just like the other!' said Flora. Kit stood, smiling, panting, not saying a word, and looking at him, Hopewell felt an unexpected twist of the heart. This child was as devoted to Davy as he, Hopewell, was to Captain Wolfe; was he an apprentice in wickedness, or merely an innocent dupe? Who knew? What was sure was that, since coming to the Lost Island, the peaky little face and sly, darting eyes had been transformed. Would that happen, if he did not deserve good fortune? But then, what of Davy Jones? Had not the island treated him, a traitor, more gently than it had treated poor Captain Wolfe? Dr Bonaventure had said the island dealt with each as they deserved – but that could not be so, in these two men's cases. Then he remembered what Wolfe had said, about Davy Jones seeking to make the Captain's rightful fortune his own. Somehow, in those papers, he thought, lay the answer to these conundrums . . .

He started, as Flora blew into his ear. 'Cat got your tongue?' she said, and laughed. For some reason, Kit coloured – or perhaps because Hopewell had been staring at him. Hopewell glared at Flora, and turned away from Kit.

'*Some* of us have been working, and are weary,' he announced grandly.

'Some of us, eh?' said Flora, unconcernedly dancing around with Caprice. 'Who might that be, then, eh, Hopewell, do tell us, sweet friend! Your hands are empty, I see; you have found nothing, have you? So I am sure you were not talking about yourself!'

'Flora,' said Kit in a rather strangled voice, 'don't, please, he does look tired. Why don't you tell him the news that . . .'

'Oh, come, come, Kitty-cat, no soft words for the great Hopewell Shakespeare!' said Flora, laughing. 'He doesn't need or want your soft words, my poor dear; can't you see he thinks you are naught but a poor little half-starved alley cat, of no more consequence than that!'

At that, Kit blushed scarlet. Anger scalded Hopewell's belly, so that without thinking, the hot words boiled up into his mouth, 'You, Mistress Flora, are naught but a spoilt little shrew, who needs to be taught some manners!' he roared. 'You have no right to speak to Kit like that, or to me, do you understand?'

But his words fell on deaf ears, for Flora shrugged,

and grinned. 'As you wish, then, Master Shakespeare,' she said, and sticking her tongue out at him, she danced away with her pet. Hopewell was left with Kit in the corridor, both of them now filled with an acute embarrassment. At length, Kit mumbled, 'It was kind of you, Hopewell, to . . .' just at the same moment as Hopewell mumbled, 'I'm sorry, Kit, but she really is a little . . .' They looked at each other, in a kind of rueful fellowship that suddenly made Hopewell want to confide in the other boy, tell him everything that had happened, ask him what he thought. Two heads might be better than one, after all. But before he could open his mouth to make that potentially fatal mistake, Kit smiled at him.

'Hopewell, the Lord of Alchemists will be back tomorrow! He is returning from his travels at last.'

'The Lord of Alchemists is returning!' Hopewell stared at Kit. 'Why . . . why, that's wonderful!'

'Wonderful indeed,' whispered Kit, but Hopewell had already turned from him. He wanted to rush out that minute into the garden, to tell Wolfe the good news; but just then, along the corridor came Davy Jones, deep in conversation with Dr Bonaventure.

'Glad to see you back, dear boy!' carolled the philosopher. 'Any luck, then, in finding *Millefloria*?'

'Er, no – sir, that is, I . . . I lost my way . . . I went the wrong way, and ended up on the western shore instead. I'm sorry, sir,' said Hopewell, inventing rapidly, and hanging his head a little, as if in embarrassment. The sight of Davy Jones, with his cold stare, had made him instantly decide he did not want even a breath of suspicion to fall on him. Jones must not, under any circumstances, know that Wolfe had escaped.

Dr Bonaventure smiled benignly. 'Never mind, child,' he said. 'There will be other days. Now, I believe it is suppertime. You must be hungry, after all your galloping around getting lost, eh?'

'I am, sir,' said Hopewell, honestly, relieved that the old man seemed to have accepted the story so easily. He stole a glance at Davy Jones' face but could read nothing from it. Certainly there was no gleam of suspicion in the cold eyes.

'And you, Kit, I'm sure our little Flora has been leading you a dance all day, no?' Dr Bonaventure put his arm around the boy's shoulder, and drawing him closer, engaged him in rather one-sided conversation as he and Davy and Kit walked along, towards the dining hall, Hopewell trailing behind. For one whose assistant had returned empty-handed, Dr Bonaventure seemed in remarkably high spirits, rubbing his hands and smiling. Perhaps the imminent return of the Master of the Lost Island pleased him. What of Davy Jones, though? Did he know that the Lord of Alchemists would be back the next day? And if so, what did he think of it?

Twenty-Four

Nothing much, it seemed. For though some of the conversation that mealtime was of the return of the Alchemist, neither Davy – nor Flora, actually – took much part in it. And Hopewell noticed that even Dr Bonaventure turned from the subject rather quickly, and resumed an earlier conversation, or rather, monologue, he had no doubt been having with Davy, about the properties of various plants, and the ways in which divers nations of the world had used them. This rather silenced everyone else, as it was conducted in Dr Bonaventure's penetrating voice, well suited to the lecture room. This enforced silence suited Hopewell just fine, however; he had been dreading that Dr Bonaventure might quiz him further about what he had done, and what he had seen. A disquieting thought was agitating under the surface of his mind – if Davy Jones had been capable of the terrible torment inflicted on Captain Wolfe, what was he *not* capable of? A man of such duplicity would easily be able to fathom the disturbance of another's mind . . .

At length, Dr Bonaventure broke off from his

conversation to smile benignly at Hopewell. 'You seem weary, my boy,' he observed, not very originally. 'Too weary to read an old man another chapter of *Metamorphosis*?'

'No, sir, of course not.' Hopewell coloured, swallowed. He would be in the study, near the papers. When Dr Bonaventure fell asleep, he could . . .

'Would you like to go up now, sir?'

'Goodness, Hopewell, you *are* eager,' Dr Bonaventure laughed. 'Good stories, aren't they – even if implausible, in our day. Science can supply us with what the gods have neglected to leave behind for us, not so?'

'Er . . . yes, sir,' said Hopewell, not caring one hoot about either science or gods' gifts. He was desperately relieved when the old man, clutching his stick, rose from his chair and tapped his way out of the hall, Hopewell following in his wake. When they were nearly at the door, Flora's bright tones rang out. 'Don't forget to lock your door, Hopewell!' she called out, startling Hopewell so much by her words that he whirled around and stared stupidly at her. 'What . . . what do you mean?'

'Just that,' said Flora, gaily. 'Do your ears need rinsing out?'

Hopewell caught the looks on the others' faces: Kit's as startled as he; Flora's light and mischievous, Bonaventure's bemused and impatient; and Davy's . . . Davy's a chilling mixture of tension, mockery and warning, a chill that struck deep into his soul. He must not let it rattle him; he must keep calm and steady, for Captain Wolfe's sake. Rejoining Dr Bonaventure at the door, he left the room with as much jaunty cheer as he could muster in the circumstances.

Back in his room, though, Dr Bonaventure's own equanimity seemed to have deserted him. Far from getting ready for bed, and ordering him to read, the old man was distinctly preoccupied and uneasy; fussing around his table, he shuffled papers about, as if searching for something. Hopewell watched him with a nasty feeling beginning in his chest, but said nothing, hoping that the philosopher would soon settle down, so that he could read him to sleep. He tried to catch a glimpse of the piles on the table, to see if the oilskin package was still there, but Dr Bonaventure's back blocked him from view. He was browsing at the bookshelf, pretending to be examining the titles with great attention, when Dr Bonaventure called him, sharply.

Hopewell turned around, trying to look innocent. 'Are you ready, then, Dr Bonaventure?' His heart raced. Was the old man going to ask him what had really happened that day? The philosopher flapped a hand. 'No . . . Hopewell, listen. I want you to think clearly. To remember, as hard as you can.' Hopewell stared. 'Dr Bonaventure, I . . .'

'The ship,' Dr Bonaventure broke in, impatiently. 'The *Golden Dragon*. I want you to think on it.'

Hopewell stared even more, utterly mystified now.

'Think,' Dr Bonaventure went on, pacing around the room, but stopping every now and then to look fixedly at Hopewell. 'In your mind's eye. Davy Jones tells me you went several times into the Captain's cabin. So you would remember seeing a pile of papers on the table.

Yes?'

Hopewell's lips were stiff, but he managed to whisper, 'Yes, I think I remember seeing—'

'Good, good. Now, Hopewell, you were alone in that cabin at least once, weren't you?'

Hopewell's heart, which had quietened down, began thumping again. 'I . . .' he began.

'And like any other curious boy, you wanted to know what was in those papers, didn't you, Hopewell? Eh?' The philosopher stopped abruptly, his face so close to Hopewell's that the youth could see the coarse hairs growing in the old man's nostrils more plainly than he would have liked. He looked into Dr Bonaventure's eyes; and seeing the shrewdness there, had no choice but to nod his head, meekly.

'Good,' said the old man, with a great sigh of what sounded suspiciously like relief, bamboozling Hopewell yet again. 'What did you see, then?'

'See, sir?' Hopewell stammered. 'I . . . I could not read everything, you see . . . or even much at all . . . just the odd word here and there . . . it was in a Latin too difficult for me to understand, I really don't know what was in it, no, not at all, I could not understand it, sir, I promise that.' He *knows*, his heart screamed, silently. Davy Jones has somehow made him an ally; and now, what's going to happen to me, and to Captain Wolfe?

'Heavens, boy, I don't expect you to have *understood* it,' said Dr Bonaventure, in a surprised tone of voice. 'I hardly understood it myself,' he added with a laugh, 'though that may seem unlikely to you, of course. What I meant was – did you see how the papers were arranged?'

'Sir?' Suddenly, sickeningly, Hopewell had a vision of his arm jogging the papers off the table when the ship had jerked under his feet; then them flying around the room like a snowstorm; his quick shuffling of them together, in whatever way he could, before Captain Wolfe came back in.

'I . . . I . . .'

'Don't look so frightened, boy! I'm not angry with you. Why on earth should I be? Did you see all of them? Every *single* page?'

Hopewell licked his dry lips. 'I . . . I think so, sir.'

'Good.' Dr Bonaventure sighed again. 'Well then . . .' – and here he turned to the table, and to Hopewell's amazement, pulled out the oilskin package from under his other things – 'well, then, you will be able to tell me if *this* is what it looked like.'

Hopewell stared as if fascinated by Dr Bonaventure's busy fingers as the man opened the package, folded the oilskin back. There were the papers, neatly arranged in the middle.

'Are these the ones you saw, Hopewell?'

Should he act surprised? Hopewell decided it might be politic to do so. 'Sir! I do believe they are! But what are they doing here? I thought they went down with the ship.'

'Davy Jones rescued them from the *Golden Dragon*. Fortunately for all of us, Hopewell. He is a good man, is Davy, with more than his share of native wit. It was he who first drew my attention to the—'

'Oh, Dr Bonaventure,' broke in Hopewell, urgently,

meaning to warn the old man of Jones' true intentions, 'you must know that Master Jones—'

'Do I hear my name, Hopewell?' The boy whirled around, to find the former first mate standing at the bottom of the steps leading to the mezzanine. Davy Jones smiled, but his eyes stayed icy-cold. 'That is of interest to me, indeed.' Unhurriedly, he began to climb the last steps. 'It is said we never hear good when we come upon unexpected mention of us; is that so, Hopewell?'

'Master Jones,' cut in Dr Bonaventure, excitedly, 'you were right. The boy did see the papers, all the pages, just as you said. And so we will be able to . . . Why! Hopewell! What's the matter! Come back, boy, come back at once! What are you doing, running as if the Devil himself were after you!'

For Hopewell, with the swiftness born of despair, had taken a desperate lunge, grabbed the package of papers in its oilskin wrapping, and shoving them under his arm, sprinted away from the study – not downstairs, but up, towards the top floor, hardly knowing what he was doing, only knowing that he must get away from Davy Jones and his murderously cold eyes straight away. Panting, almost sobbing, he took the stairs two at a time, expecting at any moment to hear the man come pounding after him, to feel his heavy hand descend on his shoulder. Up in the circular room, he gazed wildly around. Ah! There was the Globe, waiting for him. He'd be safe there; he'd seen for himself that no one could open another's night door.

Now running footsteps sounded on the stairs; he had

not a moment to lose. With a wild cry, he flung himself at the backstage door. It fell open under his touch, and he pitched headlong into the darkness behind the stage.

Part Three

Thule

Twenty-Five

Hopewell lay there for an instant, his breath screaming in his chest. The package of papers was still under his arm: had he dropped any in his rush? He groped around in the darkness. No – there was no paper scattered around, not that he could feel, anyway. Clutching the package tightly, he looked around. It was dim in there, but as his eyes steadily got used to the darkness, he saw he was in a smallish, square room, where he could see vague, rectangular shapes lying on the floor – probably storage chests or boxes. The place smelt a little damp and dusty, and it was quite deserted. He got to his feet, dusting down his clothes, and called out, softly, 'Marguerite? Marguerite? Are you there?'

No one answered. What should he do? He could not open the door that led back to the stage, or at least back into the day world of the Lost Island, that was sure. Davy Jones would be waiting there, patiently, for him to emerge. No. Turning decisively, he peered into the dimness at the back of the room. Was there perhaps the outline of another door there? A door that might lead out into the London streets at the back of the playhouse? Dared he open that, and see what was beyond? But what of Captain Wolfe, left behind in the apple grove? And where, oh where was Marguerite? He found he truly did not know, and sat down on one of the chests to gather together his ragged thoughts into some sort of order.

Had he been wrong, foolish, to run from Davy Jones back then? The first mate would definitely know now that something was very wrong, that Hopewell knew something about the papers. But would he know Captain Wolfe had escaped? Hopewell tried to think of what he would do if he were in the first mate's shoes. Surely he would not go over to the cave in the night-time. He would likely keep watch outside Hopewell's door tonight, and in the morning, perhaps, go over to check on his prisoner? If it was indeed he who had imprisoned the privateer – as indeed, it must be, surely, would he not then go looking for him, when he discovered that he had gone? And what of Dr Bonaventure? Where did he fit in, in this plot? But what was the plot? Hopewell's heart tightened as the answer came suddenly to him. Captain Wolfe said he still held a secret, that Jones would not kill him till he had it. That secret, somehow, must be connected with the papers Hopewell had in his hand; must have something to do with the questions the philosopher had directed at Hopewell. What if the secret was indeed something on one of those pages – something only the Captain, who had been a friend of the man who wrote it, knew? He remembered the philosopher's strange insistence – had he seen every single page? Yes, it must be a single page that held the key to it all. Yes. It fitted. It was as Captain

Wolfe had said: he had survived the shipwreck, but had been insensible on the shore long enough for Jones to steal the papers and put him in the prison in the cave, there to be tortured, trying to get the secret.

But how? How had Jones and the galley boy survived? How did Jones know the prison was there at all? Would he not have needed help on the island itself . . . help from Dr Bonaventure? But why? Why should the old philosopher, guest of the Lord of Alchemists, help a murderer and mutineer? Maybe greed, too, had got the better of him . . . And why, oh why, had he agreed to send Hopewell over to the shore to find *Millefloria*, if he was in league with Davy Jones – if he had any notion that Hopewell might conceivably find Wolfe? Maybe, though, he thought Hopewell would simply do as he was told. He believed what Davy Jones believed about me, thought that young man with angry insight: He thought that I was a patsy, a cat's paw, easily hoodwinked. He did not know of my love for Marguerite, and my desire to search for her, nor even that she existed at all. And neither did Davy Jones, Hopewell realized suddenly. He would simply see no reason for Hopewell to go searching about. And that was quite likely as good a reason as any for supposing that Jones did not yet know of Wolfe's escape. And so he had time. He had a little time. A night, to be precise, he thought, savagely. One night, that was all he had, to discover the secret of the papers, and what to do about it – one night, before he must go back at once to Captain Wolfe and warn him. One night, and then the Lord of Alchemists would be back, and all put right.

All at once, a chill struck deep into Hopewell. What if . . . what if Dr Bonaventure was other than what he seemed? What if, in his time on the Lost Island, he had gained enough knowledge from the Lord of Alchemists to attempt his own mutiny, in his absence? And what of Kit? What was his part in all this dreadful thing? Hopewell's head whirled painfully with his confused thoughts, but one thing kept coming back to him, insistently: one night. He had one night. He could not go back through the stage door. He must open the street door, and go out into – where? He did not know. Dream London, real London? He must go out there, and hide the papers, hide them somewhere safe, somewhere unfindable, so that Jones and Bonaventure would never find them, somewhere where they would be safe till the Alchemist returned. Then even if . . . even if they found Captain Wolfe, his secret would be of no use to them, if they did not have the papers, and he did not think they would dare to hurt the privateer, right there within the Alchemist's walls, as they knew of the lord of the island's imminent return. He did not dare to think of any other possibilities, but marched with a firm step towards the door he could see faintly outlined in the dimness of the room.

When he reached it, he paused a moment, his hand on the latch. The door felt real enough, and solid, but he trembled as he held the latch. What if this was all a trick? What if the murderous sailor and his scientific accomplice waited beyond that door? What good would it do Captain Wolfe if his only ally was dead? Would the Alchemist get there in time? And where was Marguerite, dear, sweet, bold Marguerite, whose presence at his side would have filled him with courage, so much courage he could not only have fought Jones, but lions and tigers and yes, dragons as well! She was not there; but her memory still glowed in his heart. Better to die brave, and with her memory in his heart, he thought, the burning fear threatening to overwhelm him even as the bold words filled his mind, better to die thus than to crouch timidly behind a door, wishing she was there, waiting for morning to come and certain discovery.

So, teeth clenched, head reeling, he clicked the latch, and opened the door, and almost fell back before the brightness that immediately rushed into the room. He blinked, trying to adjust his eyes to the glare. Out here, it was not night, but morning, already well advanced. He could smell something definitely familiar; the stink of a great, crowded city. And yes, he was here, in a narrow alley flanked by tall houses. Just beyond was the Thames. He could smell it, and hear the yells of boatmen, the cries of street sellers, and all the other myriad familiar sounds. Hopewell blinked again, while his whole being flooded with the joy of relief. He was home! He was back in the streets of London! He had judged right, he had done the right thing ... Perhaps, the Lord of Alchemists, close by his island now, could see him, and help him. Whatever. It did not matter. Oh! He was so happy, he could have danced a jig, right there in the alley; but remembered that he had not a moment to lose. He must stash the package somewhere quite safe.

But where? He racked his brains; and then a brilliant thought struck him. Of course! St Paul's churchyard!

There, the booksellers hawked their wares; there were stalls covered in books, and a constant bustle of sellers and buyers. One more lot of papers would not be noticed amidst the mountains of literature there. He would seize a moment when one of the booksellers would not be watching his stall, and dump the whole thing; or, better still, sell it to some likely customer. A smile broke out on Hopewell's face. They'd never find it again then, never!

Just before he set off at a run, another thought struck him, and retracing his steps, he firmly closed the door he had just come through. Then he locked the latch, by inserting a piece of wood under it in such a way that it would be quite blocked. It made him feel safer. He'd remembered Flora's words about locking his door; and now they seemed full of grim and particular significance. Her father was on his way; but there was still this island night – this London day – to live through.

Twenty-Six

Hopewell hurried through the bustling streets, the package under his arm. The familiar sights and sounds were gradually restoring his usual blithe spirits, and he gazed about him with pleasure. Ah! He had missed London indeed, he realized. The island was a fine place, but not with Davy Jones on it. Only the thought of Marguerite, and of Captain Wolfe, kept him from wishing he could simply stay here and never have to go back to the island. Well, yes, but then what would he do? He could hardly go back to Master Page's, could he, or throw himself on Widow Frail's mercy? He would have to find some other work, some other way to make a living. Oh! but anything would be better than the wheelwright's shop, anyway, with its back-breaking, endless, boring drudgery. He rather fancied something more glamorous: quite what though, he had not yet made up his mind. Well! When the papers were safely disposed of, he would think what to do about it. He would ask the Lord of Alchemists to allow him to return, with Marguerite, and then he would . . .

'Ooof!' Hopewell said, as the breath was knocked out of him, and his package flew out from under his arm to land in the mud of the street, scattering its contents everywhere. He was up again in an instant, scrambling for the package, teeth fiercely bared, ready to fight for the papers . . . and found himself staring up into the startled face of a man in his mid to late thirties, with dark, hazel eyes and hair of a rich, red-brown colour.

'Forgive me, friend,' said the man. He had a low, well-modulated voice, with a familiar country accent burring it slightly. 'I did not see you; I was far away in my mind. Here, let me help you.'

He got down on his knees to help Hopewell gather up the papers, courteous enough not to stare at them too much, but obviously curious, his eyes flicking over the pages.

Hopewell mumbled, 'Thank you, it is most kind, I too was not looking where I was going,' while he struggled to reassemble the pages in a semblance of order. The stranger handed him the ones he had picked up, and watched politely as Hopewell shuffled the papers together and wrapped the oilskin around them again.

'Your book might do better bound,' he observed, at last, with a smile that had something of a wry humour in it, and something of a gentle interest. 'It seems to be a most learned work, full of most earnest Latin phrases; a pity to see it flapping about in the street, for want of a little stitching.'

'Yes, that is so,' agreed Hopewell, getting off his knees, and putting the package carefully under his arm. 'I was on my way to do that, Master,' he added, lying. Then, as inspiration struck him, 'Master, could you make out the words in it?'

The stranger looked at him, eyebrows raised. 'Oh dear! If it is an interpreter of learned Latin prose you want, I fear you have come to the wrong door. I could make out more than a few words, yes; but making as much sense to me as a blank page might.'

'Oh,' said Hopewell, rather dashed. 'Why, then, I must be on my way. Thank you, Master, again, and good day to you.'

'Good day to you, too, friend,' said the man, with a flash of that smile again. He seemed about to add something, when a loud voice from the other side of the street hailed him, a voice belonging to a stocky, fuzzy-haired fellow with a strong-featured, irascible face, gesturing urgently to him. '*There* you are! Come, Will, we are already late, confound it!'

'I was waiting for *you*, friend Ben, remember,' said the stranger, with a smile, and a wink at Hopewell. 'Well, I had better go.' A sidelong glance, and the man added, with a wry tilt of the lips, 'And best of luck to you, young friend, with the deciphering of that fiendish, crabbed book of yours. Yes, *coming*, Ben.' And, with a friendly nod, he was gone with the man called Ben, the pair of them soon disappearing around a corner of the street. Hopewell stared after them for an instant, then shook his head, and went on his way.

He had almost reached St Paul's churchyard, when he stopped dead, and cursed himself for a prize fool. It was not only the accent that was familiar to him, being of a similar part of the country to his own, but the voice, and indeed the manner. He had heard and seen both more than once – on stage at the Globe. The hazel-eyed stranger was his own distant kinsman, the famous playwright and sometime actor, William Shakespeare. And the other with him must have been one of his fellows, rising to become equally famous – Ben Jonson, former bricklayer's apprentice who was now making quite a name as a playwright, thanks in part to the kindness of his friend Will, who had introduced him to the right people.

Curse it! If only he had known! He could have asked them for their advice, he thought: Will for his quick wits, Ben for his Latin. They might even have kept the bundle with them, and then it would have been safe indeed. Ah well! It was too late to go racing after them now. And perhaps, it was better this way, anyway, for he had more than a suspicion that theatre people would likely be terrible gossips, and might pass the papers around from hand to hand, and who's to know what would happen next? No, best press on with his original plan.

There, now, was the churchyard, and there the booksellers' stalls, dozens of them, printers and stationers and clerks everywhere, customers sampling wares, gallants sauntering, ladies promenading, dogs barking . . . Hopewell slipped in amongst all the people, his package securely under his arm, wondering where it might be best to leave it. If he tried to sell it, he might run into trouble; but if he just left it, what would happen to it? Deep in thought, he walked through the churchyard and to the open church door, peering in at all the busy transactions going on there too. It had astonished him, this sight, the first time he had seen it.

Back home, churches were not allowed to be used for such blatant commerce, but here, there were all kinds of deals sealed and done; all kinds of goods passed through the doors, and out again with new owners. Hopewell had thought how shocked and disgusted his father would be, if he'd seen this; he would not have put it past him to have found himself a whip somewhere and driven all the moneylenders and cattle dealers and punks and worse, out of the church like a disorderly mob of animals. Then he'd start on the booksellers; his father had no great love of books, unless they were Holy Writ. Philosophy he could just about admit might be necessary; but the collections of poetry, and worse, plays, that were fashionable just now would be scattered like so much chaff in the wind, if he had his way. Then he'd close all the playhouses, and people like his distant kinsman would have no place to ply their dangerous trade. Will's courteous manners and ready wit would butter no parsnips with Robert Shakespeare, Puritan worthy!

Smiling to himself, Hopewell moved away from the church door again, and was about to go and approach one of the booksellers, when he suddenly remembered something that the said courteous Will had observed after helping him pick up his papers. For the second time that strange night day, Hopewell stood stock still, remembering the time in the *Golden Dragon* when the papers snowed all around him, and he'd scrabbled to pick them all up, just as he'd done in the street. He saw himself picking them all up, and putting them back on the table, in a neat pile – *all except for one*. One, which he had inadvertently ripped, and had, in panic, crumpled into a ball and thrust into his doublet! The last page. The blank page. Could it be that . . . no, it was impossible. Impossible. And yet . . .

With a strangled cry, Hopewell took off through the booksellers' stalls, scattering people left and right, the package still sweatily clutched under his arm, running as if his life depended on it, running as fast as he could, back to the Globe.

Alas! When he reached the alley at the back of the playhouse, he found the door securely locked. Not with his block of wood on the outside, but from the inside. He rattled the door and shouted, to no avail. What could he do? If he could not get into the back, he could not open the stage door, and thus go back to the Lost Island. But . . . stay . . . if he went round the other side, to the front of the playhouse, and on to the stage, and then through the stage door, would he perhaps also get through, back to the Alchemist's mansion? It was all muddled in his mind, but it seemed worth trying. He ran around to the front of the playhouse, and to his relief, found the main door standing open. Unfortunately though, the playhouse was not empty, as before, but full of noise and movement, for a rehearsal was in progress. There were a few people calling out instructions from the galleries, and actors on the stage, and sundry hangers-on sauntering about. Hopewell hesitated for a moment, but only for a moment; taking a deep breath, he careered through the playhouse, and up on to the stage. There he caught sight, for the second time, of Will Shakespeare's startled face, gave the playwright a rather desperate wave, and dived through the open stage door. He slammed the door shut behind him, and fell into the darkness of the dressing room. As he fell, he hit his head on something sharp, and immediately lost consciousness.

Twenty-Seven

There was a sweet, low voice singing in his dream, the lovely voice of Marguerite. Strangely, though he could not open his eyes, he could hear the words, quite plainly:

'Heedless as fish, man swims to and fro,
In the limitless ocean of mystery.
Knowing not even the shape of its flow,
Nor its current in all of his history,
He is deaf to the silence that is also a song,
And calls it a trick, or else dreams.'

'Marguerite!' he cried, through a thick throat. 'Where are you, love? I cannot see anything . . .'

'Hush, Hopewell, dear,' she said, and he felt a cool hand on his forehead, his burning, burning forehead. 'Hush, and listen . . .'

She was singing again:

'Man seeks to contain, for he cannot bear long,
To know he is more than he seems.
And yet, in the water, he swoops and he flies,
Taken out of the ocean, he soon gasps and dies . . .'

'That is a strange song, Margot, my dear,' he said,

gently, 'for in the water, man does not live, but drowns. Just as I nearly drowned, in the raging seas off the Lost Island.'

'There are seas and seas,' she said, 'and oceans and oceans, and fish and fish.'

'And fishermen and fisherwomen,' he replied, 'and nets of love, and nets of hate, and hooks that tear a poor fish's lips or heal his wounds . . .'

He opened his eyes quite easily now, and found he was in his room at the Alchemist's mansion, lying in bed. Light streamed in through the open window. Lying next to his hand, on the bedclothes, was the oilskin package. And sitting in the chair, near his bed, was . . . Marguerite. Marguerite, not in the night world, but right here, in the daylight, more beautiful than ever, her blue-black hair streaming out around her, all over the rich, red-velvet cloak she was wearing, wrapped tightly around her, as if she were cold.

'You are really here,' he said, struggling to sit up, then blushing a little at the thought that she had been sitting there watching him sleep, watching him fight and struggle. 'I thought you could only come to me in the night world.'

'Oh, that is so, mostly; but the need was great, tonight, and I was given leave to watch over you,' she said, more seriously than he had ever heard her. 'I locked the door tightly, and sat there and watched over you, all night.'

He could not speak. The intensity of his feelings burnt in his throat, his eyes, his chest. He could only look at her, and tremble a little. The papers, Wolfe, the Alchemist, everything was forgotten in the great rush of love and longing and joy almost too great to be borne. But with her next words, Marguerite swept all the joy quite away. She put a hand on his. 'Now I must leave you, Hopewell, dear. Now that I know you are safe, and all will be well.'

'Stay! Marguerite, no, do not go!' He jumped out of bed. 'Please. Why must you go, why, why, if all's to be well?' She did not answer, but stood gazing at him sadly, from her great luminous eyes. 'Tell me what I must do then, to keep you with me always. Anything. I will do anything.'

'I have tried to tell you before,' she said, at last. 'When I told you of the White Ship . . .'

'But I did not understand what you meant! You were not on the White Ship, were you? Not a member of her crew, or her passengers, for that was a fairy ship, for sure, a ship of doom . . .'

'Then I looked at you, out of the pond in the grove . . . I was there, with you, and you did not see me . . .'

'I looked everywhere,' said Hopewell, hotly, 'everywhere! But nowhere could I see you! There was no one!'

'No one?' she said, still with that sad smile. 'And then, the third time, I warned you, in my actor's costume, I told you, to remember me and not to deny me.'

'How could I forget you?' said Hopewell, his head in his hands. 'You fill my thoughts, my heart, my whole soul. How could I deny you? Why do you torment me so? No, Lady, no,' he whispered, desperately, as she turned to the door, 'do not go, not yet, please. Just look at me and tell me – will I ever be worthy of you? Will you not give me one clue, as to how I may win you?'

'Hopewell,' said Marguerite, with a sudden, darting smile, 'you are aptly named. And there is your answer.'

'What answer is that? Stay, stay, stay, tell me, please – were you there, on the hill, yesterday . . . did you follow me to the cave? The flower you wear in your hair . . . the little daisy . . . is that your sign . . . is that it . . .'

'Well, it may well be,' she said, opening the door, 'and that is one step. One step, indeed, my sweet friend.'

As she slipped through the door, he made a grab at her cloak, which fell a little off her shoulder, revealing part of a russet doublet, part no doubt of her actor's costume, which she was still wearing. At that, she gave a little cry, and pulling the cloak back over her shoulder so fast that he was pushed off balance, vanished through the doorway, giving the door a flick as she did so, so that it closed almost on Hopewell's nose. He wrenched it open again, and stepped out into the circular room – too late, for already she had vanished down the stairs. He raced to the stairs anyway, and clattered down them as fast as he could go, not caring who might see him. He did not even glance at the mezzanine room as he went past, but went on down, through the meadow corridor, the dining hall, down the other corridor, to the open front door, and into the garden. But there was no Marguerite to be seen there at all. Not on the gravelled walks, not in the walled garden, not anywhere. Overcome, Hopewell sank down on the grass.

How would he ever find her? She only showed herself when she *wanted* to, he thought; he could shout till he was blue in the face, and search for her till doomsday, and he would never force her to manifest herself. She would only come to him when she was ready – when he had accomplished what it was she wanted. 'To remember, and not to deny.' What did she mean? He would never do the opposite, he would love her to the end of his days, no matter what happened! And as to the 'clue' she had given him, what clue was that? She had said he was aptly named – and was she? She had said the daisy might be her sign. Marguerite was her name. Margreet. *Margaret*, in English. Margot, you could also say. And other nicknames, for it was a flower name with many petals to it. Maggie. Margot. Margy. Peggy. Peg. Daisy . . .

A daisy was her flower, a white daisy. White flower . . . Marguerite . . . a flower with many names. How many names? A thousand names? *Millefloria* . . . thousand flowers, that meant, didn't it? If he found *Millefloria*, did that mean he would find her too? Was that what she meant? But where could he find it? Dr Bonaventure had told him on the shore, in the rocks . . . it looked paltry, like a weed. He had looked yesterday, but he hadn't found it, only the little white flower, *her* flower . . . but stay! Stay! Perhaps that *was* it: *Millefloria* herself, thousand-flowered, many-named! Paltry weed, indeed! What would Dr Bonaventure know?

He'd seen the flower growing on the hill, where the dead sheep had vanished . . . and in the cave . . . he'd held it in his hand . . . it had been in his hand yesterday, crushed in his hand, when he'd found Captain Wolfe in the cave.

Suddenly, he remembered the urgency of his other task. The page! The blank page! And the package, that he'd left in full view on his bed, when he'd run out to find Marguerite . . . oh, my dear God, he thought, what have I done? He pelted back to the mansion, down the corridor, through the hall, into the alcove – only to come face to face with Caprice, the goat, peering curiously into the open storage chest. At her feet was a crumpled mass of sea-bedraggled clothes. And when she turned towards him, he saw there was something white at the corner of her mouth . . .

'Oh no! You verminous little fleabag, you're not going to eat it!' he cried. He lunged at her, grabbing for her mouth, for the piece of ripped, sodden, shredded paper that had been the blank page, the last page, the secret page. There was a most undignified tussle, but at last he managed to get most of it from her, bar one corner slimy beyond rescue. He shook his first at the unconcerned kid. 'You wait till I tell your mistress!'

A vain threat; because what would Flora do? Probably laugh. Yes, but her father, her father, the Lord of Alchemists, was coming back today. And then they'd see what was what! He said it aloud. 'You'll see what's what, Caprice! You've been allowed to run riot for far too long!'

Caprice bleated, and cast him a look that in a human could not have been described as other than scornful. Then with a perceptible toss of her head, she trotted out of the alcove, her little black hoofs clickety-clicking across the polished floor.

Hopewell stared down at the page in his hand. He could still see nothing on it, not a scrap of writing, not a secret sign, nothing. It was perfectly blank. Well, now he must get the rest of the papers and get back to Captain Wolfe before Davy Jones and Dr Bonaventure arrived on the scene. But where were they? He had not seen them anywhere. But he had no time to speculate on their whereabouts just now. Hopewell dashed out of the alcove, through the hall, up the corridor, up the stairs – the mezzanine floor still seemed empty – and went up the last stairs three at a time. He ran into the circular room, and paused for a frantic second, unable to believe his eyes.

He'd left the door of his room open – but now there was no open door, and no bedroom beyond. Nothing but the panel with the oh-so-realistic picture of the famous London playhouse. He stared at it, then threw himself against the painted stage door. Ouch! The wall was hard. He tried again. In vain! The door was not only shut, it had gone back to being just a painted one, not a real one. He stared at it, willing it to open, to resume its former magic. In vain. All he saw was a beautifully painted wooden stage door, round, with iron bands, and a latch and . . . He peered at it more closely: and there were deep, deep grooves, scratches on it, or rather gouges, in the wood. Surely they hadn't been there before? His heart was in his mouth. What had made those marks? They looked as if . . . as if some gigantic animal had hurled itself at the door, trying to force it open, some huge animal with rapier-like claws.

The picture of the dead sheep on the hill, its throat torn out by some beast in a senseless fury, came instantly to his mind. His legs felt wobbly. He remembered Marguerite's words – 'I've been watching you all night'

– and Flora's warning. What had happened in the night, out here, whilst he careered about in dream London? He found he did not really want to know. His legs felt wobbly, his throat dry. But what of the papers? Where could they be? Somewhere in the night world, in the three-dimensional shadows behind the cheat-eye on the wall? Or somewhere else? Had Davy Jones already found them? And what of Captain Wolfe . . .

He found that he was creeping slowly around the room, looking for other clues, other signs of what had happened out here. He paused at the picture of the Doge's palace, and gently put out a hand to it. But of course it was solid. Solid paint. He nodded his head, slowly, and moved on to the next panel, and there gave a little start. Had this one not been blank, previously? Yet there was a picture emerging from it, a picture of wavering outlines which he could not yet quite discern, but which looked vaguely like a great cloud on the sea, or a . . .

Suddenly, his eye was caught by a movement. A tiny movement, but perceptible. It came from the region of the last picture, Kit's picture, the one of the walled garden. He stared at it: yes, the door in the wall was open. And more than open, it was swinging on its hinges, slowly, as if someone had just passed through it. Though the hair rose stiffly, coldly, on the back of his neck, he did not stop to think twice. In one bound, he was over the room, and through the doorway into the garden.

Twenty-Eight

Outside the walled garden, it was green and shady, trees forming a kind of leafy avenue which ran to the right and left of him. Hopewell frowned. There was something familiar about this green path, but he did not for the moment know where he'd seen it. He looked left, then right. Which way? He had no idea who was here – Kit, Davy, Dr Bonaventure, or all three. And what of Flora, who as the Lord of Alchemists' daughter, must be able to slip in and out of these worlds easily, at any time? But would she not be down at the shore, waiting for her father's ship to come in? If he came in by ship – if he did not come flying through the air, that is, like any self-respecting great magician. Or floating across the sea, in a bubble?

Hopewell caught himself up. What was he doing, he scolded himself severely, standing here like a great galoot with his head full of fanciful thoughts! Come, man, you have to make a decision, he admonished himself. You must do what— He froze, for somewhere in the distance to his left, floating towards him, he could hear a voice, a lovely, low, sweet voice, singing.

'*Heedless as fish, man swims to and fro . . .*'

'No! no! No more fish foolishness!' he cried out. 'I am coming to find you. I know this place, now, Marguerite, and why it seemed so familiar to me! It was where you disappeared, the other night. That green path, where you vanished! And now I'm going to find you, come what may!' And so he plunged down the path to his left, following the voice, which sometimes floated clearly to him, and sometimes not. As he went along, disquieting things began to come to him, of just what Marguerite was doing here, in Kit's night world, and he remembered the other boy's enchanted eyes, that first morning. What was it that he had seen, in his own night world? Could it be that Marguerite was beguiling them both? No, no, surely not. He refused to believe that. He refused to . . .

The page in his hand crackled and fluttered as he walked. He would have put it away in his doublet, but for the fact that it was still somewhat wet from Caprice's attention, and needed to dry properly before being put away. He looked at it curiously, but saw it was still quite innocent of any meaning. It was a strange notion, he thought now, but the two things, finding Marguerite, and helping Captain Wolfe, seemed to be drawing closer and closer together. The day before, he had gone to find Marguerite but had found instead Captain Wolfe; and just now had run down the stairs and into the mansion garden to find Marguerite; yet there had been put in mind of his duty to Wolfe; and when he had acted on that duty, had found Marguerite again – or at least, was well on the way to finding her.

He stopped. He could hear agitated voices, men's voices, somewhere on the path ahead of him. Hopewell recognized them at once. Davy Jones and Dr Bonaventure, arguing furiously. Ducking behind the trees on the side of the path, he moved noiselessly towards them, making sure he kept hidden. When he was close enough to understand what they were saying without straining his ears too much, he stopped, and crouched down, unseen, in the greenery.

Davy Jones was pale with passion, and waving his arms. 'It is foolish of you, Dr Bonaventure! I am telling you, you do not know him as I do!'

'And *I* am telling *you*, Master Jones, he must be drawn out − attracted to the scent, for by all you've told me, he's too old a dog to be caught any other way.'

'Old perhaps, but just as dangerous as ever! I say we must find him ourselves, and make sure he can do no harm. This way is risky − and likely to fail.'

'Tut, tut, Master Jones! You are quite wrong. You will see. Anyway, it was the child's own choice. Do not be afraid.'

'How can I not be, knowing what I know? Dr Bonaventure, you must understand − you do not know him as I do.'

'Are you sure of that, my friend?' said the philosopher, softly. Hopewell, crouching in the shadows, saw a strange change come over Davy Jones' face as he stared back at Dr Bonaventure.

'You cannot mean . . .' he whispered, and then added something else, so low that Hopewell, strain as he might, could not catch it at all. But he saw clearly the mixture of emotions flitting over the first mate's face, emotions he could not understand at all.

Dr Bonaventure nodded, slowly. Hopewell saw him place a hand on the other man's shoulder. 'Come. We must not lose a moment.'

'Yes,' said Davy Jones, but not very willingly. They moved on now, past where Hopewell was hiding, and back in the direction from where he had come; Bonaventure briskly, but Jones reluctantly, with a glance or two over his shoulder back up the path. Hopewell waited until they had quite vanished from sight before emerging from his hiding place and continuing on his way, thinking about what he had just heard. They must have been talking about Wolfe, he thought; so they must know he had escaped; but they had obviously not found him. Indeed, it sounded rather as if he had found his way into this place, too; was perhaps hiding somewhere here. But who was 'the child' they had referred to? Kit? Or Flora? And what had they planned between them – a trap of some kind for Wolfe, that was clear, but what?

Remembering the fierce, hunted look of the privateer the day before, Hopewell was filled with renewed pity. Not content with tormenting him, they were now seeking to trap him, as if he were a wild beast. He was sure Captain Wolfe, if he were still at large, would at the very least sell his life dearly, if he had to. Guilt stung him now. He should have gone out to the grove to check on him, long since. He should not have left the poor man friendless, alone, having to defend himself without help. But at least, at least, he thought, Wolfe had a chance, out of the prison in the cave. He had a chance, while he still ran free, outside, or in here. And he was, as those two had so callously put it, old maybe, but dangerous. In his younger days, he had been a famous privateer, famous for his gallantry and courage. Why should that be any different now, even though unimaginable torments had twisted his frame and grizzled his hair? Wolfe still had tricks left up his sleeve, Hopewell thought with a not inconsiderable touch of pride; those two villains obviously still feared him, or they would not have spoken in the way they had. They must think still that Wolfe had the secret key to the papers; they had not yet worked out the secret themselves. And he, Hopewell, held it safe in his hand . . .

Of course! That was how they would trap him, he realized, with a sick feeling of dismay. They – or Kit – had seen the papers lying on his bed that morning, had snatched them, and slammed the door, so that it would seem as if they had simply disappeared into the night world. Then, somehow, they had lured Wolfe here, to this place, with the promise of the papers. How had they found out he was loose? It did not matter, not now. It must be Kit, Hopewell thought, Kit they were referring to when they said 'it was the child's choice'. Kit. A twist of anger gripped at him. He had thought the boy was becoming more prepossessing, when in fact he must just have been trying to worm his way into Hopewell's confidences, making sham that he was his friend. Sly indeed; he was well named, too! He must have somehow known of Hopewell's agitation; perhaps had been watching him . . . Pah! The Lost Island gave to men what each deserved, he thought, disgustedly. That was a sham, sure enough. He'd have a bone to pick with that Lord of Alchemists, right enough!

But come, his reason intervened, in the annoying way that reason does interrupt fine flights of passion. Kit had never asked Hopewell any questions about Wolfe, subtle or no. He had never pretended not to be close to Davy Jones, or spied on Hopewell – not that he knew, anyway. Hopewell heaved a great sigh. Who knew but that Kit thought he was doing the right thing, wanting to help his friend Davy Jones, just as Hopewell wanted to help his friend Richard Wolfe? Davy Jones had probably told him the thing seen his own lying way, using Kit for his own purposes, and Kit believed it, for friendship's sake, and was prepared to face danger for that friendship and trust. Though what, in fact, had Davy done for *him*? The new thought pricked at Hopewell mightily. What, in fact, had Jones done for Kit, or . . . or *Wolfe, for himself?* He had to admit, very little indeed. Wolfe had spoken much, on the ship, true, of Hopewell's great importance; but had he taken much notice of him there beyond mouthing baffling riddles at him? He had been about to ask him to do something about Davy Jones, had he not, later, but what exactly had he had in mind? And he had spoken yesterday of being in Hopewell's debt, but had acted more towards the boy as if Hopewell were his slave. Perhaps Davy had done that to Kit, too . . .

The disloyal thought smouldered in Hopewell's heart, though he tried to douse it with plenty of cold, rational, shaming water. It was not true that Wolfe had done nothing for him – he had taken him on as crew member on the *Golden Dragon* when he needed a job, he had

239

personally taken him over the ship and showed him things, he had talked to Hopewell man to man, and not like a famous privateer addressing an apprentice boy still wet behind the ears. And he had offered Hopewell a share in the fortune he would find on the Lost Island. Yes, that was so, wasn't it!

So, hotly debating with himself, he finally reached the end of the path. And there he stopped, arrested by a most charming scene. A little painted wooden pavilion of one storey, with a carved balcony on the top floor, stood, surrounded by blossom trees, beside a sparkling, ornamental lake fringed with tall reeds. Was anyone there? He could hear nothing, from where he stood. But despite its peaceful isolation, the little pavilion did not look deserted; freshly painted, sparkling in the sunshine, its bottom casement window opened wide, it had the air of being quite happily occupied. Precisely, Hopewell thought with a leap of the heart, precisely the kind of place where he might find Marguerite! Smiling to himself, he crept noiselessly forward. So, she wanted to play a game with him! Well, he would show her how well he could play!

But when he got closer to the pavilion, he saw that the window – which, oddly, had no glass in it – was just a little too high up to be easily accessible from the ground. There was, however, a little garden, bordered with rocks, growing just under it. Perhaps if he piled up some of the rocks, he would be able to reach to the window. Suiting the action to the thought, he began to pull up the rocks, and placed them one on top of the other. To do that, he had to put down his precious bit of paper, of course. Probably, he thought, it would be best to hide it . . . So, folding it carefully, he placed it under one of the flattest uprooted rocks, clean side down, and scattered the earth all around it with the green weeds that had come up with the rock. Yes; that would hide it from any casual glance. He would come back for it, as soon as he had found Marguerite . . .

He had just placed the last rock on the pile when suddenly, from within the room, he heard *her* voice, her lovely voice, rent with a sorrow, and a fear, he had never heard in it before: 'Oh, it is too late . . . too late . . . too late . . .'

He did not stop to hear more. Crying 'Marguerite!' he jumped on to his tottering pile, and lunged for the window ledge, managing to get a firm grip on it despite losing his footing. In the same instant, he discovered, very sharply and painfully, just where the window's glass had gone to: for shards and shatters of it lay all over the ledge. But Hopewell paid no attention. Though his hands bled and throbbed with the pain, he managed to haul himself up with a strength born of despair, and dropped down into the room beyond, glass falling all around him.

Twenty-Nine

But there was no Marguerite there. Instead, Kit, barefoot, clad only in his shirt and breeches, his hair tousled, his face pale as death, though with two red spots burning in his cheeks, eyes wild and staring, was backed up against a half open door.

'You vicious hellpuppy, what have you done with her?' Hopewell was on him in an instant, shaking the other boy till his teeth rattled. 'You broke in here, didn't you, and overcame her, on your master's orders! Where is she? What have you done to her?'

Kit said nothing; but his rolling eyes seemed to be staring into a corner of the room, where there was a curtained alcove. Holding him in a painful grip, his bloody hands leaving red fingermarks all over the boy's shirt, Hopewell dragged Kit over to that corner, and flung open the curtain. On the floor behind it lay something he recognized – the red cloak Marguerite had been wearing when last Hopewell saw her, and the russet doublet she had worn underneath, that he had only caught a glimpse of. The way they lay, any old how, as if they had been forced off her, suggested the very worst to Hopewell, and he turned furiously on Kit.

'Where is she? What have you done with her?'

Kit sobbed, but Hopewell had no pity for him. 'Tell me, or I'll beat you so that you will not be able to sit or stand, for a very long time!' Fury and fear blazed inside him, making him terrible, and Kit shrank from it just like a beaten puppy. Far from calming Hopewell, though, the boy's craven reaction just made him angrier, and he was just about to make his threat a reality, when out of the corner of his eye, he saw what he should have seen before: a piece of manuscript paper, lying half concealed under the cloak. At the same time, just above his head, he heard a footstep; a light footstep, like that of a woman striving to move quietly.

The hair rose on the back of Hopewell's neck. In two steps, he bent down and picked up the paper, which he recognized at once from the crabbed writing as one that had fallen from the manuscript when aboard the *Golden Dragon*. Wordless, he stared at Kit as a horrifying doubt began to worm its way into his mind. The other boy hung his head, looking at his feet. Hopewell stared at him, seeing again the disarray of his clothing, his tousled hair . . . Marguerite's cloak and doublet lying there discarded in the alcove, the paper, the light footstep above . . . He dropped Kit as if he had been scalded, and murmured, 'She has been with you, too, she dwells in your heart . . . Far from being afraid of you, she has come here, to be with you . . . And she took the manuscript, took it to give to your great friend Davy Jones . . .'

Kit tried to say something; but either through fear, or some other passion, did not seem to be able to bring the words out.

'Why? Why did she play with me? Why taunt me in this way? Why give me hope, only to betray me? Betray me with' – he lifted his head up and glared at the shrinking Kit – 'with you, you vile little weasel-faced wretch! Ah, women are indeed the most inconstant and fickle and wicked of all God's creatures . . . to take a man's heart and then break it, smash it into a thousand pieces . . . and for what? For what? What is she, that one? An evil, soulless spirit, doubtless!'

'No,' said Kit, and his voice, strangely, was almost light, almost mocking, though his eyes were blank and still. 'No evil spirit she – or soulless, ah no – but a dream, a sweet dream, Hopewell dear . . .'

All the blood seemed to rush to Hopewell's head, so all he could see was a red, boiling mist. He lunged at Kit; but this time, the other boy was ready for him. Ducking under his arm, he made a desperate dash out of the alcove, back into the room, and was out through the half open door in an instant. With a roar, Hopewell was after him. He was much stronger, bigger, heavier than Kit, his stride much longer; he would soon bring the other boy down.

But Kit's need had lent him the swiftest of wings. Hopewell could not catch him up, no matter how he tried to shorten the distance between them. They pelted down a corridor, up another one, through another room, up another corridor, and came to a spiral staircase. Kit raced up it as if this was familiar ground indeed, but it wasn't so easy for Hopewell. When at last, after several stumbles, he reached the top of the stairs, Kit had disappeared.

Hopewell looked wildly around, and listened for a sound. 'Kit! False Marguerite!' he cried, loudly. 'It is of no use hiding, for I will find you, never fear!' Nobody spoke; but just down the corridor, he suddenly saw a door that seemed somehow to have an air of tension about it, as if it had just been closed. With a low growl of satisfaction, he crept quietly towards the door, keeping a wary eye out. Nothing stirred; he reached the door in a moment, and quietly, slowly, carefully, eased the latch up till it opened; then with a yell, he sprang into the room.

'Ah, Hopewell. Here at last.' There was a figure in the room, sitting at a table, back to the door. Grey hair, choppily cut, fell about its dark-clad shoulders. Without haste, the figure turned in its chair, and Hopewell saw without surprise that it was Captain Wolfe, and that behind him, on the table, lay the oilskin package of papers. But it was not this that froze Hopewell: but what Wolfe held, in his arms. It was Kit, held not in a friend's embrace, but tightly, cruelly, with a strong arm just under the neck. And in the other hand, the privateer held a knife, wickedly sharp, gleaming, at the boy's throat: the fruit knife Hopewell had brought him. Wolfe's face was set and still, only the eyes alive in the ravaged face, and there were recent cuts and scratches on his cheeks and on his powerful hands. As to Kit, his eyes were closed, and his face was clay-grey, beads of sweat gathered on his brow.

Hopewell found his voice at last. 'Sir, I am glad to find you here! And that you have . . .' he glanced at Kit's pallid face, his skinny limbs, and wished that the wretch could have been somehow a more worthy opponent. Beating him would not have been much of an achievement, not really . . . 'You have Kit, and the papers,' he went on more strongly. 'But sir, where is Marguerite? Was it she who brought them to you?'

'Marguerite?' said Wolfe, harshly. 'What on earth are you talking about, boy?'

'Marguerite,' said Hopewell, 'a beautiful woman – beautiful, but false. I would find her – and tell her to her face what I think of her, dallying with Kit Sly when it was I who loved her best!'

The privateer smiled broadly. 'I have seen no Marguerite here, beautiful or otherwise. However, I think you may be safe from the thought that she may have dallied with Kit Sly. For, see you' – and here he grinned, toothily – 'see you, Kit Sly does not, from this moment, exist!' Quite without warning, he raised the knife, and before Hopewell could even gasp, he had brought it down in a slashing motion, ripping into Kit's shirt, exposing one shoulder and part of his back.

Now the boy, clutching at the remains of his shirt, did cry out in such terror that Hopewell, scarcely knowing what he was doing, sprang forward. 'Sir . . . no, please,' he gabbled, 'he is just a boy, just a boy, it is Davy Jones who—'

'Just a boy,' repeated Wolfe, with a mocking smile. 'Tell him, my dear – set his mind at rest, about your dalliance with his lady. Tell him, my little heart, tell him who you really are.' The knife was no longer at the boy's throat, and the privateer made no further attempt to attack him, but sat holding him loosely, a cruel satisfaction on his handsome features.

But Hopewell did not notice Wolfe's expression. His scalp was crinkling with a strange emotion. He saw Kit's bare shoulder, thin and prominent, peeking through the remains of his shirt; caught a glimpse of some cloth wound tightly inside the shirt, as if the boy were cleaving to some secret; saw Kit's face, the eyes still closed; the sooty hair, beginning to grow around the face, and his own bones felt made of marble, his blood of ice. A disbelief as paralysing as the knowledge of his own obtuseness tried to close his throat up on the words he could not, *must not* utter. But something stronger, something wiser, made him whisper, 'Meg? Meggie? It cannot be *you* . . . not you. How . . . How?'

Kit opened his eyes, and Hopewell looked into the wild stare of Meg – Meggie, the street-sweeper, whom he had long forgotten, and never once brought to mind, never seen in the eyes of the galley boy, in his quick, thin brightness. He cursed himself for a blind fool, and felt a shrinking, that she should know he had been so blind.

'You said you were going to the very gates of danger, but that no sweet maid could follow,' Meg whispered now, and Hopewell felt riven to the heart by the tenderness and the bitterness in her voice and in the small smile that flitted across her thin face. 'So, I thought – where no sweet maid could follow, a sour lad might. But still, I was not sure of how I might do it. Until I met . . .'

Wolfe, who had been listening to this exchange with a curious smile, broke in, 'Until she met Davy Jones. And she saw how she could come . . . She was willing to be part of his plot, of everything he had planned, just so she could be near you, protect you, as if she were a tigress with her young . . . funny, isn't it, how women are? She looks more like a half-starved alley cat, to me.'

Something flared deep down in Meg's eyes, and she murmured something, very low. Hopewell could not hear what she said; could not read the expression in her eyes; heard what Wolfe was saying, but scarcely took it in. For his whole being was filled with the terrifying, the incredible knowledge of her courage in following him, despite the risks, the dangers, and his own heartbreaking indifference. He remembered complacently thinking, back in London, that he had stirred something in the girl's tiger heart that would not easily be extinguished, but now the full revelation of it left him aghast. That such gallantry, such desperate courage might be expended for him, to be near him, was a shock that pierced quite beyond any of his previous self-regard. She was no innocent, he thought; she had seen so much of life on the streets, and so must have known that Davy Jones was a wicked, and a dangerous man. Yet she had been willing to go along with him, to be involved even in mutiny and possibly murder, and certainly duplicity and treachery, just for the sake of being by Hopewell's side, yet with almost no hope of attracting his attention, except negatively. This was the real thing, he thought dazedly; the real love unto death, unto the very gates of Hell. But that it should be *Meggie* who had done this was almost too great a thing to be borne. He groaned aloud. Wolfe laughed, quietly, his grey-brown eyes telling Hopewell plainly that he saw, and understood, his turmoil. 'But all's well that ends well, eh, Hopewell? I have the papers, taken from this creature; you have the secret to the fortune of the Lost Island; I will get my fortune; Davy will be defeated; oh, and yes, your Marguerite has not dallied with another but waits somewhere on the island for you.'

Hopewell stared at him. In a voice he scarcely recognized himself, he said, 'All's well that ends well, sir? Just in time for the Lord of Alchemists' return, then, and the righting of all wrongs.' His heart was so heavy now that he thought it must drag him down, crush him with its leaden weight. He did not look at Meg, for he could not, for shame.

'The Lord of Alchemists!' Wolfe laughed. 'Ah yes, he returns!' Suddenly, so quickly and brutally that it seemed scarcely believable, he flung Meg hard from him, so that she landed heavily against the wall. Almost in the same moment, Hopewell sprang forward; but too late. In horror, he heard clearly the crack as her head hit the wall; then she lay crumpled, quite still.

Ignoring Wolfe, Hopewell got down on his knees next to her. He reached out a hand to touch her sooty hair, and found to his surprise that it was soft on his fingertips, soft and scented, as if she had been a high-born lady, instead of a street orphan. 'Meg,' he whispered, brokenly, 'Meg, forgive me . . . forgive me . . .' But he could not cry, for he was beyond tears now.

'Get up. Get up, boy. Don't waste any soft feeling on

that one. She was used by Davy, but now she is dead. And there is still work to be done, if we are to defeat that Welsh devil.' Wolfe's grip on his shoulder was cruel, the grey-brown eyes filled with a savage anxiety. Hopewell rose from his knees and stood up, facing Wolfe.

How could he once have thought that this man was admirable? How could he have trusted him? Hopewell did not know the truth about him any more, no, not him, and not Davy Jones; they were as wicked as each other, the one and the other, for all he knew, or as uncaring. It had always been a thing between the Captain and the first mate, he saw that now. Always a thing to best each other – two thieves at each others' throats, two wild beasts uncaring of who got in their way, who was hurt, who was used. Nothing mattered to them, nothing, except for the fortune they wanted so badly . . . He thought of Meg, lying so still, and a terrible anguish gripped his heart, a bleakness such as he had never known before. But strangely, he found he could speak, now, and that the words were coming unbidden.

'Sir,' he whispered, 'the philosopher – who wrote the papers about the Lost Island. You said he was dead.'

Wolfe looked in impatient surprise at him. 'And so he is. Food for the worms . . . or the fish,' he added, with an infinitely cruel smile, a smile of remembrance.

'*You* killed him . . .'

'I killed him, Hopewell. He would not tell me the final secret, give me the final piece of the puzzle – and so I killed him. Poison, the powdered glass of the Italians; and his body in a sack, and dropped at sea, like a dead dog. Like the dog he was!'

'And Davy...'

'Davy knew nothing of that. He did not even know of the existence of the man – until later. I was in Venice when I came across the—'

'Venice, sir?' Hopewell felt quite numb.

'Yes, that's where I first met the fool. He was working for one of the Doge's courtiers, on some foolish hare-brained scheme of his; but also on secret papers, the ones you see right here. He was close-mouthed about it, Hopewell; but alas, a little too fond of his cups. And one night, well in them, he told me a little: a little, but enough. Enough for me to go to him the next day, and tell him that if he needed a ship, and a captain bold enough to risk all, even the shoals and reefs of the supernatural ocean, then that man, and that ship's master, stood before him . . .'

'So you befriended him, sir?' Hopewell's mouth seemed to be working of its own accord, but his eyes, though he looked straight at Wolfe, seemed to see nothing but Meg, poor Meggie, lying crumpled on the floor, unmoving . . .

'Yes, though he was afraid at first, he ended by trusting me, and so we planned to sail. But of course, I had to have a crew, and though Davy and I had not sailed together for many years, I knew him to be a clever and capable sailor, and to be trusted, as he had been my dearest friend and comrade, yet never forgot it was I who was captain. It happened he came back to Venice, too, hoping to get a glimpse of some woman who had been his love many years before, but who had married some Venetian courtier in preference to him: I tell you,

Hopewell, women are not worth the chase! At least gold never changes . . . So I knew him to be at a loose end, and I thought that his thirst for gold was every bit as great as mine, and that as long as I told him enough, but not all, he would want, too, to risk much for great gain. But I did not know how great his thirst for gold was; that it had parched his heart, so that he no longer knew his duty.'

Wolfe was clearly agitated by the recounting of his story; his hands clenched and unclenched, his eyes flashed.

Hopewell, watching, said, quietly, 'But the philosopher . . . sir, why did he not—'

'Devil take the old fool! He would not give me the final piece; he would not give me the key to it, because he said I was not worthy. Not *worthy*, the old fool! As if it was up to him to judge! But then he was stupid enough to say that wickedness like mine would never understand; that only true innocence could pierce the secret. And no innocent, he told me, in his lecturing way, would ever set sail knowingly with a gang of rogues. Fool that he was, he had *given* me the key, without even knowing it! Of course no innocent would *knowingly* come with us; but then, if he knew, he would be no innocent, would he? And so' – here he turned to Hopewell – 'I searched, and searched for that innocent who would give me the key. But I did not find him; until the day I met you, Hopewell.' Ignoring Hopewell's wince, he went on, 'I had a suspicion, as soon as I saw you, and spoke to you, noting your innocent self-regard, your heedless ways, your cheerful anger, even, but I deliberately walked away, because I must not, on any account, approach you and ask you to come with me. How happy you made me that day, Hopewell, flying after me with such a bright face, as if all the angels in Heaven had appeared to you! But I had to be sure. I tested you once, twice, and still you did not budge from your innocence, your heedlessness, your optimism.' He paused.

'Then, when the White Ship struck us, and I landed here, I believed you dead . . .'

'Who imprisoned you, sir?' Stiff lips, slow words.

'I do not know, for sure . . . but all signs point to Davy Jones, who, as you have told me, also survived the wreck. I had found my way out, once, but was captured again, and put back in the hole where you found me. Ah! When you found me, Hopewell, when you found me, I knew for sure, for sure, that it was all meant to be. Without you I would have died, and soon; for in the dungeons of the Lost Island, time passes at ten times the speed it does in our own world. You proved your innocence, your friendship, by that action. And now, we are at the end, and you will give me the final key. I will not ask you, for I know you will give it freely, in your innocent kindness, as a friend. Believe in the best, Hopewell; that is your great strength. It is the strength of innocence, that knows all's well that ends well. Come, boy, give me the key, the answer to my problem.'

He put a hand on Hopewell's shoulder, and clasped it warmly, and Hopewell felt the burning pain of it even through his numbness.

'Sir,' whispered Hopewell, finding the words from he

knew not what desolate reach of his soul, 'sir, I would, if I could – but, oh, sir, the philosopher said it must be an innocent giving it to you.'

Wolfe frowned. 'So? There you are.'

'Oh, but sir,' said Hopewell, beginning to shake now, 'sir, I am no longer innocent, see you. No longer, sir. No more. I know too much, sir, now, too much. Oh sir! You should not have told me all this. For now I know too much, and so the key is lost, and can never be found. Never.'

Wolfe stared at him. Then with a low, deep growl, he grabbed Hopewell by the throat. 'Are you trying to tell me you will *not* give it to me? Take care, boy; you do not know what I am capable of, what I *am*. You do *not* know all. You do not know the strange places I have been in all these years, the strange men I have met, the strange power that has become mine . . . You hardly know even a half of it.' The eyes burned into Hopewell's own, the white teeth snarled in the open mouth, the grey, wild, choppily cut hair seemed to glow with a kind of unearthly light; the hand under Hopewell's throat seemed bigger than was natural. Hopewell saw all this, and remembering the broken glass, smashed by a massive body hurtling through, remembering, too, the deep gouges cut in the stage door of the Globe, and the torn and bloody flanks and throat of the sheep on the hill, should have burnt with hopeless terror at the sight. But, strangely, his real attention was elsewhere, the terror arrested by a tiny tremor of an incredulous hope, a hope that . . .

'Sir!' he managed to croak, through the choking grip

on his throat, 'spare me, sir, spare me! I will take you to it, sir . . . I will give it to you . . .' He contrived to roll his eyes terribly, as if he were hideously frightened, as indeed he was, and Wolfe, seeing this, slackened his grip. The beast-like snarl vanished, the eyes still burnt, but with a more human urgency now, searching Hopewell's own.

'Take me to it? What do you mean?'

'The garden, sir,' Hopewell babbled, 'the garden — I left it there . . . outside . . . the window . . .'

The privateer made an impatient gesture, and picked up the oilskin package of papers. 'Very well, Hopewell. You will take me there, and give it to me. But beware, if you are trying to bluff me or trick me, I shall have no mercy. None. Is that clear?'

'No sir, I mean, yes sir,' gabbled Hopewell, trying not to flinch, or look back, when Wolfe grabbed him by one ear and led him out of the room.

Thirty

Outside, everything was as it had been. The sunlight still poured down on the pretty pavilion, sparkled on the ornamental lake, gleamed on the pile of rocks Hopewell had left under the window. Wolfe made Hopewell stop for an instant, and looked around warily, almost sniffing the air. But it was utterly quiet, utterly still, and at last, he growled, 'Where is it, then?'

'Sir,' said Hopewell, a little shakily, 'it's just over there . . . there . . . a rock . . . I put it under a rock.'

Wolfe grabbed his ear again. 'I will go with you. I do not trust you.'

'Oh, sir,' said Hopewell, meekly, 'it is a pity, and a surprise, indeed, that you do not trust my innocence.' But all he got for his attempt at wit was a ringing blow on the head for his pains, and Wolfe snarling, 'Don't think I would hesitate to kill you, given half an excuse, Hopewell.'

Hopewell said nothing. He knew that the privateer spoke perfectly sincerely, and that in any case it was possible Wolfe would kill him, anyway, once he had what he wanted. And he did *not* want to die. He so much did not want to die. But that was not the only reason he went as slowly as he dared, dragging his feet, and pretending to look about for the rock where he'd put the paper, when he knew well which one it was. Time, time, oh please, time, slow down! he thought, desperately, as inch by inch Wolfe forced him to the place where at last the whole wretched secret for which he'd killed and betrayed and used people, would be revealed to him.

'So? Where is it?' Wolfe's eyes were burning again, his breath on Hopewell's neck was getting more fetid, and the young man knew that it would not be long before the beast within the privateer would burst its bonds of will and fall on him, if he did not do exactly as the man wanted.

'Here, sir, I believe,' said Hopewell, with a look of gormless fear which he hoped might stave off the evil moment a little while. 'Oh dear, sir, I am so muddle-headed, truly, I thought I'd put it here . . . no . . . there, sir, there . . . yes!' Wolfe leaned forward eagerly, as slowly, very slowly, Hopewell pushed up the flat rock that had covered the paper, flicked away the weeds that had been crushed by it, and whose juice had stained it a little; and carefully, carefully held the paper in his hand, at the far corner.

He looked up. 'This is it, sir, but—'

But Wolfe did not wait to hear the rest of Hopewell's sentence, snatching it from him with such force that Hopewell fell over. Wolfe stared at the well folded paper; then with a look at Hopewell that boded no good for him, slowly began to unfold it, moistening his finger with saliva to make the turning of the paper easier.

Hopewell held his breath. For Wolfe was *reading* now; his lips moving soundlessly over words that were obviously written on the paper. Written on the paper! But it had been a blank page, when Hopewell had put it under the rock! The tiny tremor of hope was growing, growing in his bones, creeping up like a green flowering tendril. He was afraid Wolfe would be able to read his emotions on his face. But he need not have worried; the privateer paid him no attention at all, wholly absorbed as he was by his reading.

Quietly, Hopewell got to his feet. But Wolfe saw *that*; and instantly leapt at him. 'Not so fast, my dear friend!' The man's eyes were full of a feverish pleasure, now; the snarling beast had retreated again. 'If what this paper says is true, the fortune I am seeking will not be found here, but in quite another place altogether. We will go there, you and I.'

'But sir . . .'

'No buts, Hopewell, I already told you that they are fit only for malmsey,' said Wolfe, with the ghost of his old charm. 'I will not take no for an answer, my friend. You will come with me.'

Hopewell opened his mouth to speak, then thought better of it. Out of the corner of his eye, he had caught a movement, down in the reeds of the ornamental lake; and the back of his neck prickled with a sense of the nearness of the pavilion window. It was best to go, yes, to take Wolfe away from here, so that she might have a chance, a chance . . . He did not know what would happen to him, he did not dare to think what the privateer might do later, but he would worry about that when the time came. Oh, please, please, please, he prayed, inwardly, time, time . . . slow down, slow down . . .

* ★ *

Up the path they hurried, Wolfe in firm control, almost back to being the gallant sea captain, the legendary hero he had first seemed to be. He spoke quite expansively, of his plans for the future, of how the fortune he would gain would be used to equip not one, but a fleet of fast ships, which would ply the seas of the world, laden with goods of trade.

'And sometimes, Hopewell, just for old time's sake, we might come unawares on a Spanish galleon, waddling cumberously under the weight of the gold she carries, and come home laden e'en more than when we set out! And then, indeed, I will be knighted: Sir Richard Wolfe, I'll be, and more, more: for no one will then be able to refuse me, no one will be able to tell lying stories about me to the Queen, and thus deny me my right, and my honour.' His lip twisted in bitterness. 'Do not trust noblemen, boy; they say they will protect you, but once you have got the gold for them, they turn their backs on you, and will not even give you the time of day. Worse, they send the guard after you, and fling you in the dungeon, on a story of misappropriating moneys; moneys which were *due* to you!'

Hopewell, wisely, said nothing. So this was what Wolfe's bitterness had been about, and his falling from grace, years ago! What the real truth of the matter was, whether Wolfe's patron had indeed been unjust, or the privateer was lying; and what had happened to him afterwards, Heaven only knew; or perhaps Hell, given his dark hints of meddling with sorcery. But Hopewell was not much interested, at this stage. It was not Wolfe

259

that was his concern, not at all, but Meg. Meg, poor, dear, brave, gallant Meg – seen truly for her own self, far, far too late . . .

By and by, they were there, in front of the closed door in the wall. Wolfe looked at Hopewell. He did not relax his grip on his arm. 'Open the door. Just a crack.'

Hopewell carefully eased the latch up. Carefully, he pulled open the door, just a fraction, and peered out, not into the painted garden, but the circular room of the mansion of the Lord of Alchemists. He gave a little gasp.

'What? Who's there?' Wolfe pushed him away, had a look himself. He drew back. There was a funny smile on his face. 'I can see why you love her, Hopewell. She is lovely. Poor Meg, eh – didn't stand a chance.'

Hopewell said nothing. Wolfe patted him on the shoulder. 'Fair love-struck, aren't you, my dear? I told you she'd be waiting for you, Hopewell. All's well that ends well, eh?' He opened the door wide, and stepped through the doorway, dragging Hopewell willy-nilly after him. At the last moment, Wolfe paused, and, with a cruel smile, slammed the door shut behind them. It shut with a most final clang.

As they came into the circular room, Marguerite moved forward – and from behind her, in the shadows, stepped Dr Bonaventure. At sight of him, Wolfe gave a strangled cry, and stumbled, dropping Hopewell's arm. But Hopewell did not try to escape; he could not stop thinking of Meg, whom he had thought, back there, to have moved, feebly, when Wolfe was not looking. But even if she was alive, which he was more doubtful of, now, she was there, shut in, alone. And he was here . . . here, when he should have stayed there, should have tried to escape Wolfe somehow, to help her, make her see that she was not alone, that he cared for her, that he admired her courage, her spirit, her . . .

But Dr Bonaventure was speaking, in his usual cheerful voice. He at least seemed not at all surprised to see Wolfe. 'Why, good morning, Richard Wolfe. It's been a long time.' Wolfe stared at him. When the philosopher attempted to approach him, the privateer took a step back. 'No . . . no. You're dead . . . I saw you die . . . I saw you . . .'

'You saw me lose consciousness, yes,' said Dr Bonaventure, still just as cheerily. 'But the poison you had bought, my poor friend, was not what you thought it was.'

'It was powdered glass – a deadly Italian poison. Deadly, always!'

Dr Bonaventure nodded, comfortably. 'Dear, dear – the untruths some people will tell! And no doubt you paid good silver for this potion?'

'But I had you put in a sack – dropped at sea—' Wolfe was sweating, his eyes staring, somehow looking diminished, no longer savage and terrible as he had looked back in the other world.

'So you did,' nodded Dr Bonaventure. 'But the sea can be kind, you know, especially if . . .' He caught sight of the package Wolfe still carried. 'Oh dear, is that what you wanted so badly? It is useless, my friend, useless because . . .'

'Because I do not have the key?' Slowly, Wolfe's equanimity seemed to be returning to him, though he still looked wan. 'You old fool, you haven't changed. I have it now; Hopewell found it for me, just as you said. It is here, safe in my doublet. You don't believe me? Ask Hopewell. That's so, isn't it, Hopewell? Hopewell understood. He found the one page that made sense, Bonaventure. The one you had thought to hide so cleverly, in your whole thumping useless manuscript . . .' And so saying, he dropped the oilskin package at the philosopher's feet, scattering the papers far and wide in the room.

'Dear, dear,' said Dr Bonaventure, rather sadly, but making no move to pick it up. 'That was so much work. So much. But perhaps, you'd better let me see the paper. See if it really is the same one?'

'Do you take me for as big a fool as everyone else here?' said Wolfe, grinning. 'I suppose you have managed to hoodwink Davy Jones too, eh? Where is he? Keeping him on tenterhooks, dancing to your tune? Too late for that now, friend. The fortune of the Lost Island is *mine*. And only mine.'

'Oh dear,' said Dr Bonaventure again. 'Take care, Dick. The master of the island, the Lord of Alchemists, who made the potion you thought was powdered glass, who saved me from the sea – he may not agree, you see, I fear.'

Wolfe threw his head back and laughed. 'You think to still hoodwink me with that! Friend, I have *read* the secret paper. I know now that *the Lord of Alchemists does not exist*. There is no master on this island. It is ruled by an illusion.'

Now, in all this while, neither Marguerite nor Hopewell had made a sound, nor even glanced at each other. But now, Hopewell's startled glance flew to Marguerite, then to Dr Bonaventure, and finally to Wolfe. He cried, 'How can that be? Dr Bonaventure, tell me it isn't so! The Lord of Alchemists will return, will he not? Or else, how can things be put right?'

'How can they, indeed?' Marguerite spoke for the first time. Her glance, emerald-bright as ever, was not, somehow, as fascinating to him any more. She was dressed now exactly as he had wanted to see her, in gorgeous women's clothes, a dress of cloth of gold, and the rich, red cloak over it, and slippers with seed pearls sewn into them, and her long, black hair entwined with white daisies, yet he could hardly bear to look at her. She was too lovely, he thought sadly; she was *too* beautiful, otherworldly, unfitted for a grimy, ordinary human such as himself. The eyes he wanted to look into, to beg forgiveness and ask if friendship might be given, despite all, they were not there, looking into his. The girl he had known too late – she was not there, despite the hope he'd had, back there. She was gone – gone for ever into a shadow world where he could not reach her again. And so he could not bear it, and turned away.

'Never mind, lassie,' said Wolfe, with a touch of swagger. 'No need to wait for him to answer. You'd wait long enough. Yon lad's not very bright, you know. Doesn't understand the easiest thing. Now, then.' Quite at ease again, somehow, he moved away from the garden panel and walked around the room, tapping at each of the other panels. 'Venice. No, I don't think so, eh, Dr Bonaventure? The Globe. No, I want more than mind seas and airy adventure, unlike our little friend here. Ah – now that, that's a sight.'

On the last panel, the one that had been blank, that Hopewell had last seen with a vague picture starting to appear on it, now was painted a magnificent galleon, with bright, red sails, flying serenely over a calm, blue sea. A picture that was familiar indeed to Hopewell: for he had last seen its smaller twin hanging on the wall of the Captain's cabin of the *Golden Dragon*!

Thirty-One

'You see,' said Wolfe to the silent – and in Hopewell's case, at least – stunned assembly. 'The secret was that it was under my nose all the time, wasn't it, Dr Bonaventure? It was you who gave me the picture to hang on the wall of the cabin of the *Golden Dragon*. It is here that the fortune is to be found, in the hold of this lovely ship! Magically held and hid; but real enough, in good, ringing gold.'

'It was given to me in Venice, you see. It was painted by a great artist indeed,' said Dr Bonaventure, in a dreamy tone. There was an odd note to his voice, thought Hopewell, puzzled; almost, he might have thought, one of warning. But Wolfe took no notice.

'Spare me your ramblings,' he said. 'It's here, and whether you are quick or ghost, *you've* failed to hide it from me, and Davy to take it. That's all that matters. Hopewell, you have done me proud!'

'Poor child,' said Dr Bonaventure, sadly. 'You have destroyed a precious thing, Wolfe, in your mad greed for gold.'

'Pah! Everyone must grow up, sooner or later.' The privateer's spine had straightened, his head lifted, his eyes flashed. No more was he the beast or the diminished thing that he had been. He looked like a man in command of his destiny, and about to achieve the desire of his life. Not so Hopewell, in whose mouth was the taste of ashes, in whose heart was the breath of winter.

Wolfe saw his expression, and clapped him on the shoulder. 'You're a man, now, Hopewell, and that means knowing that life is not always a pretty thing, aye. Your innocence is gone – but now you have experience, which is worth more. In the long run, you'll thank me. A man must put away childish things, eh? If you hang on long enough, and know what you want, boy, and stop at nothing to get it, then you will achieve exactly what you want.' He bowed, mockingly, to the three of them. 'Now, friends, farewell. I will set sail on the *Golden Dragon* again – as she should be, as she always will be. A never-forgotten legend, to resound through time.' And so saying, he took the paper from his doublet in one hand, and reached into the picture with the other, towards the deck of the great ship, which tilted towards him, under his hand. And as they watched, Wolfe grew smaller, smaller, until at last he was of a size exactly appropriate to the ship. He grasped at the timbers to haul himself up, and turned once more, waving the paper at them, smiling in triumph.

But as he did so, Hopewell moved, faster than he had ever done in his life, faster than he would ever move in his life again, except once – and hauled Wolfe by the legs, right off the ship, out of the picture, whilst the paper fell from the privateer's hands and tumbled into the sea, there to be lost immediately from sight. Hopewell said nothing, but hung on grimly to the privateer, as screaming and cursing, Wolfe twisted in his grip, first tiny, then small, then bigger. And as he grew bigger, his shape changed, shortened, fattened, coloured . . . and in a shorter time than it takes to say it, a *sheep* was lying on the floor at their feet. A mangy, worm-eaten, most unthrifty-looking sheep, yet bleating in a hoarse, peremptory tone . . .

'Stop that, you vile creature.' Flora came sauntering in, with the inevitable Caprice at her heels. She kicked out with a disdainful foot. 'You've bothered me long enough. No gratitude in being saved from the sea, just give me, give me, give me, I want, I want, I am, I am, don't you know what I am, and other such threats! The torture you said you suffered was self-inflicted, for here's a creature who makes a hellbroth of his own belly, my friends! The bit of sorcery he'd learnt, to make himself seem like a werewolf, he thought that would startle me, threaten me! Well, from being a wicked wolf, let's see how he likes being a silly sheep.'

Hopewell stared at her. A strange feeling crept over him. Flora looked just as she had always looked, and yet . . .

He found his voice. 'Flora . . . Lady Flora . . . are you . . . did you . . .'

She smiled cheekily. 'Did I what? Am I what? Why are you looking like that at me, Hopewell?'

'Wolfe said there was no Lord of Alchemists,' said Hopewell, slowly. 'That it was ruled by . . . by an illusion. But I don't think that's right. Or not quite right . . .'

She folded her arms and looked at him. Near her, Dr Bonaventure and Marguerite stood silent, listening.

'Well, Hopewell Shakespeare, are you going to explain yourself?'

Hopewell groped for the words. The revelations were coming slowly to him, yet naturally, easefully, as if somehow in some part of his mind he'd always known. 'This is the island of metamorphosis . . . And just as those plants I thought were weeds turned out to be the elusive *Millefloria*, revealing the words on the secret page . . . thus we are being revealed, one to the other, to see the secrets in our hearts . . . And you, Lady Flora, you have the greatest secret of all. *You* are the Lord of Alchemists.'

There was an intake of breath in the room; but Flora said, quite lightly, 'Really, Hopewell? Is that what you think?'

'It is what I *know*,' he said, seriously. 'And more than that . . .' He gulped, then went on, more strongly, 'It was *you*, back in London, the beggar child on the wharf, who gave me the bit of glass that brought me here; you, who captained the White Ship; you, who imprisoned Wolfe; you, who has made all the rules here, from the beginning . . .'

Flora held up a hand. 'It was not I captained the White Ship,' she said, decidedly. 'The White Ship has no captain. It is a phantom that marks the way to the Lost Island. A phantom arising from the sea. How it is dealt with determines the fate of ships. I can only deal with the results. But as to the other – there *is* no Lord of Alchemists.'

'No lord, no master, then, but a mistress,' Hopewell

whispered, staring at Flora. 'A young mistress, indeed; a magician so powerful, so easeful in her powers that she uses them to play – like a child.'

Flora grinned at him, her bright dark eyes sparkling. 'Hopewell Shakespeare, you will make me blush.'

'Hardly, Lady Flora,' broke in Dr Bonaventure. 'A great artist never blushes.'

Hopewell looked at the pictures on the wall, and back at Flora. 'You painted these,' he said, without surprise. 'It was your art, your magic, that made them come alive.'

Flora shrugged. 'It helps to pass the time.'

'Dr Bonaventure,' said Hopewell, 'you knew, did you not, that . . . that the Lady Flora, was, in effect the so-called Lord of Alchemists?'

The old philosopher had the grace to look uncomfortable.

'Yes, dear boy,' he said, at last. 'But I only understood that here – never in Venice, where I had first met her, without understanding who she truly was. "Everyone must come to these things by themselves," Flora told me. "You had to understand things on your own," she said. And one does not argue with *her*.'

Flora laughed. 'One *does*, and often, Doctor,' she retorted gaily, though her glance was a trifle frosty. Turning to Hopewell, she said, 'But tell me, friend, how did you guess what had to be done, just then? No one gave you a secret formula, or clever trick; so how did you work it out? For it was a most quick-witted thing to do.'

Hopewell said, low and without any pleasure, 'I remembered that Dr Bonaventure had said *Millefloria*, the flower of metamorphosis, looked like a paltry weed.'

'You read my notes!' said Dr Bonaventure, in some surprise, and Hopewell nodded, slowly, not caring who knew any more. 'And I remembered the supposed weeds I had scattered on the paper; and how the paper, that had been blank, suddenly had writing on it. I saw that Captain Wolfe had licked at his finger, the finger that had touched the so-called weed, which was already flowering, and so sweetly scented, though he did not notice . . .'

'No man in thrall to gold notices anything like that,' said Dr Bonaventure, sadly shaking his head.

'And so, I thought it was just a matter of time, if it was truly *Millefloria*, the flower of metamorphosis, whose juice had sprayed on the paper, and on Captain Wolfe's finger. I did not know what would happen, or if there was enough time, or anything . . . And I . . . I thought Meg was still alive, that she had been only stunned, not badly hurt; that she would follow . . . But then he slammed the door, and she wasn't there, and I saw he was about to leave, about to get his fortune despite everything, I could not bear to think that . . .'

'He would *not* have found his fortune,' said Flora, grimly; and pointed to the picture, where the calm, blue sea had turned huge and black, the sky purple, and the ship was tossing frail as a walnut. 'He would have been wrecked again – and this time, there would have been no saving him. You rescued him from *that*, Hopewell, even though he was quite willing to make you perish – for if Davy Jones and Meg had not been there to protect you, on the *Golden Dragon*, he would have sacrificed your innocence in the way he knew, through his incomplete mastery of the black arts. Yes, Hopewell, on that night of full moon, he intended to kill you, to throw your body overboard, to see if your innocent blood would make a path to the Lost Island . . .'

Hopewell could not speak.

'But even Davy and Meg could not have saved you from that, if I had not been there.' Flora smiled, rather complacently.

'You were there *too*?' he repeated, stupidly, finding his voice. Flora made a face at him, pursed her lips, narrowed her eyes, opened and closed her hands, extending her fingers like claws, and miaowed, very softly. Hopewell gaped, understanding at last. 'The ship's cat!' he exclaimed. 'You came on as the ship's cat!'

Flora nodded, briskly. 'Yes, that very same one. And lucky for you that I was there,' she repeated, and Caprice bleated in agreement. Hopewell smiled nervously. 'Lucky indeed, yes,' he echoed. He glanced quickly at the cowering sheep at Flora's feet. Why, then, did . . .

Flora frowned. As if reading his mind, she said, rather sternly, 'I told you, Hopewell, I cannot control the passage of the White Ship, only its results. It is fair to say Wolfe deserved to perish as he tried to make you perish, and Dr Bonaventure. As he killed my poor innocent sheep, on the hill; as he brought death and disaster on his crew, mere pawns in his mad game. Still, I play chess better than he did,' she said, with satisfaction, 'and this –' prodding the sheep with her foot again – 'is less of a grand and worthy end for him. No one will think to sing the legend of the great Richard Wolfe, turned into a mangy sheep! On the Lost Island, he will have to slowly expiate his crimes – if he can!' She paused. 'So, are you glad the wicked has been punished?'

Hopewell shrugged indifferently. It little mattered to him now, what had happened, or would happen, to Wolfe. He felt no hatred or anger even, just sadness, a great, great, numbing sorrow. 'Meg . . .' he began, quietly. 'What of her?'

'Bah,' said Flora. She was frowning rather darkly. 'Meg's gone, but what of Marguerite? Isn't that what you wanted, Hopewell? Isn't that enough, to give you the woman of your dreams? Or do you need a fortune as well, in good, ringing gold?'

He looked swiftly over at Marguerite. The girl had her head bent, and had almost, it seemed, shrunk into herself. A great pity flowed over him, for the being, whoever she was, who had had to come and go at Flora's commands; at the lovely otherworldly creature who had no will of her own, but must move to Flora's tune. She *was* a great magician, this child, or whatever she truly was, he thought, and playful, like a child; but cruel too, like a child, heedless in her innocent savagery. He would not like to cross her, he thought. No one would, in their right mind. He should placate her, say the right words to her; but the right words would not come, his throat rebelling at them. Instead, from his mouth came words he had never intended to say.

'Lady Flora,' he said, 'it seems I have been wrong all along. I have been chasing illusions from the beginning. The woman of my dreams is just that, a sweet dream, great Lady, just as the legendary privateer of my admiration was nothing but a cold-hearted scoundrel. As to the fortune – I had all the fortune I needed, in my hands, in my wits, in my heart, and did not even know it.'

'I see,' said Flora, folding her arms. 'So – is there *anything* you want from me, Hopewell?'

He looked again at Marguerite, and then away. 'Two things, Lady, if you would.'

'Two things?' Flora tickled the little goat under the chin. 'Did you hear that, Caprice? He wants not one, but two things! A little greedy, don't you think?'

'Two things,' went on Hopewell, determinedly, knowing that this girl – this woman – this ancient being, whoever she really was, had the power to turn him into a toad, or a stone, or a . . . a sheep, or anything she pleased, anything, just like that, for a whim. 'Two things, Lady Flora, for I know you can do exactly what you want – please, let Meg go back to her own place, her own home, instantly, and let her think all that has happened is a dream, except for this – that on the ground next to her, when she awakes, she finds a little bag full of silver, and gold, enough to keep her comfortable and free of want for the rest of her days.'

'Quite a touching scene!' said Flora, tweaking at Caprice's ears. 'But do go on: what is the second thing?'

'The second thing . . .' Hopewell swallowed, once, then faced Flora boldly. It was strange, but this little slip of a thing, with her bright eyes and red gown, could strike more real fear in him than anyone ever had. 'The second thing is, will you please allow Marguerite . . . this lovely, lovely fairy woman to go back to her own place too, to be free of . . . of being a dream, with no life of her own. Or if she is a dream only,' he hurried on, seeing Flora's brow darken ominously, 'if she is but a dream, let her go back to the limitless ocean of mystery where she came from.'

There was a silence. Flora pulled thoughtfully at her lip. Dr Bonaventure rubbed his hands nervously together. Marguerite kept her head down, and did not move. Hopewell waited, holding his breath.

At last, Flora spoke. 'But then I'll have no friends to play with,' she said, very crossly. 'No one to play hide-and-seek with, or chasings, or hopscotch, or anything.'

Hopewell managed a smile. 'Oh, Lady Flora,' he said with an effort, 'there'll still be me. You can play with me. I will stay, if you let the other two go. I will be your playmate, and do just as you wish.'

'Hopewell . . .' began Dr Bonaventure, but Flora hushed him with a wave of her hand. 'You and Davy both?' she observed. 'He's promised to stay, too . . . if I let you and Meg and Dr Bonaventure go. He doesn't know about Marguerite, you see,' she went on, confidingly, 'he hasn't seen her yet.'

Hopewell stared at her. '*Davy Jones?*'

'You can ask him yourself, if you don't believe me. Davy!' she called, loudly. 'Master Jones! Come here!'

'Yes, Mistress Flora, here I am.'

He must have been waiting on the stairs, out of sight. His face was even more deeply creased, and more villainous-looking, than ever. Somehow, Hopewell had been expecting him to look different: younger, perhaps? Kinder? Seeing Hopewell, he gave a rather mocking

274

bow. 'Surprised to see me, then, friend? Agreed, then are we? Don't think I'm doing this for you, incidentally, or that fool of a Meg, or even for the good doctor – but, see you, this is the only place where I can go back to Venice easily – *my* Venice, the Venice when Lucia loved me.' His eyes softened, and Hopewell remembered the glint of long golden hair in the shadows of the Doge's palace.

Hopewell did not answer, for his throat had choked up. Davy Jones looked at him, smiled, then bowed again, this time to Flora. 'So, are we all agreed?'

Suddenly, he caught sight of Marguerite. His eyes widened. He looked at Flora. 'Lady, I did not know you had a sister . . .'

'I have no sister,' snapped Flora. 'This is Marguerite.'

'Lady Margreet,' said Davy Jones, bowing. 'Lady Margreet, I am pleased to meet you.'

'She is about to go,' said Flora, waving an airy hand, 'aren't you, Marguerite?'

The shining head nodded. Silently, the girl turned, and began walking away towards the stairs, her rich cloak swirling around her, her black hair like a cloud about her face, and Hopewell found he could not bear to watch her go, but turned away.

Flora was regarding Davy Jones, with a funny smile. 'See that sheep, there?' she said. 'I want it put on the hillside. It needs fattening up,' she added, evilly, and laughed when the sheep bleated its peremptory, hoarse bleat under Davy's obedient, restraining hands.

Hopewell had thought his heart was wrung already dry, that no emotion could touch him; but the strange gentleness with which the first mate put the sheep on its feet, and herded it towards the stairs, made the tears start in his eyes. He remembered that Wolfe and Jones had, once, been great friends; and thought that the first mate, though he did not know all that had happened to Wolfe, knew that he was here, on the island. Who knew what he had intended to do, in the end? He thought back to those whispered words he'd overheard on the ship, and thought now that he had probably been mistaken, that Jones had not necessarily intended mutiny but had known something of Wolfe's plans, because of what Meg, or Flora, had told him. Perhaps, in his own way, he had even sought to protect Hopewell. Or perhaps not. You could never be sure, with an old pirate like Davy Jones . . .

'Farewell,' he called out, suddenly, as Jones and the sheep were almost out of sight. 'Farewell, Davy Jones, and may peace come to your heart, in this lovely place!'

The first mate stopped. He turned around; and smiled again, his crooked smile. 'Farewell, Hopewell. You are well named; don't lose your fortune, which is your good nature, your cheerful, hopeful soul.'

But Hopewell had stopped listening, after 'you are well named'. For suddenly, with a great leap of the heart, a wild cry of joy, he was running again, the second fastest time he had run in his life, running after Marguerite, almost knocking over Davy and his charge as he went, and calling out, 'Sorry, sorry, but I can't let her go, not this time!'

Thirty-Two

This time, she did not vanish, but stopped on the last step, one hand on the banisters, her head no longer bent, but held high, like a queen's. She said nothing as Hopewell fell at her feet at the bottom of the staircase and stammered, 'Forgive me . . . forgive me – I am the biggest, most utterly stupid fool that has ever walked the earth . . .' Looking up at her, he saw that her glance was quite steady, though perhaps even brighter than before, and he could not read her expression. His own face fell, his heart sank lower than the marble floor.

'Marguerite – Meg, Meg, my dear, please tell me you'll forgive me, one day, tell me you might let me . . . Look!' he said. 'I'm turning around, so you can kick me, kick me good and hard and proper as I so richly deserve, for denying you and not remembering you and not seeing lovely-souled Meggie in lovely-bodied Marguerite . . . go on, Lady, kick me, hard, beat me about the ears, whatever you want, whatever . . .'

'You *are* a great fool,' said Meg, at last. 'Turn around, Hopewell, I don't want to speak to your bum, see? Pretty as it is,' she added, sternly.

Slowly, he turned around, struck by the severity of

her tone – and saw that her green eyes, which were both Marguerite's and yet Meg's, were sparkling, her mouth smiling, and that she was having difficulty in containing her laughter. He looked at her, mouth a little agape, eyes wide. Oh, the beauty of her . . .

'Quit staring at me like I was some vision,' snapped Meg's London voice. 'You make me jumpy, you do. I'm just Meg, despite the rig, the metamorphthingy, see, courtesy of Flora's tricks: just Meg, mere Meggie from London Town, Hopewell Shakespeare! Away from here, that's all I'll be, see? So don't get your hose in a knot, expecting a dream to come true, and all!'

'There's nothing *mere* 'bout you,' said Hopewell, chuckling, 'you little tiger-cat, with the heart of a great queen!' And so saying, he jumped up and caught her joyfully in his arms, before she could so much as squeal. 'Will you, will you, dear, sweet Meg, will you deny that you care for me, just one little bit?'

'Ha,' said Meg, a little indistinctly, for she was clasped to Hopewell's chest; 'ha! Did I *ever* deny that, one little bit, Hopewell Shakespeare?'

He looked down at her bright, lively face, and touched it with a gentle finger. 'No my dear, you never did; because you saw things more clearly than me, who is just a fool, and blind.'

'That's quite enough of that,' she said, sternly, poking him in the chest, her Marguerite-voice returning. 'It's a form of arrogance, see, Hopewell Shakespeare, to constantly berate yourself. You've been a fool; but then so have I. We have been fools together. Does that make you feel any better?'

Hopewell stared at her. He was about to ask her *how* she had been a fool, when he thought better of it. Instead, he said, quietly, 'What is a kiss, Meg?'

It was *her* turn to look startled. 'If you don't know *that*,' she began, then stopped abruptly, colouring, colouring, her wild green eyes softening, her mouth opening on a whisper, as Hopewell's lips bent to hers.

Neither of them saw the interested audience watching them from above; but when, slowly, dreamily, they emerged, it was to a burst of clapping and cheering and hooting and bleating from Flora and Caprice and Dr Bonaventure. Smiling shyly, Hopewell and Meg held tightly to each other's hands, their faces coloured with the same emotions, as the young girl and the little goat and the old philosopher came down the stairs towards them.

'What is a kiss, indeed, eh, Caprice,' said Flora, gleefully, to Caprice. 'Did you ever hear the like love stuff, my friend? And he thinks he's a fool, indeed!' The kid bleated, indignantly agreeing. Dr Bonaventure nodded. His eyes were suspiciously shiny, and he kept touching at them. 'Sorry, sorry,' he said, crossly. 'Dust — it's a terrible thing, indeed.'

'Dr Bonaventure,' said Flora, warningly, 'it's very naughty of a philosopher to tell untruths, now, isn't it?'

'Er . . . er . . . just as you say, my dear,' said Dr Bonaventure, hastily.

'Tell them, tell them, tell them!' said Flora, dancing around Hopewell and Meg, Caprice tripping as ever at her heels.

'Tell them, my child? Er . . . perhaps they might not

. . . they might be insulted if I . . . I'm not sure it's a good idea any more,' stammered Dr Bonaventure. 'Perhaps a bit of time . . .'

'No, no, now, now, straightaway!' pouted Flora. 'There's no time, now, the Lost Island will soon be lost again, you see.'

'Oh,' said Dr Bonaventure, rather blankly. 'But er . . . I'm not sure I'm ready, and . . .' He caught the expression on Flora's face, and hurried on, 'Yes, I'm sure you're right, my dear.'

Turning to the bewildered couple, he said, 'I . . . wanted to ask if . . . you see, I do not have a family, no children, no kin to delight my advancing years, though, in Venice, I have still property and money which is mine, which trusted friends were administering for me. And I know Meg does not have a family. I was wondering if . . . if . . .' He looked at their aghast faces, with a kind of embarrassed despair, took off his spectacles, and rubbed at them so hard that they heard a crack. 'Oh, dear, that is, I meant that only if . . .'

'Dr Bonaventure,' said Meg, very quietly. 'Are you saying that you . . .'

'You see,' gabbled the philosopher, 'not only do I not have a family, but I have no one to help me in my work. And I thought that . . . you see, Hopewell has proven to be so good at deduction, at discovery, at understanding things, that I thought . . . well, why could we not combine it all, combine our strengths, as it were? I could . . . er . . . adopt you, Miss Meg, formally, you know, and so on, and Hopewell I could take on as my researcher, my assistant, my friend . . . and perhaps, in due . . . er . . .

course, he could take over my whole work. And er . . . Meg, you could do whatever you wanted, what would you like . . . er, maybe to learn to read, to write, to paint? Yes? We could . . . er . . . I have a nice house, in Venice, not very big, but I think we can all fit in, even if children . . . er . . . and . . .' His shoulders slumped. 'But forgive me; this is a shock, and I am going too fast. I know you will have many plans yourselves, and I—'

He did not finish his sentence, because Meg had flown to his side, and flung her arms about him. 'Dr Bonaventure, you are a genius!' she cried, happily, planting kiss after kiss on his round cheeks. 'A veritable genius! Isn't that so, Hopewell, my dear?'

Hopewell stared at the philosopher, then at his love, now dancing hand in hand with Flora. 'I . . . er . . . that is . . .'

'I know, I know, my boy,' said the philosopher, who had emerged rather red-cheeked and panting, but sparkly-eyed, from Meg's embrace, 'women are hasty in making up and changing their minds. You'll want more time, lad. I understand. But I want you to know that this offer of mine for you to work with me, is genuine; that I am not just making it to make you happy, though, well, h'm, of course that's nice too, but because I really, really want you as my assistant. You, Hopewell Shakespeare, have the potential to be a great philosopher, a true scientist with the open heart and mind to know wonder, to follow dreams, to love life and the world for its own sake. So settle your heart – this is a real offer, not pity or anything.'

'I . . . er . . . thank you . . .' said Hopewell, colouring

a little at the old philosopher's praise. 'But . . . but it's not that, Dr Bonaventure.'

'You have other work in mind, perhaps?' the old man said. 'I understand if that is so. You have a bright future ahead of you, Hopewell, dear. You and Meg both. Of that I am sure. Allow me then at least to give you a gift, for your wedding, and to start you up in whatever business you . . .'

'No, Dr Bonaventure, dear friend,' said Hopewell, smiling. 'It is not that, either. I am honoured by your offer, by your generosity, and know you mean it from the depth of your heart. And I should like very much to accept. But you see . . .'

Flora and Meg had stopped dancing around and were watching him too; Meg with a slightly anxious expression, Flora with an expressionless face. Only Caprice still capered about, her hoofs clicking merrily on the floor.

'You see,' said Hopewell, walking to Meg and taking her hand, 'I do not know what Meg thinks, sir, but Venice . . . well, it's a fine city, sir, and I should very much like to know it. But see you, my poor parents will be thinking I'm dead, perished in the sea. And I should much like to set their minds and their hearts at rest. They will be angry I broke my apprenticeship, like, but I will make it up to them, and I think the Pages will have found another boy to work for them, and will not seek me. I think my parents will be happy knowing that I have a good master to work for . . . that is, sir, if you agree.' He squeezed Meg's hand. 'I should also . . . like to have them meet Meg, and see how much I've changed . . . and—'

He paused, and added, quickly, 'That is, if Meg agrees, of course.'

She said nothing, but kissed him softly on the cheek, to Flora's evident delight.

'Oh,' said Dr Bonaventure, a trifle blankly. 'I see. Yes, of course. I . . .' Then his forehead cleared. 'But why should that be an obstacle, indeed? Why should we live in Venice? I can sell my property, and we can live in London! Yes, indeed! I think I should like to get to know that city again – and they tell me there are many fine sights to be seen there now, fine indeed! And people interested in philosophy, too, and new schools of thought sprung up. Why, Hopewell, I think you told me of one school – the Globe, I believe? We could go there, and engage the scholars of the Globe in discussion. What say you, Hopewell?'

'I say,' said Hopewell, grinning at Meg, whose face was alight with glee, 'I say that will be a fine thing indeed! There's a master of that school of my own name works there, see you, Dr Bonaventure. William Shakespeare is his name. We will have to have many discussions with him.'

'Wonderful, wonderful! Yes, yes, it does seem all settled then,' said Dr Bonaventure, rubbing his hands. 'Ah well, then, all's well that ends well, is that not so?' Surveying the smiling assembly, he addressed Flora. 'Now then, Mistress Flora, if you'll be so kind – I think we have much to do, back in England. Will you not send us on, right away? What time has passed, there, since these two came?'

'A month, I believe. Why, Dr Bonaventure, such haste! I thought you were not ready,' said Flora, lightly.

The old man shrugged. 'I'm as ready as I will ever be, with your permission, Flora dear,' he admitted.

'As you wish.' Flora's voice was brisk – but was that a tiny bit of melancholy in her smile? 'Meg, Hopewell – are you, too, ready to go?'

'We . . . that is . . .' began Hopewell, but Meg said, softly, 'Yes, Flora, we are.' She put a hand gently on Flora's shoulder, very briefly. 'And . . . and thank you, great lady, thank you, more than I can ever say . . .'

Flora looked into her eyes. 'I and my island can only ever bring out what is truly inside a person, whether that be beauty or ugliness.'

There was a small silence, then Hopewell rushed in with words. 'If ever there is anything I can do to repay what you have given me, Lady Flora, then I will do it gladly, and willingly, and immediately. You have only to ask.'

'Bah!' Flora said, shrugging, 'I want no talk of payment, or repayment. To do what I have done is in my nature; I am the mistress of the Lost Island, the lady of the night world, the artist of dreams. See you: I do it for play, for my own amusement. Isn't that so, Caprice?'

The little goat waggled her ears in agreement.

'As you like it,' said Hopewell, smiling. 'But do not forget that I am ready to repay, if ever you change your mind.'

'And I,' said Meg.

'And I, too, of course,' said Dr Bonaventure hastily. 'You have been a great friend to us, Lady Flora, and we will ever . . .'

'The door through the Globe shuts in two minutes!'

broke in Flora, impatiently. 'If you are not through it within that time, then it will be too late. For already, I hear another doomed ship drawing closer to the Lost Island – and in just two minutes, I will have to paint three new pictures! So go – go!'

Without waiting to hear any more, Meg grasped Hopewell's hand, and they pelted up the stairs, Dr Bonaventure panting after them. At the top of the stairs, he hesitated. 'Oh dear, my notes, I've left them all behind, whatever will I do?'

Hopewell and Meg glanced at each other, then at the picture of the Globe, whose outlines seemed to be wavering before their eyes. 'We have no time to go back,' said Hopewell, firmly, 'but don't you have most of your work locked in your mind?'

'Yes,' said Dr Bonaventure, 'but . . .'

Hopewell glanced down the stairs. Flora and Caprice still stood there, Flora an oddly vulnerable little figure, despite his certain knowledge of her great powers. He swallowed, and raised a hand, in salute and farewell.

'Go!' she called, sharply. 'Go!'

'Dr Bonaventure . . .' Meg tugged at him. 'You can make a fresh start, in London!'

The old man stared at her, squared his shoulders. 'You're right – I must make a fresh start! Come on then, my children! What are we waiting for?'

'You, sir,' smiled Hopewell, herding him along. But the old man wasn't finished yet. Just as they reached the picture of the Globe, he paused again. 'My books!' he wailed. 'My Ovid. I've left them all behind!'

'Dr Bonaventure,' said Meg, taking his hand, and

squeezing it tightly, 'do not fear. We will get you new books. A new Ovid. Everything. You must come.'

'Yes, yes, plenty of books in St Paul's churchyard, hundreds, thousands, and cheap,' gabbled Hopewell desperately. The galleries were beginning to vanish, the lines of the theatre to blur, to disappear into the wall. The stage door was open; but it was beginning to swing shut.

'Young man,' said Dr Bonaventure, drawing himself up, 'I have never bought a cheap book in my life and I'm not going to—'

He never finished his sentence, for Hopewell and Meg, working together as one, lifted him up and thrust him bodily through the doorway, racing through themselves in the split second before the door shut behind them with a mighty clang. 'Farewell! Farewell!' came Flora's voice, thin and far away; and then they were falling into the shadows behind the stage, where all was quiet, and dark.

'Oh dear,' said Dr Bonaventure, at last, from the darkness, 'oh dear. I do hope that someone can use all my books, and my papers. I do hope.'

'I am sure they will, Doctor,' said Hopewell, gently, understanding the old man's melancholy. Meg spoke what he thought: 'And Flora will be just fine, Doctor. I am sure it is not the last you – or we – have seen of her. Didn't you say you had met her before, in Venice?'

There was a silence from the old man's corner, then a little snort. 'Ha! You are doubtless quite right, Meg my dear. That Flora – she will turn up again to pester us all, never fear.'

'Never fear, indeed,' echoed Hopewell. 'Now, Dr

Bonaventure, will you take my arm, and Meg's? London is a busy and crowded place, these days.'

'Young man!' said Dr Bonaventure, with some dignity, 'I will have you know that I am no country bumpkin, but well used to great and crowded cities indeed! However – you each may take my arms, for I would appear in London as I wish to continue, side by side with my family and friends!'

'Right you are, sir!' said Hopewell, flinging the street door open, so that sunshine and noise poured in. Dr Bonaventure peered out, exclaiming a little under his breath. But Meg, stepping to Hopewell's side, murmured, 'Right you are. Right *we* are, indeed, Hopewell Shakespeare.' He saw that though they were back in their own world, their own place, she was still lovely; not with the supernatural beauty of Marguerite, but that lovely, lively intelligence and spirit that had always been Meg's. For her metamorphosis had been no mere spell, no mere formula, no mere supernatural trickery, but the emerging into sunlight of her own soul. The beauty had always been there, within her, needing only opportunity to flourish and become visible. He saw all that in her, but not in himself, though Meg did, and loved him the more dearly for it.

'Meg, my dearest . . .' He took her hand, and held it. 'Meg – oh, Meg, are you ready?'

'As ready as I'll ever be, Hopewell,' she said, with a wry, happy look.

'One last thing,' said Hopewell, 'the walled garden in the picture, in the Lost Island: where was that, Meg? What was your dream?'

A heartbeat of silence, then she smiled and said, 'Oh – that's the garden we will have at our house, of course. The garden where I shall write the poetry I have always had in my heart. You will be a man of science, dear Hopewell; but I will be a woman of letters! Now then, Dr Bonaventure – your arm, sir, if you please.'

And so the three of them stepped out into the London street, into the cheerful noise and summer sunshine of a new beginning.

A great while ago the world began
With hey, ho, the wind and the rain,
But that's all one, our play is done
And we'll strive to please you every one.

(from *Twelfth Night*, William Shakespeare)

Author's Note

The Tempestuous Voyage of Hopewell Shakespeare was inspired directly, of course, by two of William Shakespeare's plays, *The Tempest* and *Twelfth Night*. With their mixture of romance, adventure, humour, mystery, melancholy, magic, mistaken identity and metamorphosis set around a voyage and a shipwreck, they have always been amongst my favourite Shakespeare plays. I have also used various allusions to other Shakespeare plays, as well as events in his life. For instance, Kit Sly's name comes from a character in *The Taming of the Shrew*. And Davy Jones' name not only refers to the old description of the sea as 'Davy Jones' locker', but also it is associated with perhaps the first acting troupe Will Shakespeare himself might have come into contact with. This was the amateur acting company of Davy Jones, who lived near Stratford when Will was young, and who was a cousin by marriage of Anne Hathaway, the woman who eventually became Will's wife.

Elizabethan England was a time of enormous change. People were moving from the country to big towns like London, medieval ways of life were slowly fading as religion was transformed. In art and literature and music wonderful things were being done, new learning in science and philosophy spread, explorers discovered new worlds, such as America. New influences came from abroad: Italy and its culture, in particular, was very much in fashion in England at the time. Not only contemporary Italy with its wealthy and powerful city-states such as Venice and Verona, but also ancient Rome, as the Latin classics were read by an increasing number of people. Ovid's *Metamorphoses*, for instance, was one of the most influential of Latin books. It inspired many writers of the time, including Shakespeare. Yet there was also uncertainty, tragedy and conflict as well as excitement. Many people took the loss of the old ways very hard. Religious turmoil sometimes threatened to plunge the country into civil war, especially trouble either with die-hard partisans of 'the old religion', Catholicism, or the extremist Protestant sect known as the Puritans (because they liked 'purity' in everything). An exciting but terrifying time in which to be alive: and this was the unstable, rich soil in which William Shakespeare and his contemporaries grew.

Other great stories influenced my novel – the medieval Arthurian story of Sir Perceval, whose humorous, romantic and action-packed journey from heedless youth to thoughtful man is one of my great favourites; the marvellous Greek story of the sorceress Circe's island of metamorphosis in the *Odyssey*; and a little bit of Robert Louis Stevenson's *Treasure Island*!

And Hopewell's name? Well, it sounds like a good Puritan name (Puritans were apt to give their children names such as Praise-the-Lord, and God's Grace and other such things), but it also came in a lovely serendipitous moment. I was discussing possible names for the novel's hero with my husband, when he said, 'You remember how when my sister was teaching the plays of Shakespeare, the version of the plays she used at the school were published under an imprint called Hopewell Shakespeare, and one of the kids thought that was the name of one of Shakespeare's relatives? Well – why don't you give him the name Hopewell Shakespeare?'

Yes, indeed! There he was, conjured up before me in an instant: bright, cheerful, brave, heedless Hopewell setting out hopefully on the tempestuous voyage of his life!

CARABAS

Sophie Masson

They hated her. She knew that. She could see it in their eyes, their twisted faces.

When the people of her village discover Catou's unusual gifts, she is banished forever with only Frederic, the miller's son, as company.

But now she is free to follow her true nature, to turn her gifts to her advantage. Before long, she and Frederic had found their path into the opulent Court of Tenebran, to its strange powers, its mysteries and its terrifying challenges . . .

'Masson's narrative is resplendent with surges of lyricism.' *Reading Time*

'A captivating narrator . . . who knows how to hypnotize her readers.' *Lollipops*

'A sophisticated and timeless tale of magic and human nature.' *Weekend Australian*

CLEMENTINE

Sophie Masson

There is something I must tell you. The romantic secret of it has burned brightly in me, the dream thrilled in every pore of my skin. So bear with me, and come with me, into a place long ago and far away . . .

Aurora, daughter of the Count of Bois-Joli, and Clementine, the woodcutter's child, have been friends for sixteen years. Until, one day, they stumble on a castle they never knew existed . . .

A century later, Lord Arthur, a young scientist, feels himself strangely drawn into the legend of the sleeping castle of Bois-Joli, and finds that science is no match for a magic that has lain untouched for over a hundred years . . .

'an elegant fantasy romance full of delicious eighteenth-century detail and an exquisite French setting.' *The Times*

'the detail of court life and ways is enthralling. A fabulous novel . . .' Adele Geras, *TES*

THE BURNING

Judy Allen

His image slithered across an old cottage window, his thin white hands were reflected briefly in the glass, and somewhere inside, in a dark quiet place, the smallest imaginable tremor moved the air. It was not like a full awakening. Not yet. But something that had lain in such deep peace that it might almost not have existed was now a little nearer the surface than before . . .

To Jan and Kate the changes are gradual but disturbing. An attic opened after years left sealed. A stranger seeking answers to family mysteries. A bonfire kindling on a village green that bears the scars of a terrible fire decades ago. Below the surface of their village, something has begun its search — for somewhere to feed and grow, for someone to embrace and use its slumbering power . . .

'The insidiousness of evil is beautifully handled in Allen's exploration of jealousy and revenge' Janni Howker in *TES*

'The writing style is exceptional . . . readers will be riveted till the very last page' *Fiction Focus*

'The writing is tense and the complex plotting assured, which adds up to an exciting, imaginative tale . . .' *Books for Keeps*

LORD OF THE DANCE

Judy Allen

'There be a witch closed in this bottle. Let her out and there be a peck of trouble.' He picked the bottle up and rolled it gently from one hand to the other. Then he held it up to the light. The glass was cloudy and scratched. It wasn't possible to see if there was anything inside.

Mike knows it can't be true. Reckless Helly has them all worked up over some silly antique. But Lee's fear is real. And so too is the choice Mike finds himself having to make.

Caught between his calm, responsible brother, and his impulsive sister, this is his chance to make an impression. Just make the right decision, choose the best ally, then surely everything will be all right . . .

'A fascinating book which will not remain long on the shelves but should certainly be available for young teenage readers' *The School Librarian*

'An intriguing and well written psychological novel' *The Northern Echo*

STORM-VOICE

Judy Allen

'I'm wet and cold . . . There are black things in the air above me – they might be snakes. A man comes at me – he swoops towards me – He's pulling me by the arm, he's shouting, his mouth is so wide open I think he's going to swallow me. I can't get free and I can't breathe properly and I think I can't scream . . .'

Night after night, Katie's mum wakes screaming. Her dream is always the same. Is the reason hidden somewhere in her childhood in a seaside town she has never revisited? Desperate to stop her mother's terror, Katie is determined to take her back . . .